14

4

7

17

John Burke had several short stories published before winning an Atlantic Award in Literature from the Rockefeller Foundation for his first novel. He is now a full-time author and has had more than 140 books published. John Burke lives in south-west Scotland.

HANG TIME

What objections could there be to plans for developing an abandoned East Anglian airfield into a theme park commemorating the American presence during World War II and the Cold War? Captain Craig, an eventful military career behind him, is a partner in the family's wine and beer distribution business. Unexpectedly drawn into mysterious undercurrents in the theme park project, Craig grapples with his own problems in a passionate affair with the wife of an MP. Gradually however, he realizes that someone with a long borne grudge has been manipulating events, leading to his being charged with abduction and possibly murder . . .

JOHN BURKE

HANG TIME

Complete and Unabridged

ULVERSCROFT
Leicester

First published in Great Britain in 2007 by
Robert Hale Limited
London

First Large Print Edition
published 2008
by arrangement with
Robert Hale Limited
London

British Library CIP Data

Burke, John Frederick, *1922 –*
    Hang time.—Large print ed.—
    Ulverscroft large print series: mystery
    1. Airports—England—East Anglia—Fiction
    2. War memorials—Fiction 3. Revenge—Fiction
    4. Suspense fiction 5. Large type books
    I. Title
    823.9'14 [F]

    ISBN 978–1–84782–247–5

Published by
F. A. Thorpe (Publishing)
Anstey, Leicestershire

Set by Words & Graphics Ltd.
Anstey, Leicestershire
Printed and bound in Great Britain by
T. J. International Ltd., Padstow, Cornwall

Women sometimes forgive those who force an opportunity,
  never those who miss it.

— *Talleyrand*

The vultures had been circling ever since I left the courtroom. Now and again there would be a lull, when a few of them went off to scavenge somewhere else; but they were soon back. One bright spark tried climbing up to the kitchen window with the aid of the drainpipe. When he slipped and fell back into the narrow garden of the basement flat I could only hope that he had done himself a painful injury.

The phone rang for the fifth time in the last half-hour.

'Mr Craig?'

'Yes.' If this was another reporter, I would slam the phone down.

'Look, I'm speaking from Flat 7. Immediately above you.'

'Yes, I know. And I can guess — '

'You've got to get rid of them. My wife is scared to go out. Every time she sets foot on the front step they're pushing and shoving and asking how well she knows you, and whether she approves of the verdict. It's got to stop.'

'I'm only too anxious for it to stop,' I

assured him, just the way I had assured the other two residents. 'As soon as I can persuade them there's nothing to be learned here, they'll be off.'

'If you can't do something about it right away, we shall have to lodge a complaint with the housing association. The terms of the lease are perfectly clear. This kind of anti-social — '

'I know, I know. Don't you think I want to be rid of them just as much as you?'

I'd have to go out and face them. Get it over with. I was a free man, wasn't I? Free to walk out when it suited me, free to go to the shops or the pub. And right now, the pub seemed a good idea. I was entitled to as much fresh air and as many pints as the next man, without being hounded every inch of the way. I'd been found innocent, hadn't I? Or at any rate the prosecution had decided it hadn't enough evidence to proceed.

The moment I opened the front door they were twittering in from all sides, not so much like vultures as starlings who have just noticed that someone has scattered large chunks of bread on the bird-table.

'Mr Craig, how does it feel — '

'Did you expect the whole thing to be dismissed like that?'

'Since I wasn't guilty,' I said, 'of course I expected that.'

Two bulbs flashed in my face.

'If I could meet you inside for a confidential talk . . . '

I pushed past them. They trotted along the pavement, dodging in front of me, one of them chattering away about money.

Of course. Money. Early on, one of the papers had offered a fair old sum to tell my story in grisly detail, which they would undoubtedly embroider before it appeared in print. The offer probably didn't stand at the same figure any more. Confessions of a brutal murderer were one thing. Reminiscences of an innocent man were far less valuable.

But they still hoped. 'Now that it's over, Mr Craig, and they've thrown in the towel, aren't there just a *few* pointers you could give us?'

'Such as, where's the corpse?' chimed in a little man with a microphone clipped to his tie. 'You must have *some* idea.'

One idea I had was that if they badgered me enough and made enough nasty suggestions, I might cash in on a slander or libel suit.

We reached Gloucester Road and I waited at the pedestrian crossing with the pub looming invitingly at the far side. The sun struck harshly back from the pavement. I lifted my right arm to shield my eyes, and a young woman slipped her arm through mine. 'We're thinking of a television documentary, Mr Craig. One of our unsolved crime series. Only it'll be more a dramatization than a straight factual programme. All about the clumsiness of legal procedures, especially in cases like yours. If you could come to our office, we can start talking terms. I mean, it's illegal for a criminal to make financial profit from reminiscences of his crime, but of course that doesn't apply in your case, does it?'

I would have been prepared to bet that if I had in fact been found guilty, there would have been ways of getting round that little legal snag.

'And incidentally,' she wittered on, 'is that name of yours hyphenated? I mean, when we heard it in court — Craig Sinclair Craig . . . '

'No hyphen,' I said.

'Makes it difficult to know whether one's using your Christian name or your surname, doesn't it?'

'I can always tell,' I said, 'when it matters.'

Just as I was dragging my arm away from hers, and a Jaguar was reluctantly stopping so that I could step on to the crossing, a police car swung in to the kerb beside me. I heard a babble of protest from the carrion crew as the police began warning them about the way they were blocking the traffic, or the pavement, or creating an unseemly disturbance, or something. I didn't look back, but reached the far pavement and dived into the hospitable shadows of the pub.

At this hour there were only a few men in it, huddled against the cool far end of the bar as if to keep well away from daylight.

I ordered a pint of bitter. The barman wasn't the landlord, who would have greeted me with a coarse joke and a welcome-back grin. Or would he? But the lad behind the bar must have served me sometime or other, and recognized me. He stared, wondering whether to say anything, and then simply handed over the change and turned his back to fiddle with some bottles on the shelf.

I settled into one of the alcoves that had not been done away with during a recent pseudo-Irish refurbishment, and took a leisurely look around. It was second nature to relate the place to our own establishments and play the familiar game of assessing its probable turnover, its profit ratio, its tie-ins with a brewery chain or a family business like Craig and Hebden. It was time to get back to work: time to get to grips with the real world again.

After maybe another pint I would have to go down the road to the delicatessen, then to the wine shop, and maybe buy a newspaper or two just to check on the coverage of my last day in court. Or maybe there wouldn't be anything until next morning's editions.

The door from the side street opened, and a shadow added itself to the others at the end of the bar. When it had acquired what looked like a large gin and tonic, it didn't settle on a stool but drifted towards me and sat down on the other side of the table.

'Well, Mr Craig. Pleased with the result, I suppose?'

'And evidently you're not.'

'Wouldn't expect me to be, would you?' Detective Chief Inspector Plant put his glass down and stared across the table as if hoping that even now, when it was apparently all over, the suspect would suddenly crack and confess and tell him he'd been right all along. 'All that hard work, and it all gets thrown out.'

'Better luck next time,' I said, 'with somebody else. And something more substantial.'

'Such as a corpse.'

'With a name like yours, I'm surprised you didn't get round to planting one.'

'Thank you, sir. Yes, it's been quite a joke

among my colleagues. A very long-running one.' He sighed and returned to his drink.

'But you're still trailing around after me?'

'I just had a hunch you'd be back in here at the first opportunity. This being your usual watering-hole.'

'One of the many useless details you've painstakingly accumulated?'

The light through the coloured panes along the top of the window threw a purplish stain on Plant's left temple like a mottled birthmark. Shadows dug deep into the crinkled lines along his forehead. Even deeper shadows down his cheeks gave his flesh the appearance of uneven linenfold panelling. With his heavy jowls and thick lips he looked like a sad dog past its prime — but still a dog with his full set of teeth, capable of violent, unpredictable attack.

He stared into what was left of his gin. 'You wouldn't believe it, Mr Craig, but even in my spare time I read a lot about crime. Factual books, famous trials, that sort of thing. Keeps you up to the mark, you might say.'

'Busman's holiday reading?'

'Nineteenth-century mysteries — that's been my own speciality.'

I wondered how smoothly I might do my shopping and get back to the flat without being intercepted.

'Adelaide Bartlett, now,' Plant was continuing. 'You'll remember what the lawyers said after she got away with *her* murder charge?'

'I'm sure you're going to tell me.'

'Adelaide Bartlett. The lawyers said that now she'd been acquitted of poisoning her husband with chloroform, and couldn't be tried again for the same offence, she owed it to medical science to tell the world how she'd done it.'

'Yes, I've read that, too. In the Bartlett case, there was a corpse. Loaded with chloroform. In my case, there's no corpse,' I reminded him.

'No, it's baffling, isn't it? But there has to be a corpse *somewhere*, hasn't there? Where d'you suppose it might be?'

'I wish I knew.'

'When the body does turn up, Mr Craig — '

'You'll try and pin a murder rap on me?'

'I didn't say that, Mr Craig.'

'You didn't need to.' I finished my bitter. As I stood up, he looked at me with a sideways glance which he must have thought was very knowing and would leave me feeling uneasy.

'And what would you be thinking of doing next, Mr Craig?'

'I'm thinking,' I said, 'that if you continue wasting my time and police time, Chief Inspector Plant, I might lay a complaint of harassment against you.'

I was on my way to the door when he said: 'One thing I do promise you, Mr Craig. I'll find her. There's no such thing as a case abandoned, you know. I'll find her. However long it takes.'

★ ★ ★

The girl in the wine shop gawped as I came in, then hurriedly looked away and began rearranging a small cigar cabinet on the counter. I knew she was watching as I wandered from shelf to shelf. Did she suppose I was going to strangle her and help myself to a couple of bottles of brandy? In the end I settled for two decent clarets and one Chilean sauvignon. She held my two banknotes up to the light and was disappointed not to find they were forgeries.

Mr Gupta in the corner shop gave his usual little grin, and said: 'Nice to see you again, Mr Craig.' I was sure he meant it.

I bought a loaf, some butter, and a couple of packaged meals for the microwave, then looked at what were left of his newspapers.

'The evening paper is sold out,' he said

with a little chuckle. 'People are all very interested.'

I went back to the flat by a roundabout route. There was no longer a posse staking the place out. Maybe they had all been called away to a gun battle in Notting Hill.

Pouring myself a BNJ, I switched on the television news, to be confronted by myself striding down three steps and shouldering my way between a cluster of cameramen and reporters. It was eerie, seeing that figure from outside. If it had been a stranger I was watching, I'd have had difficulty in assessing the man's character and whether he looked guilty or not. This dark-haired man on the screen was just under six feet, holding himself very erect, with a slightly swaggering military bearing. Had I really been putting that on without realizing it? Quite impressive — from outside.

Five minutes later, the entryphone buzzed.

Another assault from the predators of Canary Wharf? I was ready with a brisk dismissal, but the voice this time was a familiar one. All too familiar.

'Craig, old lad. Let me in. Time to celebrate, eh?'

I could have told him I wasn't in the mood. Least of all for any sort of celebration with *him*. Or I could simply have replaced the handset and left him out there on the step.

But sooner or later we would have to come face to face.

I pressed the release and opened the door into the hall.

Barry was beaming, his right hand thrusting forward. 'Well, what a turn-up, eh? What a blessed bloody relief.' He was pumping my arm.

'I wasn't expecting you,' I said. 'Didn't know you were in town.'

'Didn't think I was going to shun you, did you? Didn't think I'd pretend not to know you any more?' He was walking on into the flat. He strode towards the sitting-room, a padded carrier bag and a folded evening paper in his left hand. 'Done you proud, haven't they?' He went booming on in one from his extensive repertoire of declamatory tones. ' 'After the judge had declared him a free man, Mr Craig left the court with the proud, upright bearing which harked back to the days of his distinguished military career. He was every inch an officer leaving a court-martial, his face stern and unyielding, after being acquitted of conduct unbefitting an officer and a gentleman.' Thinking of selling your memoirs for a vast sum, old son?'

'I've got better things to do.'

'You can say that again. Let's face it, a lot's

been going on since you've been . . . well, out of action, like. We've got to accept a lot of challenges. And obviously you have to come into it.'

'Obviously.'

'Whatever little problems we may have had in the past' — Barry had switched to being condescending and tolerant — 'the old man thinks there are things we ought to sort out just as quickly as possible. For the sake of the firm. For the sake of our good name, right?'

Whatever little problems we may have had in the past.

You had to hand it to him. Such an airy way of dismissing his part in all that had led up to this.

PART ONE

VIN PÉTILLANT

1

Whenever good old Barry, fellow director and good old mate Barry, came to London from the fastnesses of County Durham for business discussions and to follow up contacts, Maureen and I had got into the habit of offering him a bed for a night or two. After all, we were partners, and it saved the firm extra expense. Our house was only half an hour from Charing Cross, or an hour and a half if you were mad enough to drive in; and our friendship went back quite a way, didn't it?

It was only after a fair number of such visits that I realized he was spending some afternoons in that bed with my wife.

I had driven home a bit earlier than usual. It was a mild, drowsy afternoon. Daffodils were golden all along the avenue, hardly stirring in only the faintest of breezes, and there was a bright cluster of crocuses in the ceramic pot beside our driveway.

Maureen looked startled to see me. She came out of the spare bedroom in a rush, and made a big business of kissing me and hugging me and telling me to sit down while

15

she brought me a whisky and finished getting the bed linen into the washing machine now that Barry had left. I wasn't in the habit of drinking Scotch at this time of day. Instead, I went past her into the bedroom, offering to help with turning the mattress.

In the wine trade you have to have a discerning nose. Right now I didn't like the smell on the sheets.

When I told her what was too bloody obvious, she let out the sort of outraged scream she had practised to perfection in so many local dramatic society productions.

'Craig, are you out of your mind? I'll just pretend I didn't hear that.' She was all of a whirl, opening a cupboard, fussing from the spare bedroom to our bedroom and then into the bathroom. 'Look, *do* keep out of my way. It's my evening for the clinical study. I don't want to get there out of breath and all shaken up.'

'Couldn't you have told Barry that — asked him to be a bit less strenuous in his performance?'

'Oh, don't be so crude.'

On stage with our local Tithebarn Players she had always been one for running up and down, gasping, flitting from one member of the cast to another whether that was in the stage directions or not. Now she was tingling with a sort of gloating twitch over someone being keen enough to have it off with her, and the perverse thrill of having been found out.

I said: 'Anyway, I think that today you could give your medicine men a miss just this once, while we — '

'Craig, please don't be difficult. I do have to dash.'

I had learned, also, how she could make the most of her part in the research project she had volunteered to attend each month. When telling friends about it she revelled in the cadences of its description — 'a multicentre, randomized double-blind placebo-controlled screening programme to evaluate a new antidepressant designed to eliminate deleterious side effects'.

I heard her Micra scrape against the flower tub as she drove off.

When she returned she was flushed with a pleasure which suggested that by now she not merely was herself as the key figure in the entire research programme but had been telling the nurses and psychologists exactly how to run their investigation. Thinking that on the drive home she would have been rehearsing some emotional lines, swinging between remorse and proud defiance so that whatever I said she would be ready for it, I had intended to take up the Barry matter right away. But she was on a different high.

'Do you know, the study nurse says I've got the blood pressure of an eighteen-year-old! And they've never known anyone go through the memory test so fast, and so accurately. Oh, and the clinical psychologist' — she drew a deep, ecstatic breath — 'thinks it would help them if I would take part in some individual screening at the end of the year.'

It would be too clumsy, too much of an effort, to crank up a calculated row at this stage.

Sooner or later it would come to a head of its own accord.

★   ★   ★

My father had set up Craig's Vaults in London in the 1980s, building up a steady trade in the supply of wine to a chain of hotels and pubs. When commercial rents in the capital began soaring, he was one of the first to see the potential of importing direct through the growing container port of Felixstowe, and had a stroke of luck when he found a large warehouse with deep cellars only a few miles away on Deben Head. The promontory had housed a secret radar research station during World War II and the years of the Cold War. When the Iron Curtain

18

rusted away, the military had been only too glad to find a buyer for something that was of little use to most people but suited Craig's storage and distribution needs admirably. It had its own wharf, and proved an even better buy when cross-country road links to and from Felixstowe were upgraded.

By the time I quit the army and came into the firm, there had been so many brewery and pub chain mergers that we began to see clouds drifting over the whole enterprise. Every time there was a take-over of some hotel or pub chain, everything had to be centralized according to accountants' calculations of overheads and profit margins, and small groups and specialists had to be bought out or cut out.

At this point Barry Quirke introduced me to his father-in-law.

I had met Barry not long before emerging from my military career into civvy street. Maureen and I were spending a week in a Lake District hotel where Barry had been chasing up some deal with the proprietor. We got drawn into a pub quiz on the second evening, with Maureen sitting on the sidelines, well aware of Barry's gaze on her and enjoying it, just as she enjoyed the same sort of attention at mess parties at Camberley or Andover.

Barry insisted on lavishing drinks on the two of us afterwards. We found then that we shared one common interest. We were both keen on steam trains. After the holiday ended we kept up a desultory correspondence and met once or twice at steam rallies. Also he began calling on us when he happened to be in our neighbourhood, enjoying the ritual of presenting himself at the guardroom and asking for Captain Craig. Whenever Maureen was present, he preened himself and talked suggestively and more loudly than when just the two of us had a drink together. When she wasn't there he hinted with a lot of nudging and convoluted asides that right now he was trying to make an impression on his boss's daughter. It worked. Maureen and I were invited to the wedding, which had some sticky moments when he clearly enjoyed kissing my wife more than kissing his own bride. But he was always confident in his own ability to do whatever he fancied doing at any given moment, always the hail-fellow-well-met, booming salesman anxious to show his skills as a fixer for everybody's mutual benefit.

After my discharge and entry into the family firm, he became matier than ever. 'It's time we pooled our resources, old lad. Now you're in our own line of business, it's high time we set up together — a marriage of talents, hey?'

My father was suspicious of any kind of merger. In spite of current problems he thought we could soldier on alone, relying on my organizational background as a Transit Co-ordinator in the Royal Logistic Corps to tighten up our own distribution network. As for myself, I too wanted us to be in control of our own destiny. After the constrictions of military red tape, it was good to be really in charge of an enterprise, making things work, solving problems without having to cover your tracks.

Then my father and mother died in an air crash on the way to a holiday in New Zealand, with which he hoped to combine a business trip to the Hawke's Bay vineyards. Barry pounced. His pushiness almost put me off, but I agreed to attend a new alcopop promotion in Harrogate and meet his father-in-law again.

Walter Hebden was a thickset man with thinning sandy hair and a coppery face pitted with little black flecks as if coal-dust had settled permanently in every pore. In contrast, the glaring brightness of his eyes always suggested that he was alert for anyone likely to give him offence. During our previous encounter at Barry and Rhona's wedding he had been hospitable and sentimentally expansive. This time he was in a quite different, quarrelsome mood over this concocted drink we were each being urged to stock.

'Coloured piss, that's all it is. No wonder they're growing up nowadays with no taste for real beer.'

He had been a pitman in County Durham. Injured in a coalface collapse and invalided out, he was found a job running the bar in a local miners' club. He soon discovered that he had a flair for stock control, keeping things flowing smoothly and keeping staff on their toes. He became manager of a string of clubs across the region. Then as pits closed, and miners became redundant and the clubs declined, he acquired a string of pubs for himself and bought an interest in a small brewery at Hesketh-le-Street on the borders of Durham and Northumberland. After five years' hard work he took it over and set up a new sign boasting of the purity of HEBDEN'S FINE ALES.

Like ourselves, he was now finding himself in danger of being squeezed out by too many take-overs. Pubs which he had once supplied individually became part of some fat conglomerate, buying everything from a linked Northampton group because they were told to do so by the group's accountants. Bulk supplies were in the hands of fewer and fewer distributors. None of them was interested in shipping small quantities of beer from any company outside their own group, in spite of the government ruling that all landlords should be free to offer a guest ale as well as their owners' obligatory keg product. The owners had soon found a way round this. They bought up a number of real ale breweries and claimed that supplying one of their products was, in strictly legal terms, supplying a 'real' guest ale. There was little choice.

Hebden was too set in his ways to adjust to contemporary wheeling and dealing. He had no intention of selling out so that his brew could be sucked into an insipid lake and sold under a name that no longer had any real meaning. He needed to find other outlets, but lacked the know-how to reach them.

We talked together, and pooled our ideas. Two months later we set up a clearing house outside Wolverhampton from which individual hotels and pubs could order individual casks of real ales, and small quantities of wine. Within six months we were doing well enough to branch out with four main delivery and despatch centres, two in the Midlands, one in London, and one in Hebden's base of Hesketh-le-Street, with wine imports still coming into the warehouse on Deben Head.

We made a virtue of the differences between the individual styles of small local breweries when supplying to small groups of pubs and hotels, or individual premises which could otherwise never order just a cask or two at a time from different breweries or keep up a direct intake of small quantities of wine from individual vineyards.

Barry was a glib, fast-talking sales manager. His brashness made him good company for other reps and contacts in the trade. And hadn't I found him good company, too, in a limited way?

Now the limitations had been overstepped. The next time he phoned, I made it clear that he wouldn't be offered any further hospitality and told him why.

'Oh, come off it, aren't we taking this a bit too seriously?'

'Seriously enough to make sure it doesn't happen again. You're not denying you've been shagging my wife?'

'Well, old lad, what can I say?' Like Maureen, there was a slight snicker in his voice as if he found guilt enjoyable.

'You could try saying it's not true.'

'Not much good in that, eh? Obviously you *know*. Women! Can't help blabbing, can they?'

Maureen had been listening eagerly to my end of the conversation, and now sauntered along the passage with eyes demurely downcast but maybe ready to play her part in a scene of being swept off her feet by my fit of jealous, masterful rage. I was going to have to disappoint her. This wasn't a scene from a Tithebarn Players' production in our local Community Centre.

Perhaps I should have realized long ago that she'd be an obvious target for a compulsive swaggerer like Barry. Always one for obsessive self-contemplation, she longed for someone to play up to her daydreams and contemplate her with equally rapt adoration. Maybe they had been at it much earlier than I thought — while I was away for a few weeks in Northern Ireland, and that advisory fortnight I'd had to spend in Kuwait before demob.

During the next couple of weeks we managed to live in the same house without inhabiting the same world. She was wrapped up in rehearsals for a cosy comedy thriller, and I had reasonable excuses to stay in town for a seasonal rush of work, and to stay some nights in a hotel near the Deben Head wharf and warehouse. At home, I moved into the spare bedroom.

'Aren't you being a bit silly?'

'I don't think so. This way I won't interrupt you reading your lines in bed, and you won't be bothered when I get back late.'

Maureen could never be happy with indifference. One evening when we were at home together and had actually eaten dinner together, she must have been summoning up the determination to turn any idea of guilt away from herself and towards me.

'I've done my best to be the kind of wife you expected. Given things up because of you. You do realize I could have made a career in the theatre if I hadn't married you? Once I had lost Mike' — pause for dramatic effect — 'I ought to have made a new life for myself instead of listening to you. There was that wonderful opportunity at the BBC which I gave up because of you. So soon after Mike's death . . . I was so vulnerable. When I think . . .'

I had heard it so often before, and was good at switching off.

'All right,' she went on, 'so I've made other mistakes as well. But you haven't even got the guts to beat me up.' Her reproachful tone was the one she used when rehearsing some particularly fraught scene from the local

26

production of some well-worn melodrama.

'Not quite my style,' I admitted.

'Just doing everything according to Queen's Regs. Always keep your cap badge polished, and make sure everybody salutes you. But never give anything back.'

All at once, quite dispassionately, I knew it was time to call it a day.

★ ★ ★

I found a small ground-floor flat in a row of Georgian houses behind Gloucester Road, along with a lock-up garage in what had once been the mews when each whole house had been a separate entity, and told Maureen I was moving out. I'd keep in touch, and we would work out some sort of financial arrangement.

'You're not serious?'

'I'm trying not to be too serious. No point in having any unpleasantness. Just take it as it comes.'

'But Craig . . . just because I gave way just this once because I was . . . well . . . I felt so *lonely*.'

'Ten or a dozen times, more likely. Maybe a lot more.'

She still could not repress a little flush of glee, then tried to look very, very earnest. She put her right hand on her left breast in quite a pretty gesture. 'But Craig, I mean, after all we've been through together.'

I tried to think of anything important we had been through together, but after the first year or so of enjoying her admittedly sleek body, I couldn't think of anything very spectacular. And even then she'd had the knack of putting the dampers on. 'You're not to feel guilty about making love to me, Craig,' she gushed one night. 'Just because of poor Mike, you mustn't feel shy about me. I *do* want you to enjoy me.'

'Let's work it out reasonably,' I said now. 'It's not as though we've got kids to worry about.'

'So that's what this is about?' I had carelessly offered her a wonderful cue. 'That's what's really behind it.'

'No, what's behind it — or right up front — is you and Barry.'

'Just because I haven't had any children, I'm no use.' She had latched on to one thing she thought she could concentrate on, and was swiftly acquiring a reproachful tone which identified me as the guilty party, not herself. 'Is that it?'

'I've never worried about that. Never blamed you for it.'

It was true, but now her reproach became a

squeal. 'It's not as though it was all my fault. It was . . . it was *you*. Psychosomatic, that's what's been wrong with you.' She could pick up misheard jargon from any specialized field and regurgitate it like a bird bringing goodies back to the nest. 'After that last quarter's psychological assessment on my screening programme, Dr de Haan said that from what I'd told him, you were the one he ought to be seeing.'

Yes, from what she had told him . . . I could just imagine how her version was put across. I held my tongue, though.

Maureen had been a slim, pale girl with very pale blue eyes and hair that was almost flaxen. This pallor made her look fragile and china-doll pretty. I wondered if her pet psychiatrist had been shrewd enough to notice that nowadays the little lines in the corners of her mouth had tightened to suggest something a lot tougher; and her voice had hardened from practice at project-ing it at impressive volume on stage.

She switched to that harshness now. 'She's back, isn't she? That's what it's all about.'

'Back?'

'Oh, don't play the innocent. Lisa. That was her name, wasn't it? You think I didn't see through all that pretence of military consultations, and then afterwards just happening to bob up to inspect your new premises. It was pathetic. And now she's back, and this time you want it to be for keeps?'

'I haven't seen Lisa for years,' I said. 'Haven't seen her or even thought of her.'

Except once or twice, vaguely. Something that had never come to anything. Something that had no reason to linger. Too shadowy for even Maureen to flesh out into a drama.

I could almost have predicted the moment she would begin to cry. Her timing was pretty reliable. It sounds callous when I put it that way, but I really had been through it all before, through so many scenes and acts, so many hysterical flourishes, over and over again.

This time I wasn't going to wait for the curtain calls.

★　★　★

In the early hours of Monday morning I woke up in the strange surroundings of my new home feeling absurdly conscience-stricken. Had I been cowardly, waiting all this time for an excuse to get out, even welcoming this shabby unfaithfulness? There ought to have been some other way of coping. If only I had been more masterful from the start and slapped down those mannerisms and pitiful exaggerations — all that pathetic daydreaming. Oh, sod that. I could be decisive enough in scheduling troop movements or, nowadays, consignments of wine; but not the type to play strong-arm tactics with my wife.

All the same, a bit humiliating for poor Maureen. Losing her first husband in the service of his country was an uplifting idea. Losing the second one not to another woman, but just having him walk off, was quite different. Of course she would find some way of telling her friends a plaintive story. The thought of how well she would manage, how touchingly she would wear that hard-done-by look, and the sympathy it would generate, did something to assuage my guilt.

All right, so I went on feeling guilty just the same. The older you get, the more things you have to feel guilty about, because of the past you've accumulated. I would just have to live with it.

There had been a threat of some delay in getting me a phone number at my new address; but the pace quickened when our fiercely efficient Diana in the office set to work with her usual blend of cajoling and fuming. I was less grateful when the first person to ring was Barry. Of course the two of us would have to meet again, sooner or later. Phones and e-mails were all very well for day-to-day running of the enterprise, but every now and then there were policy decisions which needed face-to-face discussions, preferably without somebody listening in. But I was in no hurry.

His voice was as breezy as ever. 'Just dug out your number from our darling Di. Quite a girl, eh? Anyway, I'll be in town tomorrow, old lad. Have to have a shot at doing a deal with those peanut and crisp people. Wouldn't want to tread on your toes, though. So we ought to sort something out, right?' He waited, then: 'Maybe we could meet for a drink.'

'No, thanks. If there's anything important, we can meet in the office.'

'No chance of a bed in your new pad?'

'None.'

'You're not still peeved about that business with Maureen?'

'Not peeved,' I said. 'Just not terribly sociable. Getting choosy in my old age.'

'Oh, come on, you know you haven't got on with her for ages. She told me quite a bit about that while we . . . I mean, when we . . . '

'I'll bet she enjoyed that. The chat, I mean.'

'Really, I've done you a good turn, if only you can face up to it.'

'I'm supposed to be grateful?'

'Look, it's a bit silly getting huffy with me. I mean, you know, she did quite a bit of the come-hither.'

'And you just had to oblige her out of politeness?'

I put the phone down. He didn't come round to the office, but a few days later sent me a screed of stuff about the fantastic deal he had set up with an up-and-coming firm which had every chance of putting Walker's and Smith's out of business. I made a note to investigate this fairly soon, before he made a fool of us.

Two days later there was a call to my direct office line from Walter Hebden. For a moment I thought that perhaps he was going to ask me what was wrong between Barry and myself; but Barry, sensible in this at any rate, had evidently decided not to risk his father-in-law getting wind of his behaviour. All Walter had to say was: 'You haven't forgotten the Trade Fair next month?'

'No, I haven't forgotten.'

'See you up here, then. Everything all right at your end?'

'No problems,' I said.

At the end of the third week of my new life, someone else set about making me feel guilty from a different angle.

2

Rhona had a breathy, piping little voice which became even more shrill on the phone, always sounding reproachful or apologetic even when she had nobody to reproach and nothing to apologize for. Today she sounded even squeakier than usual, rushing a few words and then faltering over the next few.

'Sorry to ring you at the office, but I didn't know your new home number, and I . . . well, I didn't really like to ask Maureen. A bit embarrassing, with you . . . well, I mean . . . I understand you've — er — gone away for a while.'

'For good. Surprised?'

'Look, Craig, this can't go on.' The tone had become plaintive.

'It's going on smoothly enough, right now.'

'Craig, I know Barry's a louse — he's told me everything.'

'A bit stupid of him.'

'I knew there was something wrong. In the end I got it out of him. And I can't be doing with it. Craig, I just can't be doing with him snivelling about the place every day.'

'Snivelling?'

'He keeps moaning about how he's been a bloody fool, he's lost the best friend he ever had in the world, and he just can't go on.'

'High drama seems to be contagious.'

'Look, couldn't you just have a drink with him? Have a bit of a laugh at it all?'

'I didn't find it especially funny, though I'm sure he was giggling all the way through.'

'You're both still part of the company, so you'll have to meet to discuss things. Craig, I know he's been silly. Awful. But *you* don't have to be the same. Next time he has to come to London, perhaps you could — '

'No,' I said.

But the next time he came to London, Rhona was with him. She was the one who phoned me again, told me the hotel they were staying in, and insisted that I come and have dinner with them. She was very insistent.

Cunning old Barry. Sly salesman's technique at work again. Getting his wife to make the call, because it was much more difficult for me to be dismissive towards her.

Weakly I said: 'Well . . . '

'No chance of Maureen joining us?' She was determined to show how insouciant she could be. Not that she had ever had much time for Maureen, or was likely to have much now.

'So Barry can play footsie-footsie with her

under the table?' I said. 'No, I think not.'

'You haven't got . . . er, I mean, there isn't anyone else you'd like to bring along?'

'No,' I said, 'there isn't. And I'm in no hurry for there to be anyone.'

Rhona managed a worldly-wise laugh. 'Well,' she said brightly, 'we'll see you at seven. Right?'

★ ★ ★

I had taken a deep breath before crossing the hotel foyer into the bar, determined not to be conned by the two of them or either of them. But it wasn't just Barry and Rhona waiting for me at a table in the corner. There were three of them.

'We thought we'd make a foursome of it.' Rhona began twittering right away, trying to make everything jolly and uncomplicated. No question of us quarrelling in front of somebody else, was there? 'Fran, this is Craig. Craig, this is Fran — Frances Leith. Like yourself, she's at a bit of a loose end at the moment, so we thought — '

'I'm just taking a sabbatical from my husband,' said Frances Leith. 'So they thought I'd be available. Which I am, I suppose.'

She had probably had a couple of drinks by

now, and most likely said it out of sheer bravado. But she had a very slow, well-controlled voice, and her smile was calm and self-contained rather than suggestive.

Barry was on his feet. 'Great to see you, old lad. Oh, and Fran — Craig isn't just Craig. He's Craig Craig. Sounds as though this place has quite an echo, eh? Double-barrelled, sort of, but not hyphenated. Right, old lad, what's it to be? The usual large malt, eh?'

Rhona said: 'Looking after yourself then, Craig?'

Rhona was a small woman who had grown podgy after having two children in quick succession, and never lost the extra weight. Her hair was slightly wavy, of such an ordinary brown that it was difficult to describe it as other than just that — brown. She wore glasses in very large oval frames. On some women they could have looked fashionable. On Rhona they made her look goggle-eyed and permanently startled. As if to keep up this image, she tended to chatter like a wide-eyed child, intermittently glancing at her husband as she might have glanced at a parent to see whether she was allowed to get away with what she was saying. This evening, though, there was more than a touch of defiance in it. After what she had learnt about

Barry, maybe she was ready to be less subservient.

The woman beside her could not have provided a more striking contrast. Frances Leith had hair so black that where the light fell on it there was a glow as blue as a raven's wing. Her skin had a warm olive tinge, and in the centre of each of her almond eyes was a fleck of burnished bronze. Unlike Rhona, who was forever shifting on her seat, moving a beer mat on the table a fraction of an inch in one direction and then back to where it had started, she sat very calm and still. She looked straight at me and smiled as if challenging me to look away.

I didn't want to look away. She made a very attractive picture.

Behind me I could hear Barry's voice at the bar. He could never have been taken for anything else but a rep. Ordering a drink, he assumed a clipped, bossy accent, and was a great one for raising a peremptory hand at waiters or clicking his fingers at a barman. With a barmaid he would lean on the counter and coo, 'Dear lady, when you have a moment.'

'Well. Well, here we are.' He was back, setting my whisky down in front of me, and spreading himself expansively on the banquette. 'Here we are, hey?'

There was a silence that went on a bit too long. It had to be broken with something bland and banal. I saw that Frances Leith was looking down into her drink with a little flicker of amusement. I wanted her to look up at me again. I said: 'What might your line of business be?'

It was a bit silly, really, after what she had said a few moments ago. How could she describe herself, right now, other than as a potential divorcée in waiting, marking time? I was in a similar position, wasn't I?

But Rhona came prattling in. 'Oh, she's awfully important. She — '

'Takes your breath away,' boomed Barry, taking off his horn-rimmed glasses and polishing them with a blue handkerchief from his top pocket. It was a habit of his, almost an uncontrollable physical tic, whenever he thought he was saying something particularly amusing or daring. 'Juggling two jobs at a time. Only she's decided to give one up for the time being, right?' He put his glasses back on, replaced his handkerchief, and beamed archly at her as if waiting for a ripple of applause.

Very quietly Frances Leith said: 'Very boring, all of it.'

'Oh, but it isn't,' cried Rhona. 'It must be absolutely thrilling. Have you ever met a real image consultant before, Craig?'

The only explanation for such dissimilar women being friends must be that they had been at school together. And Rhona would of course have been the gawky, slavish worshipper.

'I am also' — there was a touch of flippant self-denigration in it — 'the wife of the MP for Alderthorpe. Which has been even more boring.'

'Alderthorpe — in the Lincolnshire Wolds?' I said.

'You know it?'

'We supply a small hotel chain in that neck of the woods,' said Barry proudly, as if I needed to be told something I knew perfectly well.

'Tory or Lib Dem?' I asked.

'Labour, believe it or not. Since the last election but one. Wouldn't want to bet on the next one. And neither is Toby. I'm by no means sure he quite believes he's Labour, either. Just a chance that came along, and he adjusted his principles and took it.'

Barry snapped his fingers at a passing waiter and asked for the menu.

When we had made our choice, Frances Leith said: 'Shall we change the subject? I'm sure you want to talk your own sort of shop.'

I wanted no such thing. I was much more

interested in her. The light fell on the string of small pearls around her throat, and each time she moved there was a different, shifting glint on her skin.

I said: 'Barry can come into the office in the morning and go through things, just the two of us.'

I hadn't meant it to sound like a threat, but I saw Barry wince, and he began talking even more rapidly than usual. He avoided my gaze and told Frances just how he was hoping to clinch a deal with a really imaginative whizzkid who was converting his family farm into a supplier of a special breed of potato which would produce crisps of a quality guaranteed to drive Walker's and Smith's out of business within the next eighteen months. And he, Barry, was of course securing all distribution rights for Craig & Hebden.

I would certainly have to have a frank talk with Barry in the office. When he glanced at me again, before rattling on, I could see that he had already anticipated trouble in that direction. He certainly had more to worry about than Walker's or Smith's did.

'And *your* part in all this?' Mrs Leith persevered. She was looking at me in an odd, lopsided way — a mixture of amusement and calculation.

'Simple stuff,' I said. 'Nuts and bolts. Getting things packaged up at one end and making sure they arrive on time at the other. Preferably unbroken. Routine stuff.'

'No such thing,' Rhona breathed. 'Craig used to be terribly important, moving troops around, or tanks and guns or something. Top secret stuff, before he came out into the ordinary world.'

'Nuts and bolts,' I said again. 'Supply transit co-ordination in the Logistic Corps. Much the same as things are today, only now it's casks and bottles instead of troops, vehicles and ammo.'

As we ate our way through dinner by the light of candles in tall smoked glass cylinders in the centre of the table, Rhona's glasses flashed reflections from one side to the other as she asked every few minutes if everything was all right, if my saltimbocca was just the way I liked it, and if Frances's sea bass was as good as it looked.

Over coffee and brandy, Barry's mobile tinkled out a few repeated bars of *Blaydon Races*. He smirked, made an apologetic grunt and further grunts in answer to whatever was being communicated from the other end, said 'Will do, will do,' and shoved it back in his pocket. 'Damn things. Can't get away from 'em, can you?'

I had refused the brandy. I knew how much drink made sense when I was driving, and how much made nonsense.

'A good idea,' Barry said effusively to his wife. 'Great idea of yours, pet. Splendid evening.' He consulted the other two of us. 'Right place, right company, eh?'

'Thanks,' I said, 'for a delightful evening.'

When we got up to leave, Frances Leith stumbled slightly. I took her elbow to steady her. Her arm stiffened, and she looked for a moment as if she was about to shake me indignantly off. Then she smiled and whispered thanks.

I said: 'I'll drive you home.'

'No, please, I'll get a cab. I haven't got far to go.'

'It'll be no trouble. My car's just round the corner.'

'No, really. I — '

'He's got a very plush Saab,' said Barry, now able to risk looking at me with that familiar nudge-nudge wink-wink expression of his.

'If it's not far out in the Home Counties,' I said, 'I can fit it in easily.'

As Rhona took her friend away to collect her coat, I noticed that Mrs Leith had a slight limp which made her left hip swing in an odd, seductive rhythm.

I might have known that Barry would be aware of it too. 'Makes her sashay real sexy, doesn't it?' He looked archly at me. 'Better watch ourselves, hadn't we? She could be murder, that one.'

By the time the two of them returned, Frances Leith had apparently accepted — or been persuaded by Rhona, eager to stir up something to gossip about later — that I would be driving her home.

'See you in the office, then,' boomed Barry. 'And we do need to settle one or two things about the Trade Fair, eh, right?'

It was only ten minutes to her flat, on the second floor of a block tucked away in a square behind the Marylebone Road. She had some difficulty with her key, trying it clockwise and then anti-clockwise until she managed to get the door open. 'Not used to the place yet,' she said. 'It's on loan from a friend until I . . . sort things out. All mine for a couple of years. Not that I expect to take that long to . . . well . . . ' Her words drifted away like the faint musky perfume that drifted from her as I stood close to her on the step.

I didn't ask whether the friend was male or female.

And she didn't ask me whether I wanted to come in for coffee. Turning in the doorway, she said: 'Thanks for the lift.'

'Can I give you a ring? Have a drink one evening. Or dinner somewhere.'

'Nice of you, but . . . oh, I don't know. Maybe best not.'

'Give me your number. I'd like to — '

'You're still married, aren't you?'

'Only sort of.'

'Sort of?'

'I used to commute. Sometimes stayed overnight in town. Now I'm full-time in a little place off Gloucester Road.'

'I had my share of that. Only it was all week in town while Toby sucked up to ministers and their useful sidekicks, then weekends down at his bloody constituency, while he held forth at committee meetings and drooled over smelly old ladies. That's why I've gone in for some travelling of my own.' She swayed in the doorway as if thinking up another confidence, but then deciding it wasn't worth the effort. 'Thanks again for the lift.' She closed the door.

Her presence was still beside me as I drove back to the flat. There, yet still elusive. Worth following up, or just one of those casual meetings which you enjoy and then can't be bothered to pursue?

★ ★ ★

45

The morning that I set out for Hesketh-le-Street was bright but with a brisk wind that clouted the Saab on the side whenever I passed a large lorry. Quite a few of these were out today, but there were no hold-ups or congestion until I was past Newark. Then we had several unexplained slowdowns, and twice came to a halt. Traffic on the southbound carriageway was just as spasmodic.

At the roundabout just before a section of motorway, with roads feeding off to the west and east, there was a major hold-up. Police cars were edging in towards two large trucks drawn up on the verge, with a crowd milling around, waving placards I couldn't read from this angle. A small group began clambering on to the bumpers of the first lorry, trying to plaster something across its windscreen. The driver leaned out of his window to shout something. It gave a tall, lanky man with a narrow, scared yet determined face the chance to grab his arm and try to drag him out. 'You know what you're doing?' a girl was screeching as she clambered up beside him to shout in the driver's face. 'Proud of contaminating your own country?'

A small coach came weaving its way through the stalled traffic, and ten or a dozen policemen in riot gear sprang out, heading for the crowd. I saw some batons flailing, and a couple of placards on what might have been broom-handles swung in defence.

The battle lasted about ten minutes, until the demonstrators were clubbed to the ground, dragged up, and shunted towards a waiting police vehicle, or made their escape across the road and over a low hedge. One of them, cowering down to conceal himself close to the line of waiting cars, came right up to my offside window and banged on it. His lips moved like a goldfish pouting against the glass.

'Get me away from those thugs. Please.'

I leaned over to open the door, and he slid in, hunched on the seat with his head down. His whole crumpled posture reminded me of a young man I had picked up, strictly against regs, in Kosovo. I had released him in a quiet street, only to see in my wing mirror a gunman leaning against the corner of an alley and almost cutting him in half with a spray of bullets.

No bullets here; but it was still pretty ugly.

I said: 'And what exactly are you lot up to?'

'Speaking up for England,' he panted. 'The real England — not the Americans' lap-dog.'

'Americans?'

A police car came squeezing along like a sniffer dog in search of further prey. The boy ducked even lower. Then there was a peremptory blast of horns ahead. Police were directing the lorries out and round the roundabout; and at last we were all moving forward, gaining speed.

'Who else d'you think's been training those goons? Strong-arm tactics. Smashing up a peaceful demonstration.'

'Demonstrating against what?'

'Don't you read the papers? Not enough for them to build up Menwith and Fylingdales. Now they want to reopen the old air base at Skelmerby. Dragging their filthy weaponry across the country, all so we can be forced to play their bloody stupid Star Wars games. Strategic Defense Outworks — that's what they call it. And with an 's' in Defense, as well. Even have to kow-tow to American spelling.'

'Is there somewhere I can put you down?'

'And what's our government doing? Stopping them? Not bloody likely. Letting us be dragged into their grab at Iraqi oil. Yes, please, do come into our own country while you're at it. Bring your tracking devices and anything else you like. Make yourself at home. Put your missiles down wherever you want. I ask you, though — why should we be the front line of their defence?'

There was a sign for a service station half a

48

mile ahead. I swung into the lane, dumped him outside the Little Chef, and was on my way again.

★   ★   ★

Our offices and depot in Hesketh-le-Street were in a converted woollen mill above the stream. Walter Hebden lived in a house in Gallowgate built into the walls of an old monastery overlooking the stream from the town side. Like its neighbours, it had oddly angled rooms set into the heavy stone walls during Victorian times when the building had been a training college for Anglican clergy. Purists had several times tried, with the backing of conservation groups, to force the local council to strip out the living quarters and restore the walls as they would have been in the days of the Prince Bishops of Durham; but others said they were such charming relics of the Victorian era, their doors and phoney mullion windows wreathed with creeper, that they too were of historic value. Inside, the sitting-room was dominated by a large illuminated fish tank. Walter invariably sat in a stained leather armchair which creaked with every slight movement he made. At his left hand, a miner's lamp converted into an electric table lamp stood on a stumpy wooden table. He insisted on still having an open coal fire, with a large brass coal scuttle, though since his wife died the house had somehow taken on a permanent chill.

He took my bag from me and put it in the spare bedroom, where there was always one of my spare suits and a selection of shirts and underwear in the wardrobe. I apologized for the delay in getting here, but was only halfway through explaining what had happened when he burst out: 'Bloody demos. Been going on for bloody weeks. Mucking up our van deliveries, slowing things doon. Causing trouble all the time, man. One of the exhibitors at the fair still hasn't got some of his stuff through because they're bobbing up on every back road you can think of. Bloody pests. Not that I've got any time for the Yanks. Not after them turnin' doon our offer of supplies.'

The widely spaced, unobtrusive return of Americans to the Cold War air bases they had quit not that many years before had seemed at first to augur well for local business. But they were refusing to deal with local suppliers. Only their own people were allowed through the gates.

'An' still they call us their Allies.' Walter snorted. 'All good marrers when it comes to bashing the hell out of the Iraqis. How much further do we have to go? Allies — or just yes-men handing over chunks of oor own country to make sure nowt drops on *their* country.' He sounded like my young passenger down the road. 'Using us when it suits them, but offering us nowt in return. Every damn thing flown in from the States. Food, drink, the lot. Offer to supply 'em, and you're just brushed away. The waste of it!'

The Trade Fair was held in another old mill, restored as a local community and conference centre. It had a terrace jutting out above the old mill lade, with tables which by the mid-morning were cluttered with pint glasses lined with clinging froth. A couple of glasses had been knocked over into the rancid water below, to join a consignment of lager cans and sodden catalogues.

Barry was fussing in and out, doing deals or failing to do them, buying hopeful prospects a drink and in between his brief campaigns nipping out to the terrace to finish a pint and add his glass to the growing array of empties.

He bustled over to join Walter and myself at our stand just as a lean man with iron-grey hair crisply *en brosse* headed towards us after studying the Scottish and Newcastle Breweries display. His American accent made Walter bristle immediately.

51

'Now which of you gentlemen would be Mr Craig and which Mr Hebden?'

Before either of us could speak, Barry chimed in. 'Barry Quirke, sales manager. And this, sir, is Mr Walter Hebden, and *this* is Mr Craig Sinclair Craig. Mr Craig Craig, actually.'

'Great. A great pleasure to make your acquaintance, gentlemen.' There was a tangle of shaking hands. His grip was firm and comradely — and would be just as calculatedly sincere and comradely for everybody else, I felt. 'And I'm Foster Keating. Of Buywise Trading Incorporated. I reckon you'll have heard of us?'

We had indeed. Rumours of their movement into the British market-place had been surfacing at intervals in the trade press. In alliance with Czech and Polish brewers and distillers, they declared their intention of setting up a more flexible and even larger operation than the big Anglo-Belgian-Scottish combines. Interbrew had long been threatening to dominate the market, but Buywise, with its own chain of supermarket and restaurant outlets, proclaimed that there was still great scope for a more tightly integrated yet adjustable corporate plan.

'For ourselves,' Keating was going on earnestly, 'we are hiving off our wine interests and traditional bottlings in favour of developing own-name brands for supply to our own main outlets. Means higher margins and higher return on capital. A guaranteed market, guaranteed quantities. And we could fit your organization neatly into that scenario. Take some of the methodology off your hands. I think we're ideally positioned to do business together.'

'I divven think so,' growled Walter.

'For our mutual benefit, Mr Hebden? And with our contacts' — he lowered his voice coaxingly — 'there's a strong possibility that this would give us — give *you* — an entrée to the American military bases in this country.'

'Now you're talking,' said Barry.

'I guess you've been just a bit irritated by some of the restrictions our military folk have been imposing on . . . well, what you might call outside catering, right?'

'Too right,' I said. Walter muttered something to himself.

'But with a strong American element in your company, there'd be ways of getting round that. I'm telling you, gentlemen — we already know there'll be an opening. We do have our contacts.'

'All run from America?' grunted Walter.

'An association of equals, Mr Hebden. With a healthy influence in every outlet.

Fingers on any number of pulses.'

'Globalization,' said Barry eagerly. 'You know, we do have to go along with it nowadays. Either go along with it or get swallowed up whether we like it or not.'

Foster Keating beamed. 'Well put, Mr . . . er . . . Quick.'

'Quirke. Barry Quirke.'

'Mr Quirke. But *quick* on the uptake, huh? Yes. Look, why don't we all get together later and talk this through? Or you talk it over and then make contact, and we'll sit down and thrash it out between us. Put our cards on the table — both of us. Not playing a game of poker or anything underhand. Make it a date soon, right?'

Keating's gaze strayed for a moment, appraising the neighbouring displays and a distant banner.

When he had gone, Barry said: 'It's got to be a good idea, you know. Otherwise we get squeezed out altogether.' He tried a solicitous family line. 'You know, Pa' — I had never heard him address his father-in-law this way before — 'you won't want to go on forever. That osteoarthritis of yours isn't getting any better, is it?'

'I can still get around to the places I need. And I'm in no mood to see our company colonized by the Yanks.'

54

Barry realized this was no time to pursue the matter. He waved to an imaginary acquaintance and bustled off. I had a hunch that he would contrive to bump into Mr Keating again.

Abruptly Walter said: 'Do you think our Rhona's Barry is reliable?'

'He's got a good salesman's technique.'

'But as a director of the firm? I divven na. If I was to stand down and let these take-over boys in, they'd run rings round him. Fleece him. And then finish the firm off when they've taken what they need.'

'Asset-stripping?'

'Why, aye. Sounds like what I've read.' He eyed me warily. 'And just what was that recent business between you and him? There *was* something, wasn't there? Not that I blame you for not wanting him around.'

I was saved by an old friend, a retired master brewer, coming up and pumping Walter's hand, then plunging right into some mutual reminiscences.

As I made a move towards the bar, I found the American already there as if, having finished with Barry, he had been waiting for me.

'Mr Craig. Like to try one of our liqueurs?'

'No, thanks. I'm a wine or malt man myself.'

'Mr Craig. I realize your older partner is
. . . well, shall we say he's getting just a bit old
for this sort of market? I do think, though,
that *you* ought to think seriously about your
future. *Very* seriously.' It sounded almost like
a threat. As we parted, he gave me one of his
earnest handshakes. 'I'd appreciate it if you'd
give me a bell when . . . well, let's say when
you're ready. OK?'

When the Fair was over, with no sign of
Barry on the premises, I collected my bag
from Gallowgate and thanked Walter as usual
while he gripped my hand affectionately as if
he needed to be sure of having someone on
his side.

'Haven't called in on Rhona this time,' I
apologized. 'Give her my regards. And the
family.'

Walter snorted. 'Jason and Jasmine. What
sort of names are those for kids?'

★   ★   ★

Back in our Blackfriars office I spent a couple
of hours going through a sheaf of faxes and
e-mails. Once upon a time you could read
through letters and orders and sort things out
at a reasonable pace. Nowadays if you don't
respond to a fax or an e-mail within fifteen
minutes, the sender's on the phone asking if

you've received his message, and if so, why haven't you come up with an answer? I dealt with a complaint about one of our delivery men, one about some corked wines — which I knew was a con trick but which wasn't worth contesting — and an approach from a small grocery chain querying a deal offered them by Barry Quirke.

Just as I was contemplating going out for a quick lunch, the phone rang. I nearly waved through the glass to Diana that I didn't want to take it; but I weakened and picked it up.

Diana said: 'There's a Mrs Leith on the line. Do you want to speak to her, or shall I say you've just left?'

Mrs Leith? A fraction of a second when I didn't remember the name. Then I conjured up a picture of that casque of dark hair and the gleam of bronze in those disconcerting eyes.

And I was eager to pick up the phone and hear that level, faintly amused voice again.

She said: 'Craig? Mr Craig — or was it just Craig?'

'Just Craig,' I said. 'Frances?'

'I wanted to apologize for that silly thing I said the other evening. I didn't mean it to sound that cheap.'

'I don't remember anything particu-larly — '

'Saying I was available. It must have sounded so tawdry.'

'I realized it was only a joke.'

'That's sweet of you. But . . . look, would you care to come round for a bite to eat one evening? I'm tired of cooking for myself, and I don't fancy eating on my own in these tinpot restaurants round here. And I don't care to be picked up halfway through a dismal plate of penne by some prowling chancer.'

Even as I said yes and we agreed on the following evening at seven, I was wondering what had prompted her to ring me. And I went on wondering after I had put the phone down. Why on earth should she think it necessary to go to the trouble of finding my number — finding it from the business pages of the directory, or from Barry? I hoped it wasn't the latter. Ringing me to apologize for an inconsequential remark about being available, and then asking me out with the implication that she was in fact available and fancied some non-committal entertainment? Or just to show that she could offer me a civilized evening without being available?

Either way, I wasn't reluctant to find out.

She could be murder, that one.

It's a phrase I've often thought back on.

3

Frances Leith was wearing a silk shirt in a shade of terracotta which seemed to run on into the rusty red of her velvet slacks. As she held the door open for me to pass her, she gave off that faint yet intense musky smell I remembered from that previous moment in this same doorway. She closed the door very quietly, and her dark brown mules made no sound along the polished floor as she followed me into the sitting-room.

It was in fact a sitting-room cum diner, with a two-leaf table opened up and laid for two against one wall. She waved me towards the beige leather couch dominating the opposite wall, and poured me a large Lagavulin. Obviously she had made a mental note of what Barry had bought me the other evening. When she had poured herself a vodka and tonic, she came and sat beside me. Even without touching me she exuded a startling warmth: not the heat of sweaty exertion, or of a recent hot bath, but a natural physical glow.

'How are you filling in the time?' she asked. 'Finding it heavy on your hands, now and then, when you're . . . well, wondering what to do next?'

'I've got plenty to think about. Regarding the firm. And listening to music.'

'Watching telly?'

'Hardly ever. And you?'

She prodded a slice of lime against the side of her glass and squeezed it with her forefinger. 'I've been treating myself to the theatre. Toby could never sit still for more than ten minutes in a theatre. Always looking round as if there might be an influential cabinet minister in the stalls. Or a journalist who could report his interest in serious drama.'

'So you've been having a wallow?'

'Rather a disappointing one. Last night it was supposed to be a comedy. A fashion model adjusting to marriage to a minor duke. I don't think the author had ever met even a minor viscount, and the actress gave a better performance at the curtain calls than during the play. In the story she was meant to have a lot to learn, but she really ought not to have needed to learn walking across the stage. That woman could never have been on a real catwalk in her life.'

'Is this the image consultant giving a professional opinion?'

'Oh, dear. I do give myself away, don't I?

Please steer me off any of that nonsense for this evening, anyway.'

'Just what is this image consultancy business? It's a new one on me.'

She was studying me in just the way she had studied me that evening with Barry and Rhona. Her lips parted very slightly as if reluctant to smile. I wondered if she knew how sensual they were.

'I'll tell you one thing. You're in no need of it.' She got up and walked towards the door. 'Must just see how things are in the galley. Ten minutes, I think.' She nodded towards the bottle of Vouvray in a cooler on top of the cocktail cabinet. 'Can I leave you to take care of that?'

While she was in the kitchen I made a brief study of the surroundings. A painting of a naked woman, made up of a mosaic of tiny lozenges in mauve, green, orange and mother-of-pearl, was too large for the narrower end of the room. Pretentious and rather silly — not her sort of thing at all. A coffee table with a tinted glass top had three or four art books laid out on the rack below in carefully casual fashion so that there should be no hint of vulgar display. The couch I was sitting on was too large for the room and too deep for comfort. Behind it, the maroon wallpaper was incongruous. But then, Frances was only occupying the place while her friend was away, so there was nothing here to define her own tastes.

When she came back, she caught me contemplating the curlicues on the door of the cocktail cabinet. 'No,' she said, 'I don't think I'll want to stay here too long. Hilary's tastes don't quite match mine.'

Where, I wondered, did she fancy going next?

We had a spinach roulade with mushroom filling for starters, followed by scallops on a bed of creamed potatoes. Halfway through the main course she said, as if to tidy up any loose ends: 'Of course, Toby and I have a flat in Pimlico as well as our place in Alderthorpe. But it's a pretty soulless little dump.'

'And you're not going back there?'

'Probably not. And you're not going back to Deepwood or wherever?'

It was an odd question. Not *Are you thinking of going back to your wife?*, a subject which had at least been mentioned between us, but in effect *Are you thinking of going back into the Army?*, a background of which she surely knew nothing.

'I've done my time,' I said. 'Served my sentence. And had my fill of it.'

'I wouldn't have thought they'd have

wanted to let you go. And nowadays, aren't there all these private defence groups crying out for trained officers?'

'Mercenaries,' I said.

There was a silence while she waited for me to expand on that theme. I broke it by asking how she had come to meet Rhona. At school, as I'd guessed. Walter Hebden had insisted his daughter went to a place where she would meet posh people and pick up their manners and mannerisms, even while he continued to detest them.

'And this Hilary was one of your chums there, too?'

The tip of her tongue dabbed at her lower lip. 'No.' It could have been a gentle taunt, knowing what I was angling for. 'And your friends? And your job? I've only met Barry a couple of times, and he makes it all sound very grand but isn't too good on the details.' Her eyes were sizing me up, and she seemed to make a decision and then relax, her voice becoming a languid purr. 'You're a wine connoisseur, the man who sets the standards, while Barry's the eager work-horse whose sheer energy keeps the whole thing rolling along.'

'A bit of an over-simplification. I like the job because I like good wine and I like other people to like it. But as far as the business itself goes, I'm a bit of a work-horse too. Or at any rate a hard-worked shipping clerk.'

'And your wife?' Here it came at last, the inevitable subject between a man and woman tentatively sparring with each other. 'She's been an enthusiastic partner in the business? Or just a loyal spouse in the background?'

Her glass was almost empty. I refilled it to give myself time to wonder how much I should confide, or how much I should dodge.

'We muddled along, the way people do,' I hedged. 'Until the muddle became too claustrophobic.'

Still she didn't ask whether I thought of going back. I wondered whether to take my turn and ask about her husband, but as if to counterbalance her own questions about Maureen and get the subject out of the way, she said of her own accord: 'Toby has his city job as well as his seat in the Commons, of course. To keep him busy in the mornings.'

'Something in a big advertising agency?'

'Nothing so demanding. He's an invest-ment bankruptcy adviser.'

'Sounds impressive.'

'Nice work if you don't mind getting your hands dirty. Not by lifting heavy weights or twisting words and phrases. Just twisting figures. Simply wait for someone to get into financial trouble and then get them into an

even worse financial state by charging over the odds to get them out of it.'

'I hope I'll never need that kind of advice.'

'I fancy you make your own decisions. And stick with them.'

Yes, I had been accused of that more than once, especially by senior officers who hadn't meant it as a compliment.

Over coffee we sat in a companionable silence. Nothing awkward about it. When there was something to say, I was sure it would be said. Somehow we were in a comfortable suspension where time was standing still, waiting for one of us to make a move.

I suggested that I give a hand with the washing up. No. She would stack it all in the dishwasher. I gave her a hand to load the dishwasher. As we stooped and loaded, she brushed against me, and I saw that her nipples had hardened and were rasping against the silk of her shirt. And when she stood up I realized that not merely was she not wearing a bra, but that almost certainly she wasn't wearing anything else underneath.

So it was up to me to make the move. Leaving the kitchen, I took a stray step towards the closed door beside the sitting-room door.

'No,' she said. 'Not in there. I haven't made the bed yet.'

It didn't seem like her. She wasn't the sort to leave a bed unmade until this time of the evening. But I took the opportunity and said: 'All the better. You won't have to make it twice in one day.'

She could still have shrugged that off as a distasteful hint too far. Instead, she led the way back into the sitting-room. At the couch she turned to face me. Her whole body seemed to have slumped an inch or so, as if waiting to collapse very slowly and gently. Her lips were parted again — slack, quivering very slightly.

I said: 'Fran.' It was the first time I had used that name. It sounded too familiar on such a short acquaintance; but I knew now that familiarity was going to be all right. I touched her cheeks with the fingertips of both hands, and tried it again: 'Fran.'

She was trembling. 'Craig, you . . . somebody's giving off electricity. You or me?'

'Must be a loose connection.'

'Better make it tighter.'

The depth of the couch made it more comfortable than I would have expected, but one of its arms twisted us into a position so complicated that we both began laughing, and the laughter grew hoarse and more and more steadily rhythmic. Suddenly she grabbed me by the hair and dragged my head back so that she could stare into my eyes as she nibbled me deep down and then tightened to bite deep inside. And all the time she was talking with those hidden, greedy lips, the mouth I could see was quite calm, and her eyes contemplative rather than demanding. Then she turned her head away, dug her nails into my back, and we both laughed and gasped in fierce unison.

Afterwards she disentangled herself, climbed over me with a graceful flick of those legs that I was reluctant to let slide away. I tried to pull her back, but she calmly drew clear and stood up. It was a briefly awkward movement. For a moment I glimpsed the odd twist of her left hip, then she was pulling her slacks and shirt on and running her hands over her hair to smooth it down. I began collecting my scattered clothes and putting them back on. As we collided against the end of the couch, I kissed her. Her response was no more than cool and mildly affectionate.

'I enjoyed that. We must do it again sometime.' Her tone was that of a polite hostess arranging a bridge party.

I said: 'The sooner the better. I can give you a hand with making the bed. And with getting breakfast.'

'I'm not very good at breakfasts.'

'All right, I'll go hungry. Apart from — '

'No, Craig. Another time, yes, but . . . well, when it suits us.' She was tidily plumping up a cushion on the couch where she had so recently been so ravenous. 'Care for a drink before you go?'

When it suits us — or did she mean 'When it suits *me*?'

There was a smidgen of wine left in the bottle. We shared it, and I said: 'Come and have dinner with me tomorrow?'

'No, I don't think . . . no, not tomorrow.'

'Thursday?'

'I'll think about it.'

'Think about it now.' And I added: 'I do have a reasonably sized bed, and I promise it'll be made up properly.'

Her frown was no more than a tremor of fine lines across her forehead, still faintly moist. 'Craig, I can't bear anyone being too possessive.' She looked full at me as if wanting to see if she could shock me. 'I do have appetites, and every now and then I like them to be satisfied. It doesn't mean I want to be served by the same waiter every time.'

'But Thursday?'

She laughed wonderingly. 'You didn't hear what I said, did you?'

'I did, but I'd like to think your appetite for this particular dish hasn't been sated all at one go. So . . . Thursday?'

'I'll have to think about it.'

I went back to my own bed and lay awake hoping she was thinking about me as intensely as I was thinking about her.

But would her thoughts become as tangled as mine? Why should these awkward, vague questions start nagging at me? It had all happened so quickly, and yet there had been those moments when she seemed not to want it to continue — or not to happen at all. Yet she had been ready for me, ready to be swiftly naked for me. And that odd question about going back to Deepcut — why should that keep fidgeting at the back of my mind?

And had I really been so desirable? Worth preparing an evening for, and dressing — by no means over-dressing — for the occasion?

Stop arguing. Most men would be happy to believe that of themselves, with such a beautiful creature responding the way she did.

But first go off? And just for a one-off?

Why should that matter? Be grateful. Why argue?

★   ★   ★

On the Wednesday morning there was an urgent message from Deben Head. George Goffin had reported an accident near the new building projects around the old airfield. One of our delivery lorries had been hit by a 5-ton truck, severely enough to dislodge cases of wine and smash bottles all over the road. It was surprising that half the population wasn't there, down on their knees.

I rang him back. 'Georgie, you can cope? The usual routine.'

'I think you'd better come down, Mr Craig.'

It wasn't the first time we'd had an accident on one of the byroads, making a delivery to Snape Maltings during the music festival or some sponsored weekend. Little Georgie Goffin was a first-rate transport manager who knew everybody and everything in the region. It was unlike him to need me down there personally.

'There's something fishy about it,' he said. 'Some bossy type calling himself a liaison officer says he's got to talk to somebody in authority.'

'As far as I'm concerned, Georgie, you have all the authority that's needed.'

'He won't talk to me. Says I'm not to do anything about any insurance claim, or reporting to the police, or discussing any

70

details with anybody until he's had a word with' — his slow Suffolk voice tightened with offence — 'someone *in authority*.' He drew a deep breath. 'There's something fishy about it,' he repeated.

After I had rung off, Diana was on the line. 'Mrs Leith calling,' she said, 'again.' Through the glass she looked as impassive as usual, but I thought I detected a quiver of curiosity in her voice.

Frances said: 'Craig. I thought I'd accept that date for tomorrow. If the offer's still on.'

'Tomorrow? Oh, damn it. Thursday's tomorrow, isn't it? Something's cropped up. I've got to go down to our depot to sort out a spot of bother.'

'The story of my life, you might say. Business always raising its ugly head just when one is . . . thinking of something more interesting.'

I saw that Diana had left her switchboard to fetch a drink from the machine. 'Look, could we switch it to Friday? Or maybe I can wrap the whole thing up and get back by tomorrow evening — '

'Why don't I come down with you?' she said unexpectedly, even quite eagerly. 'I can do with a day out in the country. And you can show me some of your background. Man at work, that sort of thing.'

71

'And tell me how to improve my image?'

'I've no criticisms so far.'

'Look, the business shouldn't take me too long. I do know a quite agreeable hotel on Felixstowe seafront. We use it for business visitors. A bit square, but it's comfortable enough.'

I half expected a hesitation, while she turned over the implications. Instead she said: 'Separate rooms?'

'That doesn't sound very inviting.'

'Twin beds, then.' So calm and cautious, unlike the wild thing I'd had difficulty holding steady in my arms. Was she playing the image consultant, even at this time of day fashioning her own image to disguise what she was really like underneath?

'That's not madly romantic, either,' I said.

'Better for recuperation. Getting one's breath back.'

'To get your breath back, you need some exertion first.'

She laughed. 'All right, where do we meet?'

I thought of just where and how our bodies would meet, and I was impatient to get this day over and done with, and on to tomorrow.

Unexpectedly she rang back an hour later.

'Glad I've caught you in. I thought I'd better swot up the background of where we're going, so I've just been skimming a tourist brochure for the region. There does seem a rather nicely isolated place called the Old Manor House Hotel. Rather took my fancy. Do you know it?'

'I know of it, yes.' A hazy memory drifted back, and I thought what a hell of a coincidence. All I could say was: 'You'd prefer that?'

'You sound a bit dubious. Something you don't like about the place?'

'No, not at all. If you think it sounds preferable, fine. I'll make a booking.'

'Just that it sounds more inviting than a busy seafront.'

'Let's accept that invitation, then.'

Coincidence, yes. But that one previous occasion had been a nothingness. A long-forgotten date with Lisa which had come to nothing.

It wasn't going to be like that this time.

4

George Goffin was a small but tough, wiry man whose father and grandfather had been fishermen. Two of his brothers had followed the family tradition, but after the drowning of her husband and both boys in their own boat, Georgie's mother had insisted that her youngest found himself a job that would never take him closer to the sea than Felixstowe docks and eventually our Deben Head wharf. Georgie had gone almost bald in his thirties, with only three strands of hair like thin tarred rope to drag across the top of his head. His face was as dark as a walnut, weather-beaten as if he were still out on the North Sea with his brothers, and he had that stubborn jut of jaw which anywhere along the Suffolk coast would provoke the grunted confirmation, 'Oh, he's a Goffin all right.' Even at his most cheerful he had an evil grin, as if always expecting the worst and enjoying the prospect. He was utterly loyal and utterly reliable. His twisted grin grew even more crooked as the years went by, due to his reluctance to spend money at a dentist's: when a tooth grew wobbly he would tie one end of a piece of string to it and the other end to the knob of an open door, and then slam the door.

When Fran and I arrived, he looked disconcerted for a moment. He was uneasy in the presence of any woman. He had never married. Whether he looked after his widowed mother to a greater extent than she looked after him was the subject of regular jokey debates in local pubs. But anyway there were just the two of them in their council house. I sensed now that he didn't approve of Fran being here. In spite of his awkwardness he had been amiable towards Maureen on the only occasion they had met. She had been in one of her most winsome moods as she condescended to visit the warehouse with me for a staff Christmas party, and somehow latched on to Georgie. Afterwards she told me that she had always had this instinctive affinity with real working-class people, and ought really to have considered an executive career. She was convinced that she would have made a wonderful personnel manager.

Fran could have lounged around in the hotel while I sorted out the situation, but she had made it clear that she wanted to be shown round our operations rather than just mark time.

'And charge us a consultation fee for

suggesting improvements to our image?'

'I'll promise to keep very demure and respectful.'

George would have been the ideal guide, if a somewhat taciturn one, but I needed to listen to what he had to tell me.

'Young Pennington,' he suggested. 'He's good with the chat.'

True enough. There had been an awkward incident between Archie Pennington and the wife of a pub landlord outside Framlingham, but I didn't imagine Fran would have any difficulty coping with him. Might even offer him some advice on his image, which at present was too crudely on the macho side.

When we were alone, George said: 'Our driver's out of hospital. Sid Carter. And we've been told to tell him to say nothing until there's been a full inquiry.'

'A police inquiry?'

'They want to avoid that if possible.'

'Who the hell are *they*?'

'Something to do with the development company. You know, all that stuff about a theme park and shopping centres. Blust, you'd think we were going to get a whole new city round here.'

Of course I knew what there was to know so far about the proposed theme park. The local newspaper had been full of it for months, and we had been deluged with glossy handouts and copies of planning applications for our information and, it was hoped, approval. Theme parks were all the rage nowadays. Here some entrepreneurial group was planning to buy up the remains of an old airfield and transform it into an open-air museum of coastal history — of which there was plenty around these parts. Invading Angles, the Dutch wars, Martello towers, the secret radar research on Orford Ness, American bases during World War II and during the Cold War. And it was all to be done in conjunction with a supermarket and a couple of restaurants — one smart, one self-service. Plans for a large filling station and supermarket on the main feeder road had aroused predictable opposition from local traders, but planning permission had gone through. An exhibition in Debenbridge Town Hall included a video showing the layout of the accompanying supermarket, together with diagrams and models of three exhibition halls along the perimeter of the old runways. Somewhere in the background was an American adviser trained in Disneyland but, it was reported, with a history degree from Princeton. I had found some of the hype a bit puzzling. Was the catchment area really large enough? To me it had seemed from the start that the whole scheme was too ambitious, yet it was all going through with remarkable speed.

'That Mr Agnew from the development company visited Sid in hospital and told him not to worry, they didn't want to bring any charges. Provided he didn't talk to anybody else about what had happened.'

'Particularly if the blame was on their side anyway. What do the police have to say about it?'

'They've been told that no charges have been made so far by either side, so they aren't taking any action yet.' George leaned across the stack of invoices on his desk and lowered his voice, although there was nobody else in the office. 'One of them containers that rolled off. It had a skull and crossbones. Warning about poison, right?'

'Usually is.'

'And then there were letters and a number. I only saw them upside-down, but I think they were FX213. Or it might have been — '

'One letter wrong,' I said, 'and one digit missing. But I think I can guess where that came from.'

He waited, expectant. But although I knew he was too reliable to go in for gossip, I didn't fancy revealing something quite that alarming to him. The contents of that canister were poison all right. Lethal stuff. Possibly a left-over from the Pentagon's chemical warfare plant at Fort Detrick in Maryland. But why had it ever got here?

'Was the canister full or empty, d'you know?' I asked.

'Couldn't say. But it looked heavy enough.' The internal phone on his desk began buzzing. He picked it up, and nodded at me. 'I told their Mr Agnew what time you'd be here to see him. Right on the dot.'

Agnew was a lean, bony man with the sallow face and bleakly appraising eyes of an Inland Revenue inspector. Even at first glance you were sure that if he smiled it would only be after he had pulled a fast one on you. His charcoal grey suit was immaculate, without the slightest sign of a crease or stain, and the knot of his dark blue tie sat perfectly shaped, perfectly centred.

'Mr Goffin.' It was no more than a coolly polite acknowledgement of their earlier contact, and made it clear that he was not going to indulge in any further conversation until George was out of the room.

Then he held out his hand to me. 'Martin Agnew.' His grip was firm and confident. Too calculatedly reassuring. 'Captain Craig.'

'Not any longer,' I said. 'Not for quite some time, in fact.'

'No, but we still think of you in that light.'

'We?'

It turned out that he did not represent the development company — nor the Inland Revenue — but was from the Ministry of Defence, liaising with the US from the days of their Cold War occupation of Heathwaters airfield and its mysterious silos. He rattled the information off in staccato fashion as if reciting cut-and-dried orders rather than explanations.

'An irritating business, this. I'm sorry we've had to drag you out here, but we wouldn't be happy dealing with anyone else.'

'Where exactly do you come into this?'

He winced slightly at this. I knew people like Agnew of old. They liked to stick to their briefing, not answer awkward questions. 'None of us would care for any misleading publicity over this incident. My masters' — at last he allowed himself a little grin of complicity, implying that we spoke the same arch jargon — 'want to clear up this awkward situation for our allies as tactfully as possible. Your man Goffin wanted to go straight ahead and report to the insurance company.'

'Quite right. The correct thing to do.'

'Yes, in the normal run of things. But in this case we'd prefer to settle matters without too many other factors involved. We don't want the incident to go to court. Dangerous driving, or anything like that.'

'Or carrying dangerous chemicals on the public highway?'

He took a hissing little breath. 'That's what we're afraid of. Somebody getting the wrong idea.'

'And what exactly would the right idea be?'

'Look, Captain . . . Mr . . . Craig. You know how one bit of gossip can be inflated out of all proportion. We've been trying to keep a low profile. Obviously I'll have to be honest with you, though.'

And obviously it would hurt. I waited.

At last he cleared his throat and said: 'Our driver was one of a number bringing things away from the site before the developers take over.'

'Things?'

'I'm sure that the MoD cleared this place of yours before letting you move in and convert it into a wine warehouse.'

'It was empty,' I agreed. 'And clean.'

'Just so. And we want to make sure the old Heathwaters complex is left just as good and empty.'

'Empty,' I suggested, 'of things which the public didn't guess were there in the first place?'

'You could put it that way, Mr Craig.

Rather cynical, though. Let's just say that it's a matter of getting rid of — ah — sensitive material which ought never to have been left there. Very slipshod. Crates and canisters rotting away in a couple of sheds. Probably safe enough by now, but we're taking no chances. A bit like mine-sweeping. Checking old underground fuel tanks. And the old silos for possible radioactivity. Tidying up the mess left over from a violent bit of history.'

'And meanwhile there's the little matter of tidying up the damage to our vehicle.'

'Yes, of course. And really, I'd like to make it clear that in return for your discretion we would be prepared to reimburse you for whatever damage was done. And to pay for any additional treatment your driver may need.'

'And bribe him to keep his mouth shut?'

'Glad we've had this meeting, Mr Craig. I think we understand one another.' With only the slightest change of tone to suggest a *quid pro quo*, something in return for his frankness, he said: 'While I'm here, I suppose there's no chance of my having a little conducted tour of your premises? I'd be fascinated to know exactly how you've adapted them.'

'I'm afraid there are strict rules regarding security in the bonded warehouse section.'

'Odd. I thought as I came in that I saw a young woman being escorted around the premises.'

'A consultant,' I said glibly. 'Offering us some technical advice on other aspects of our operation.'

'And those other aspects?'

'Sorry. Commercial confidentiality.' It was a glib phrase used by everybody nowadays. I had always regarded it as a cop-out, but for once I didn't see why I shouldn't join in the chorus.

His grudgingly assumed friendliness was ebbing. 'Of course. Like our friends at Heathwaters. You know, there are confidences you might profitably share with them. Once their complex is up and running, there could very well be some deal for your company to supply them with some of your produce. I'm sure you could reach an agreement. If everything goes smoothly.'

Meaning, I sensed, that the smoothness had to begin right now. And there was an odd echo of the approaches that had been made to the Hebdens and myself at that Trade Fair.

'So,' he went on, 'may I take it there'll be no awkward repercussions from that unfortunate collision, and we agree no further action is necessary?'

'I have a hunch that things would be made

difficult for us if I insisted on following normal legal procedures.'

'Hardly worth the hassle, is it?' He was on his feet, handing me a visiting card. 'Do send your claim for damages and any additional expenses to this department.' Casually he added: 'And how is your lady wife these days?'

'We're separated.'

'I'm sorry to hear that.'

I had a creepy feeling that this wasn't the first time he had heard it.

'Don't you ever feel sorry that you didn't sign on for an extended period?' he asked. 'You'd have been just the right sort of liaison for all the logistics involved in co-ordinating US and UK missile defence systems.'

'Star Wars?' I said. 'Dangerous kids' games played by retarded adults.'

'And you were never tempted by offers to lend your expertise to any of the PMFs? A lot of them have been making a fortune in Iraq. Better pay than the Army ever offers. I can't believe you weren't approached.'

So he knew that as well.

'Private Military Forces — mercenaries?' I said. 'Not my scene.'

'You prefer moving casks of booze around?'

'At least the Logistic Corps qualified me for that. And a lot of peaceful folk get a lot of pleasure as result.'

When George, who must have been watching from the warehouse floor, came in with a sullen expression which dared me not to tell him what was going on, I gave him a watered-down version. 'Simply removing old rubbish that ought not to have been left behind in the first place. Not wanting to let on in public that they were so negligent in the first place.'

'But that's not right,' said Georgie. 'The way I saw it, I don't think they was bringing things out. They was on their way in.'

★ ★ ★

At that moment the door was held open with a gallant flourish by Archie Pennington. It was difficult to make a sweeping gesture with a creaky old door like that one, but he managed it. Fran gave him a dazzling smile as she passed him.

Ten minutes later he was standing by the loading bay, pretending not to watch us. You couldn't blame him for feeling envious. She was so sleek and elegant in blue-striped shirt and dark blue slacks. He could only guess at what I knew: that within that smart austerity was yielding softness.

Driving away from our buildings, I asked

Fran what she had made of her conducted tour.

She said: 'If I were making a promotional film for you, we'd have to shovel all those scruffy overalls out of the way. And straighten out that bent logo above the loading bay. And we'd have to feature you as a steely-eyed executive running up charts and routes and sales figures on a computer, timing your vans and lorries every inch of the way, instead of chalking things up on a board in the warehouse. Only you're not like that, are you?'

'You think I ought to be?'

'I think you inspire great devotion in your staff.'

Then she put her head back and watched the landscape of the Suffolk saltings roll past.

I always enjoyed coming here. The sky seemed higher than anywhere else in the country, and the clouds more adventurous, sometimes scudding restlessly, sometimes piling up in great white sprawls, marred only by the sullen lump of Sizewell power station. I never got bored with the sight of ships coming in to Felixstowe or Deben Head, or the assured rhythm of container lorries rolling off, the swift marshalling of convoys. It was more rewarding than the embarkation or disembarkation of tanks, personnel carriers, and ration wagons. It could be especially heart-tugging at night, with the lights on every deck, the flags catching the light and flapping in and out of dark spots, accompanied by the build-up of throbbing engines.

Now, in daylight, once we had left the coast we were on a road where I always waited with keen anticipation for the long arc around one particular village green which appeared on so many picture postcards. The tall pole carrying the inn sign, creaking in the breeze which never quite ceased in these parts, was the axis of an almost too perfect scene of mown grass, tiny flowerbeds behind picket fences, and half-timbered cottages which yet never staled. The pub bought small but regular quantities of wine and individual casks of real ale from us. I usually stopped for a chat; but not today.

The Old Manor House Hotel had its own moat dug out of the heavy Suffolk clay. The stableyard had become a car park, from which a wooden bridge crossed the moat through an archway into an inner courtyard like that of some coaching inn, though in fact the whole building had gone through conversions from an early medieval grange to a Tudor hall-house and then a Georgian manor. One side of the building was still jettied and half-timbered, the main frontage narrow red brick.

There was no lift. We climbed a staircase magnificent enough for a house twice the size, to a bedroom with one double bed and a single bed under the window, overlooking a fringe of gardens along the edge of the moat. I studied Fran as she leaned against the end of the single bed, looking out. She looked cool and remote in that crisp shirt and dark blue slacks with their sharp crease. I was hungry for the nearness of her, eager to make a mockery of that remoteness.

Much hungrier than for the dinner, excellent as it was. The dining-room was mercifully free from the jangle and thud of the pop rubbish which seeps out of the woodwork in most places nowadays. Here the only sound was a quiet murmur of conversation and the click of knife against fork, spoon against crockery. Three middle-aged couples occupied the window tables. A young couple at the far end of the room kept reaching across the table to touch each other's fingertips, then looked archly around to see if they were being observed.

I felt almost as silly and besotted as the young man.

After coffee we strolled through the narrow garden and a few steps up on to the terrace. From one angle the wind shrilled faintly through my teeth. Then when I turned away from it, the lowering sun was too bright. We found a seat on a terrace tucked into an L-shaped wing to the west of the house, sheltered from the wind. There seemed no need to make conversation. We watched the clouded horizon begin to swallow the sun.

At last Fran said dreamily: 'You're so still.'

'You think we ought to be taking a brisk walk, or looking for a local disco?'

'Not what I meant, no. Just that there's a ... oh, a steadiness, a stillness, about you.' Her laugh hid an uncertainty I had not sensed in her before. 'It's so easy being with you.'

Easy? No challenge, nothing to disturb her — was that the best impression I could make?

'I'm sorry,' I said. 'I'd rather you felt all a-tremble when I'm around.'

Her hand strayed on to mine. Her fingertips did not so much stroke the back of my hand as press gently into it, communicating without words.

The sun had only just gone down, but it was time to go to bed.

At first she seemed cool, almost indifferent, as if waiting for me to prove something. But when she began laughing very quietly, I could feel the pulse of that laughter deep inside her as she nibbled and then clamped upon me, and all at once she was wide awake and greedy. No shrieks of phoney orgasm, but catches in her breath and an uncontrollable rhythm through her entire body.

Afterwards, lying wide awake, I stared at the ceiling. What was she really like? What did she really want — and for how long? It was all too easy. Nothing in life could ever be this simple and rewarding, with no strings, no problems.

Fran said drowsily: 'What are you thinking about?'

'You.'

'Don't let it keep you awake.'

But for a while it did keep me awake. Fretting with absurd half-formed suspicions again. Hadn't it all been too neatly planned and satisfying? Tidy. Almost, you might say, a cosy trap.

Oh, for crying out loud . . . who'd be stupid enough to argue over the pleasures I'd just tasted?

Just before dawn I woke, somehow aware in the uncertain light that I was being watched again. She had slid into the other bed and was lying on her side, looking thoughtfully at me. When she realized I was awake, before I could ask what she was thinking about she had slid from her bed and under my duvet, and her hand began making an insistent demand. She kicked the duvet off and climbed on to me, a pale ghost with pale breasts dancing in the beginnings of the morning light. But a very solid, demanding ghost.

At our last gasp she began breathing out a keening sound that was half singing, half a cry of long-held pain.

At breakfast she smiled amiably across the table like a long-married, unassuming wife. 'What's the programme for today?'

'Explore the countryside?'

Looking at her hand as she reached for her napkin, I thought how enticingly it had explored, such a short time ago.

On our way out, a man reading the morning paper looked up, stared, and looked away again. But somehow the back of my neck told me his gaze was following us as we went out into the sunshine.

'I had a feeling somebody there recognized you.'

She shrugged and took my arm. 'I can cope.'

'You don't think your husband might have set a private eye on to you, to get evidence for a divorce?'

'No,' she said, 'I don't.'

We drove around without any particular route in mind, turning our faces towards the wind off the sea, the tang in the air, the sense of isolation from the rest of the world. It was that isolation which had led to the whole area being chosen in wartime for secret activities so remote that nobody was likely to pick up shreds of information about what was going on.

Only once did I allow business concerns to intrude. We visited a vineyard near Framlingham and tasted two excellent Muller-Thurgaus. Just the sort of thing we could distribute through our retail outlets. The young man in charge of the shop was very keen, even though he complained how difficult it was to keep going. 'What other country taxes its own produce at the same rate as imports? And talks about free and fair competition while turning a blind eye to takeovers and destruction by the big boys?' It was a familiar moan. I took his vineyard leaflet and price list, and promised to be in touch.

As we drove away, Fran said: 'You find it everywhere now, don't you? Talented specialists waiting to be taken over or driven out of business. Doesn't it worry you, too?'

'I've fought worse battles.'

'What would it take to make you surrender?'

'Are you doing one of your character assessments on me?'

92

'I have to admit I'm becoming fascinated by you.'

'Good,' I said. 'Keep at it. I won't offer much resistance.'

We went into Debenbridge for lunch. There had once been a preponderance of American voices in the bar. Today some had apparently come back, maybe revisiting old haunts. They all had cameras slung round their necks, looking like tourists. Or making a big thing about looking like tourists. Why should I have thought that? The old prickly sensation in the back of the neck, instinctively wary, suspicious.

On our way out, we had to edge back over the narrow pavement to make way for a large van similar to the one that had hit our truck. It could have been heading towards the building site on the edge of the town.

Reluctantly turning back towards London, on impulse I made a slight detour around Heathwaters. Much of it was simply a long stretch of fencing enclosing a stretch of abandoned runway, with the humps of sunken silos along the perimeter. Two men in hard hats emerged from a squat brick building, looking up at a line of concrete wall. One was carrying a clipboard. Their heads turned to watch our car. I even had a momentary glimpse of what looked like a tiny camera being lifted below the clipboard. What was I getting so neurotic about? Old instincts playing up for no good reason.

We said hardly a word during the rest of the journey. There was no need to talk. But why should I still get this weird feeling that things were happening too fast, out of my control? I drove more slowly as we approached London — not because of the traffic, but because I was in no hurry to bring the day to an end.

When we stopped outside her block of flats, I was still in no mood to let her go. As I opened the passenger door for her and she brushed past, she gave me that sideways glance of hers, maybe not so much checking on me as on herself. Almost reluctantly she said: 'Care for a night-cap?'

I went in, and we made love again, and then she told me in a pedantic little voice that it was time for me to go home.

'I feel quite at home where I am,' I said.

'Home? I don't think so. Not here. This is just a . . . well, a sort of staging post.'

I wasn't sure whether she was applying that notion just to this flat or to our whole relationship.

'If you don't like it here,' I said, 'you know you can move in with me. In fact, I think that would be an ideal solution.'

'I don't think so. Far from it.'

I said: 'Fran, seriously — '

'No. Please, Craig, no. Seriousness is something I can do without.'

'But what's all this been about?'

'Pleasure. Isn't that enough? When I'm hungry, I like to be fed. But I thought I'd made it plain: it doesn't mean I want dinner, bed and breakfast with the same man every time.'

I tried to stop her reaching for a bathrobe, but she dodged away with the clear hint that I should leave while she went into the shower. Yet there was something in her face, something almost desperate, denying the airy remark she had just made.

I tried again. 'We do need to talk over what's happening to us.'

'No. No, Craig. Please don't get too intense. For your own sake.'

I drove back to my own flat and lay awake again, wondering, doubting, tossing and turning.

★ ★ ★

Next morning I rang Walter to report on the Deben Head incident. He heard me out, then said: 'Man, there's something going on, isn't there? Those two we met at the Trade Fair have shown up again. Pestering me. And just happening to bump into Barry again. Such a coincidence! And him so ready to listen.' His exasperated breath spluttered in the phone. 'But I can tell fine it's not Barry they're really after. It's you. You're the one they'll have to break down.'

'Who says I'm ready to be broken?'

'Not me, bonny lad.'

'But what gives you that impression, anyway?'

'I feel it in my bones. And don't laugh. That's what bones are for.'

Early in the evening I rang Fran's number. There was no reply. I thought I'd noticed that she had an answering machine, but she must have forgotten to switch over.

I tried again on the Sunday, and then on Monday morning from the office. Still no reply.

At home that evening I poured myself a stiff Caol Ila, and switched on the six o'clock news.

The main story was of two big clashes between demonstrators and police at Menwith Hill and near Alderthorpe in Lincolnshire. The Lincolnshire item led on to a doorstep interview with the MP for Alderthorpe, starting with a summary of the bare facts and then getting a bit more aggressive.

'And isn't it true, Mr Leith, that questions have been raised about a possible conflict of interests between your constituency duties and a retainer being paid to you by a leisure and catering group linked with American interests in this country?' Oh, dear, I thought. Another dreary cash-for-questions scandal. 'I believe tomorrow morning's papers are producing evidence of some hidden income from an undeclared directorship.'

'Newspaper gossip. I have declared any personal financial interests in the Parliamentary register in the usual way. None of them affect my Parliamentary work or my obligations to my constituents.'

'Not if these interests of yours threaten their own businesses?'

'Local suppliers will benefit from approaches I have made — perfectly proper approaches — to the United States authorities responsible for commercial and defence procurement in this country with a view to encouraging their purchase of food, drink and household goods locally rather than importing them from the States.'

'After which, the local suppliers will be taken over by an American-based chain, and the whole thing steamrollered through the Monopolies and Mergers Commission?'

Toby Leith tried a disparaging smile to

make it clear that the question was too tawdry for him to answer. He had a puffy, complacent face, and every word oozed sincerity like an after-shave moisturizer. But I noticed that even when bothering to trot out a glib answer to the interviewer's questions he was smirking at intervals without relevance to what was being said, and looking over the shoulders of passers-by. It reminded me of something Fran had said about him; and of something I had encountered before, when visiting my own MP at the House of Commons to discuss prohibitive rates of tax on home-produced wine — that very question raised in Suffolk. It was a tic acquired by all MPs: eyes forever straying, assessing passers-by, ready to wave at someone more important than oneself, ready to say, 'Ah, good afternoon, Minister' and to smile ingratiatingly.

Then on the screen Toby Leith did smile again and put out a hand to draw somebody closer to him.

There she was. Fran. Frances Leith. Mrs Toby Leith. Looking very cool and collected, every inch the perfect constituency wife.

So she was just that — the loyal little wife who had decided to abandon what she called her sabbatical, and go back to her husband?

5

I usually looked forward to my trips to the Dordogne, but this time I had only half my mind on the job. And for once I wasn't immediately cheered by the sight of Jean-Pierre's broad smile cracking that sun-varnished face of his.

I was supposed to be concentrating on the quality of last year's bottling now ready, and discussing new terms for our contract with the vineyard. Instead, part of my mind was fretted by questions about Frances Leith. I had to dismiss them. And her. Get her out of my mind. She was obviously not worth the trouble.

But she was haunting me. Travelling with me, distracting me.

I tried to make the most of the glass which Jean-Pierre handed me the moment we were in his *chai* — a ritual which never varied.

Ten years ago, Jean-Pierre Vaillant had established an estate of Viognier vines some twenty kilometres southwest of Bergerac, in the teeth of warnings from his confrères that the *terroir* was not suitable for this notoriously temperamental grape. Only the immediate neighbourhood of Condrieu away to the east could hope to produce the real thing. Vignerons world-wide had already refuted this with some success, and Jean-Pierre's own defiance had produced a classic varietal, a white wine of aromatic beauty which we had little difficulty in selling throughout Britain. The only complaint we ever had was that there wasn't enough to go round. He had been a pioneer of ageing his wine in small oak barriques rather than the more familiar large foudres; and again, after an agonizing wait, had proved successful.

I dipped my nose into the glass, gave the deep golden wine its ritual swirl, and was rewarded with a bouquet of peaches and apricots. 'Mm. A gem.'

'The bouquet of such a wine is more appealing than the odour of a woman, yes?'

I was in no mood for such olfactory comparisons right at this moment. 'That depends.'

'Ah, I think you are in love, Craig?'

'Nothing of the sort.'

His sun-cracked lips puckered sympathetically. 'But I see it. I see you *are* in love. A pity. It can destroy one's palate. But' — he refilled our glasses — '*bonne chance, mon ami.*'

Some ten years earlier Jean-Pierre had begun the clearance known as biodynamie, cleansing the soil of the Vaillant Frères vineyards of residual fertilizers and weedkillers in order to concentrate on uncontaminated organic wine from his cherished Viognier rootstock. His neighbours might prefer to use clones — vines selected and laboratory-bred from one parent vine, giving greater scope for blending into a reliable uniformity. One vigneron had once been proud of his Sauvignon, with its bouquet of gooseberries and nettles, but in recent years had fallen for the blandishments of the 'flying winemakers' — the technically accomplished Australians whose skills as industrial chemists produced larger outputs and a bland standard flavour which the supermarkets and chain stores favoured. This sort of thing was not for Jean-Pierre.

But now he was beginning to get apprehensive. Sitting on the little bench beside the table in that favourite little cellar of his — and a familiar, favourite place of mine, too — he suddenly came out with it.

'You know they are coming here now? They — how you put it? — are closing in. The big ones. The . . . you say *congloméré* . . . ?'

'Conglomerate, yes. Spreading out their tentacles — '

'That is it. *Exactement.*'

I spoke reasonably demotic French and

enjoyed the resonance of it in my head. Equally, Jean-Pierre prided himself on his English and would insist on battling with surprising flourishes of colourful phrases and equally surprising stumbles. But in any language this story we were contemplating was too familiar. The group which threatened him owned a gin distillery, three whisky distilleries, a rum franchise, a best-selling fizzy drink, and a make of sweet biscuits. They were linked through a holding company to Buywise, the folk who had been pestering us at the trade fair. Coincidence? Not much of a coincidence, really. There were only two or three big groups in the world by now, fighting it out between themselves, grabbing what they could here, or undermining what they found awkward there.

'And what is it they know of a living wine? A living, changing wine?'

'They don't want a living, changing wine,' I agreed sadly. 'Given the chance, they'd make a blend of your wine with a Chardonnay from that computerized winery over the hill.'

'Blend? They blend my wine? And call it . . . what?'

'Your guess is as good as mine.'

We had both been long aware of the onslaught of branded wines whose names the customer would recognize: wines which would not be expensive to produce, mechanically planted, pruned, and harvested. Such product usually lacked the desired acidity, but that was added in the form of tartaric acid, usually imported from China.

'Homogenization,' I said. It came out like a swear-word. 'Aussies flying all over the place, making sure everything which might be awkwardly distinctive is smoothed out. They'll soon be giving themselves some fancy name, such as international oenological consultants.'

'And my wine?' It was gnawing away at him. 'What will they call *my* wine?'

'Something stupid but easy to pronounce, I expect.'

'And it must all be hurried, *oui*? They know nothing of the hang time, especially with the finer old vines — how the vintage will improve as the grapes ripen slowly and gain in . . . in . . . '

'In complexity. No, the subtleties of the hang time, the long waiting time for fulfilment . . . no good for producers who go in for speed and quantity.'

High street buyers in my own country, I had to tell him, had already abandoned any idea of acquiring parcels of mature wine, and now had to work to financial imperatives laid down by their accountants, not even allowing for maturing at least some of it for connoisseurs or even for themselves.

'*Ici aussi, hélas.* Our friend Malraux over the hill, he now does well with the *négociants.* He mix his wines to make what the customer is told to like. And now he build a restaurant and a . . . ah . . . *un magasin de nouveautés.*'

'A gift shop. Souvenir shop. Yes, that's par for the course. And no doubt there'll be a handsome PR budget, and contacts who will deliver free samples to leading wine writers in the more influential newspapers and colour magazines.'

'For me, no. No, no. But . . . ' He gave a despairing shrug.

'But?' I prompted.

'How am I to live? To survive if I do not join them?'

'Jean-Pierre, we bash on just the way we've always done. There'll always be room for the small groups with the right product.' I spoke with more conviction than perhaps I felt. 'We offer quality rather than quantity. We'll survive.'

He gulped, and shook my hand fervently. Then we went on to discuss shipments in the coming months, as if everything was going on smoothly as before. Discussing the celebrations planned for his niece's wedding six weeks hence, we made this an excuse to open another couple of bottles. I spent an evening with the family, and we parted in the usual way with lots of kisses and hugs and good wishes all round.

But there was a cloud over it all, and it went on hanging over me as I headed for home.

★　★　★

Driving back from Heathrow, I made a short detour. Like any lovelorn adolescent, I slowed and stared up at the windows of Fran's flat.

It was early evening, and the street lights were just coming on. Was it the reflection of one of them in a window of Fran's flat, or was there actually a light on in the sitting-room?

Somebody was just coming out at the head of the two steps down to the pavement. I recognized the swagger. It was Barry.

When he had turned the corner, I swung the Saab into one of the parking slots I already knew were available after 6 p.m., and crossed the road to ring Fran's doorbell.

After a short delay her voice crackled in the speaker. 'I've told you, nothing doing. Go away.'

I said: 'Fran, it's Craig.'

I waited for her to say something, to turn

me away or say she had a headache and she'd give me a ring or something. Instead there was a buzz which told me I could push the door open.

She was waiting for me on the first-floor landing, wearing a light green cashmere sweater and a heathery tweed skirt which made her look every inch the country squire's wife visiting town straight from the local charity fête. I wanted to put my arms round her and kiss her. At the same time I wanted to ask her what sort of games she was playing, and whether it was worth my while coming here at all. Then she put out her hand and steered me into the flat.

And all I could find to say was: 'What the hell was Barry doing here?'

'Hoping for a bed for the night.' Her sly, self-deprecating grin was back. 'Presumably because you were away, and he thought he'd try his luck with me.'

'Somehow knowing that you were back?'

Her head jerked angrily towards me. 'Don't go all possessive on me, Craig. He was just chancing it. Not the first time he's tried it. And by God, you have to hand it to him, he does try. Played up to me as an image consultant, pretending to consult me on the firm's behalf, and asking Oh-so-coyly for advice on his own image. Called me 'hinny' as if he thought it sounded endearing. Just concentrates, tries to wear you down. Many a girl would give in so that he'd stop talking and you could have a quick bash and get it over with.'

'But you didn't?'

She waved me towards the armchair. 'If I'd wanted to, I would have done.' It came out defiantly. 'I've told you about my appetite. But the taste of that one didn't appeal. I sent him away with a flea in his ear.'

'But you *have* been back for a romp with your husband. More satisfying than poor old Barry?'

She settled herself on the couch and crossed her legs with a faint rustle of nylon. 'Craig, please. Don't get too earnest about it. About anything.'

But then she gave a little shrug, smoothed her skirt over her knees, and told me the story.

She had gone back at short notice to help Toby over a potential crisis. Some of his enemies were trying to inflate rumours of a past financial scandal just before he had won his Parliamentary seat. There had been some deals with a local entrepreneur who had helped back him in the campaign for that seat. Questions were being asked about the way a consortium formed by that backer, now facing legal action into matters of tax avoidance, had manipulated him.

'As well as all this new stuff about the Americans?'

'Oh, that. Actually, there was some talk,' she said in an oddly dispassionate tone, 'of Toby standing down — for the good of the Party, as they always put it on these occasions. And someone was stirring up other rumours. Why was the member's wife absent, so rarely to be seen with him? A marital rift? His agent had been explaining my absence from his visits to the constituency by saying I was deeply into charitable work in London. But I was needed to help avert trouble. I felt I had to go back. Just for a few days.'

'And resume domestic relations? Such as sleeping with him?'

'Why shouldn't I? We're still married. It's not just legal — it's positively moral.'

'But — '

'It's all right, Craig, I didn't.' She kept me waiting, then came out with it: 'Actually, he's gay.'

I remembered that epicene appearance, and the unsteady rise and fall of his voice. And I could believe it. 'But why . . . I mean . . . '

She stared earnestly at her interlaced fingers as if weighing up whether to tell me to mind my own business or whether to come out with the truth. I was hopelessly besotted with the mere sight of her. Every slight movement of her body within those 'sensible' clothes was a denial of a cool marriage of convenience.

Yet that was virtually what she was telling me. 'That particular constituency doesn't look on homosexuality as leniently as most places do nowadays. He needed an attractive wife. A status symbol. Attending the bun-fights, sitting beside him on platforms, smiling benevolently at visitors to our little garden get-togethers. A wife to deflect any shabby gossip.'

'But what was in it for *you*? What on earth possessed you to marry him on those terms?'

Her breasts rose and fell gently. Her breathing seemed to hiccup slightly. She looked full at me, then away, then back again. Her tongue dabbed out along her lips. 'I don't know why I should want to tell you. I've never told anyone before.' Her fingers were tightening into a stranglehold. 'How much *do* I have to tell you? And why *you*?'

I waited, afraid of frightening her away into those shadowy recesses which still held so many secrets.

At last she went on: 'My father was a brute. Not a raging brute, just a cold one. He led my mother a miserable life. She died when I was eight. And then there was Nora.'

She paused again, for a long time. I risked a prod. 'Your stepmother?'

'He called her his housekeeper. When he called her anything at all. I didn't know much about mistresses then, but I soon got an idea what was going on. He never married her, though I imagine she kept on at him about it. I didn't see much of them. He sent me away to school, and in the holidays I usually went to stay with friends — Rhona, and a couple of others.'

'Hilary?' I ventured.

For a moment she looked blank. 'Hilary? Oh, no.' She hurried on.

'Then I had an accident in the gym. Broke my hip, and they didn't make a very good job of re-setting it. Father sued the school, of course. But didn't bother to take me away. Which didn't make my life there any easier.' She gave her clenched fingers a wry smile. 'It must have been then that I learned to put on an act. Became my own image consultant, you might say.'

'Your father . . . still alive?'

'No. When he died, he still hadn't married Nora, but she did get all the money.'

'Nothing for his daughter? I'd have thought, legally — '

'I didn't want it. I was making my own living by then. And I wasn't ever going to get tied to anyone. Never get snarled up in that sort of dismal tangle.'

'But in the end you did marry Toby Leith. I'd have thought that could be pretty wearing. Full of frustrations.'

'No. There was no commitment there. Quite genuinely a marriage of convenience.'

'How did you come to meet him?'

'As an image consultant. Called in by his own little spin doctor — and boyfriend. He knew Toby needed sprucing up, learning a bit more about communicating with people. In the end it was Petroc's idea that we should get married. Round off the image. As I said, no commitment. I called the tune as it suited me. One thing about being trained as an image consultant is that I can devise which image is best suited to me in any given situation.' A different, more timid smile crept through as she looked at me, then faded again. 'I've always been afraid of being found out.'

'Found out?'

'As someone . . . not up to it. Unable to cope.'

I couldn't take this in. She was so poised, so smooth, so well qualified to be consulted on anybody's image, that these words about

111

herself made no sense.

'Being with Toby meant no hassle,' she said. 'With him, the façade became the real thing.' She forced herself to unlace her fingers. 'Why don't you stop me talking all this rubbish? Come on — you do know how.'

We went to bed. Actually the bed this time. I'd thought I was exhausted by the French trip, but I proved far from exhausted.

When we had finished but were still stuck to each other by the sweat of fulfilment, she wrapped her arms round me and clung as if afraid to let go. 'I must be mad. It wasn't meant to work out like this.'

It seemed to me, jubilant, that it had definitely been meant to work out like this and that it would go on working out just as wonderfully. With the scent of her left shoulder still in my nose, I went blissfully to sleep and did not wake up until the light was bright through the curtains. Fran was no longer with me. I stumbled out of bed and went blearily through to the sitting-room. She was curled up on the couch, with a rug over her.

She opened her eyes reluctantly, staring at me with what seemed almost resentment. But when I stooped and kissed her, she gave a slight whimper and said, 'Oh, dear. I suppose you'd better stay for breakfast.'

She fetched a towelling bathrobe and ran a hand through her tousled hair. I felt closer and closer to her because she was now accepting me, not troubling to put on makeup or consider what image was most appropriate. She pottered into the kitchen and began casually laying the breakfast bar.

Over a bowl of muesli, I said: 'We must do this more often. I think I'm ripe for domestication.'

'*I'm* not. And I wouldn't have thought you were, either, so soon after your previous bit of domestic bliss.' She poured herself a mug of coffee. 'I talked a lot too much last night. But you didn't get round to telling me why *you* got married. Something romantic that just got boring in the end?'

'Sort of.'

'What was she like, this . . . '

'Maureen. Very pretty.'

'Of course. I wouldn't have supposed you'd marry an eyesore.'

'It just sort of . . . happened.'

'What's all this 'sort of'?'

I told her as crisply and impersonally as I could. Maureen had been the wife of a fellow officer, a good friend of mine. I had been due to take on an awkward reshuffle of things out in Kosovo, but I had a minor tussle with the bonnet of a truck. It put me out of action for long enough for them to need a substitute. It wasn't quite the truth, but even now, even with Fran, there were strictly confidential matters and always the obligations of Queen's Regs and a certain document one had signed. 'By the time I was untwisted, Mike had been sent out in my place. And got killed.'

Fran sipped slowly at her coffee, looking at me over the edge of the cup. 'The old officer and gentleman stuff? Goodness. The old traditions still apply.'

'She was pretty,' I repeated defensively.

'And if she hadn't been?'

'Well, I . . . but that didn't arise, anyway.'

'You felt guilty because you ought to have been out there in your friend's place. You were the one who ought to have been killed. And since you weren't, you were duty bound to look after your fellow officer's relict — that is the word, I think.'

'It wasn't as crude and straightforward as that.'

She turned suddenly towards me and locked her fingers round my arm. 'No, Craig, I'm sure it wasn't. With you, it would have to be complicated. Genuine, and honourable . . . but complicated. And now look where you are, with a whole lot more complications to cope with.'

I kissed her, and she took a long time to

draw back. 'There don't have to be any complications here.'

'Oh, but there are. So many. More than you realize.'

★ ★ ★

When I got back to the flat there were two messages on the answering machine. One was from a Sussex vintner asking me to ring him about a wholesaler who was offering better terms than Craig & Hebden; the second from Rhona, saying that her father had been caught up in a demo near Fylingdales and seriously injured, and could I come at once.

6

Walter's head was half swathed in a bandage, and his left arm was strapped up at an awkward angle. His usually dark, dour face had gone very pale, and when he tried to smile as I came towards him it was as if his lips were being dragged painfully open, still half under an anaesthetic.

It had taken me quite some time to find him. On every floor of the hospital, at the junction of every corridor, were little recesses with two young women behind a counter filling in forms, collecting slips of paper from nurses and handing out other slips. Messages flashed on screens set at an angle below the counter, and phones bleeped at short intervals. Yet there was some difficulty in locating the patient I was asking for. 'I'm sorry, I can't find anyone of that name . . . Are you sure it's this hospital . . . ? Just a minute, perhaps . . . No, I'm sorry, the supervisor's out of her office at the moment.' And then, at last, 'Oh, Walter Hebden. The one who got himself hurt in that demo?' The disapproval in her tone implied that the patient was a troublemaker who deserved all he'd got and was not the sort of person they ought to be wasting their valuable time on.

Now, looking at the edge of a purple bruise swelling out from under the bandage, I said: 'And what happened to the other feller?'

Walter was in no mood for any attempt at lightheartedness. 'Stupid bastards. What good do they think they'll ever do? And what the hell's it got to do with me, man?'

'How did you come to get involved?'

He shifted himself a few inches to one side in the bed, and winced. 'And as to that other lot, with their courtesy visits. *Courtesy* — with a back-up of outriders and God knows what else.'

'I'm not with you, Walter.'

'Some bloody American general coming on a courtesy visit to the Fylingdales installation, to see the new facilities there. As if we wanted any more of that lot stomping over our countryside.'

'I never saw you as a protest marcher.'

'I wasn't marching or doing any damn thing. Only on my way back from a supplier in Scarborough.'

'Jim Braithwaite?'

'Of course. Sally got a message on that machine of hers, saying there was something seriously wrong with three of our casks. Caused some sickness to his customers.

117

Really serious, and I'd better get there. Only when I did, he denied ever sending any such message and said he'd got no complaints whatsoever. And then on my way back there was a traffic diversion, and I found myself in the thick of it. A lot of kids trying to chuck up a quick road-block across the bloody general's convoy. And I got dragged out and beaten up.'

'Who by?'

'A policeman who got me into an ambulance said it was a gang of teenagers who set on me, thinking I was a reporter or something.'

Anyone looking less like a reporter than Walter Hebden it would be hard to imagine.

Suddenly Barry was at my side.

'What the hell, Pop? What's been going on? I came as soon as I heard.'

Walter tried to make a sensible story out of it, but he was too tired and bewildered. None of it made any sense to him, or to us. Just one of those ridiculous things that happen when, as the glib commentators say on the TV news, you're in the wrong place at the wrong time.

A nurse came in and said we really ought to leave and let Mr Hebden get some rest.

'There's a pub across the road,' said Barry. 'I think we could do with a bit natter over a pint, don't you?'

As we left the front of the hospital, a young man darted along the pavement and grabbed my arm.

'You'll have been in to see that old feller who got beaten up?'

'Just a minute. I don't think we — '

'And I remember you now. You were the one got me away from those scum down by Skelmerby.'

I remembered, too. I said: 'So you're still stirring it up? I'm not sure I ought to have rescued you that time, considering what's happened to my partner.'

'Look, I'm telling you. It wasn't us. All part of their strategy, the bastards. Pretending to be us.'

'Why would anyone want to do that?'

'To take attention away from what they may be up to somewhere else. Look, don't you see what they're at? Haven't you seen the notices — round Skelmerby, and round Fairford down in Gloucestershire? 'Use of deadly force authorized.' Authorized — who by? Don't you see? The undercover takeover by the Yanks of old airfields, supposedly for supplying Iraq. But it's not short-term. It's long-term. Now they're back, they intend to stay. And who's next? Iran . . . Syria?'

Two policemen appeared suddenly round the corner of the hospital and headed straight for him. 'Right, lad, you'd better come with us.'

'I haven't done anything wrong. I've only been talking to — '

'Causing harassment, alarm and distress outside these premises,' recited one of the officers after what must have been a number of recent rehearsals. 'You'll have heard of the Protection from Harassment Act? And paid no attention, in spite of repeated warnings. Well, this time — '

I said: 'Officer, we're not making any charges.'

'You don't have to, sir. I suggest you leave this to us.'

'Are we going for that drink or aren't we?' Barry was fidgeting on the edge of the kerb.

As we crossed the road, the young man, pinioned between the two policemen, yelled after us: 'Don't you know a put-up job when you see one?'

'And who the hell was that?' asked Barry.

I started explaining, half wanting to turn back and argue with the police, but he had pushed the door of the saloon bar open and was only half listening.

Like ten out of the twelve pubs in Hesketh-le-Street, The Ridley Arms bore the large plaque of HEBDEN'S FINE ALES. Unlike the better ones, it had a jangle of pop music from all corners of the bar. We got as far away as possible from the speakers, though I noticed that Barry was half humming one of the tunes.

He made a big thing about getting the pints in, doing his usual Jack-the-lad act with the barmaid. When we had taken our first satisfying gulp of Walter Hebden's undoubtedly fine ale, he said: 'Well, we've got some thinking to do, haven't we?'

'All we have to think about,' I said, 'is getting Walter back on his feet.'

'Look, old lad, it's more serious than that, and you know it. We've got to think of what it means to the firm if he's out of action for a long time.'

'We'll manage,' I said. 'We've still got a good team to help him.'

'I can't help thinking this is the time we considered the alternatives.'

'You mean that by trying to remove Walter from the scene, they can put the frighteners on us as well?'

'What are you on about, Craig? Letting that yobbo back there put conspiracy theories into your head?' He looked past me and said: 'Well, I'll be damned.' Then let out one of his more boisterous, cackling laughs. 'This'll fuel your suspicions, eh?'

Foster Keating made a big show of looking

as surprised as Barry. 'Mr Quirke. Mr Craig. I've only just heard the news. I was on my way here for another appointment, and — look, would it be OK for me to visit Mr Hebden in hospital? I sure would like to pay my respects. You reckon he'd be up to it?'

'Sit down,' said Barry. 'We can talk about it. We've got a lot to talk about.'

He went to get Keating a drink. 'I think your tipple's a Jack Daniel, isn't it?'

Every word, glance and movement made me quite sure that Barry had known that Keating would be here. When the glass of deep brown whiskey had been set down on the table, the two of them were looking at me as if to decide who ought to make the first move.

Finally Keating said: 'You know, don't you, that this sad business is going to make life tougher than ever for both of you?'

'A pretty hefty threat, that,' I said.

'Mr Craig. Can't you see we're on the same side? In the same business. And business means collaboration, expansion, to our mutual benefit. We really do have to discuss it. It's unfortunate that Mr Hebden has suffered at the hands of some rioters — '

'Demonstrators,' I said. 'And it's by no means certain that it was at their hands he got those injuries.'

'However it happened, the situation is that you're a senior operative short. And my organization would be only too happy to discuss mutual beneficial terms for taking some of the weight — on an experimental basis for a while, if that's the way you'd prefer it — until everything's clear.' He got to his feet. 'Look, we need a refresher, right?'

When Keating had gone to the bar, Barry said: 'You know it makes sense. We don't stand a chance on our own. Not the way the world's going nowadays.'

Over the next round of drinks, Keating said: 'Well, Mr Craig — or can I drop the 'Mister' and just call you Craig?'

'It works out the same,' I conceded.

'Fine. Craig, then. What's it going to take to tempt you into partnership with us?'

'Not big boots and big talk, that's for sure.'

Barry fidgeted resentfully, and Keating sighed. 'I do respect your courage, Craig. Believe me I do. The old British military tradition, right? But there are times in history when you've been on to a loser, and this might be another one.' His tone grew harsher. 'We want to do this in a friendly way, and I do sincerely mean that. But there might be somebody minded to go for a straight buyout and takeover.'

'Over my dead body.'
'Don't tempt fate, *Mister* Craig.'

★ ★ ★

I drove back to London talking irritably to myself. Lots of folk do that in the cocoon of their car. And I'd known some who did it outside, as well. There was one colonel who burbled away in the mess or in his office, not stopping when you left the room and still blathering when you came back.

However Barry might fancy his chances of an appointment as a well-paid and under-worked consultant, or whatever other purely cosmetic title the Buywise bosses chose to offer him, I wanted to find other ways of surviving. It was time to do a quick round-up of old friends and assess our mutual strength.

And I needed Fran. I needed to hear her voice on the phone as we arranged to meet, and needed the glow of waiting in a doorway for her to come towards me through a crowd: the steadiness of her lovely head as she walked briskly but with that hint of a limp, seemingly remote from everyone around her until she saw me. Immediately her face would brighten — not in any sudden rapture, but in satisfied recognition.

Needed the closeness of her.

Resented every moment we weren't together.

I was apprehensive about her reaction when I suggested she came with me on a tour of my French contacts. Would she be tied up with some wifely duties to boost her husband's image with his constituents? Would she be in one of those moods when, without warning, she became suddenly reluctant, telling me not to take things too seriously, didn't want to commit herself for too long?

She seemed to battle with just a moment of that reluctance, and then said that a trip to France was a delightful idea.

In bed on our first night in Calais, after a quiet, long-drawn-out, almost lazy build-up to an ecstatic climax, her head tucked itself into my shoulder and she said drowsily, as if the effort was almost too much: 'What exactly is the programme? You've got some plans to fight off the predators?'

'Rallying the outposts. Trying to draw them closer together.'

'Doesn't your wife hold some shares?'

I felt an inexplicable chill. 'How did you know that?'

'Good heavens, it's normal. I assumed it'd be the same with you.'

She went off to sleep, and I eventually did the same; but only after some twenty or thirty minutes of a lingering unease I still couldn't explain.

The next day we visited an old contact with a supermarket and a large wine warehouse on the outskirts of Calais. Then on to see the Flambards and Daviaults of Touraine and their neighbours in Anjou. Everywhere the story was the same. Nobody wanted any part in any 'rationalization' or 'globalization'; but the pressures were beginning to squeeze the resistance out of them. And everywhere, sooner or later in the conversation, the name of Buywise drifted in.

As we crossed the street towards the Saumur hotel which would be our final port of call, she said very earnestly, as if it was somehow a matter of principle to force the words out:

'Craig, you're so much at home here. You . . . somehow you sort of . . . you *belong* in France. Never thought of giving in to those predators? Taking the money, settling down here . . . or somewhere further south, maybe?'

'We're not giving in.' It was still as simple as that. But as we reached our room I was somehow unable to stop ranting woozily on about it. 'You've seen my contacts over here. Some of them in danger of selling out, all right. But the others are still loyal. We've got the making of our own combine, and to hell

126

with the Buywise bully boys. With Walter's brewery, the wine producers who still believe in their old traditions, and firm deals with two distilleries, we can fight off takeovers because we've got this loose confederation of ... well, friends with mutual interests.'

'Friends,' she said, peeling off her stockings, 'who can be picked off one by one.'

'Not when we get round to redrafting our articles of association the way I have in mind.'

She paused, looking back over her bare shoulder at me. 'Oh? Sounds interesting.'

But just the sight of her blotted out any interest in other things. I put my hand on that gleaming, sweet-smelling shoulder, and turned her fully round towards me. We made love drunkenly, clumsily, but contentedly.

In the morning she had, as usual, slipped away from me and into the other bed. I moved across and sat on the edge of her bed. 'Fran. My love. It's time we talked seriously.'

'No. No, it's not.' She turned her head away on the pillow. 'I've told you, Craig — please don't ever get serious.'

'I love you,' I said. 'We've got to make something permanent out of this.'

'Don't complicate things. Please, Craig. I told you from the start, don't get too serious.'

But there was a pathetic wavering in her voice, and when she turned back on the pillow she was looking at me almost imploringly.

★ ★ ★

There was a story in the Hesketh-le-Street weekly paper about Walter Hebden, giving background details about the well-known local brewery and its traditions, but saying there were rumours in the trade that it was about to merge with a consortium including a Calais wine warehouse and an American megastore combine. When I revisited him in hospital, he was furious. Of course not one word of that had come from him.

I marched along to the newspaper office and demanded to see the editor. He was away doing personal coverage on another violent demonstration against the presence of our American allies in places where a lot of locals didn't want them. A young woman assistant assured me that the story about Craig & Hebden had been thoroughly researched, but of course if I had other views to add, they would be delighted to consider them, perhaps in the form of a short letter.

As I left, I noticed a copy of the paper left ostentatiously open across a desk with a double-page spread advertising in full colour the opening of a new Buywise store on the outskirts of neighbouring High Rigg.

For the next few weeks I was rushed off my feet. With Walter incapacitated, I had to visit and revisit one contractor after another, assuring them that we were still very much in business, and stiffening their resistance to any blandishments that might be offered by someone with no long-term security. On the surface, Barry was still one of us, enjoying his usual busy scurrying about; but I felt that on that side my flank wasn't really secure.

Fran came back with me to France, and down to Deben Head, and, just as a break from the ridiculous treadmill of business, for two nights in the Lake District, when I swore to both of us that I would not even glance at a hotel which had been doing business with us for the last five years but had recently said it might be making 'other arrangements'.

Then she disappeared for a whole week on a commission to advise on the updating of a Leeds fashion store. I was deprived of everything that mattered most to me, and twitched like every lovesick teenager stung by suspicions of the loved one sliding away, escaping. Once she came back, I would have to hold on tight to her, or she would somehow drift away on a slowly turning tide.

At the end of the week she came straight to my flat, which she had never done before. We made love, and then, walking naked but oddly unrelaxed to the wine cupboard, she poured a stiff whisky and handed it to me as if I might need it to face a shock.

Then she said: 'Craig, I'm pregnant.'

It wasn't apologetic, or accusing, or defiant. Just a calm statement of fact. For a moment I felt dizzy, then I put the glass down and wrapped my arms round her and laughed crazily.

'Wonderful,' I said. 'Oh, this is wonderful. Now you can't argue any more. This settles it. We have to . . . what's the word? . . . regularize the situation.'

'Oh, Craig, what an awful word. 'Regularize!' But no' — she pulled away from me — 'I intend to sort it out my way.'

'Just a minute.' I still wanted to laugh at everything. 'Just what will your husband think of this?'

'I don't know if I'm going to tell him. But if I did, I imagine he'd be quite pleased. Good for his constituents' opinion of him. Squash any faint rumours of him being queer.'

'But his *own* feelings?'

'I told you how we get along. He's not going to feel physically jealous. Not going to feel cuckolded.'

'But I'm not going to let my child bear somebody else's name.'

'You won't have to. I'm going to sort this out. It should never have got this far.' Suddenly she burst out: 'Damn you, Craig. I love you. And I wasn't supposed to.'

'By whom? Look, my darling, you really are talking the most awful rubbish. Is this one of the symptoms of impending motherhood?' I tried to seize her again, but she dodged away, holding out her hands in a plea.

'Please, Craig. Please, my love. If things come out . . . when we clear this all up and you find out . . . please promise me you won't hate me.'

'Hate you? What on earth for?'

'Anything. Everything. It should never have got this far,' she said again. 'I shouldn't ever have let it.'

Suddenly she was groping for her clothes, anxious to be off home, and not wanting me to drive her there or to say another word.

Next morning I had an irritable call from Maureen, asking where the hell had I been, because she hadn't been able to contact me and had to see me. It was urgent. There was a lot to talk about and we had better get it well and truly settled.

7

Maureen had bought herself a tight white blouse and a black trouser suit. She also sported a close-cropped hairdo. Today her role was obviously going to be that of a tough businesswoman.

Swinging the car on to the short drive and stopping a few inches from the garage door was still a familiar, automatic sequence. Only usually the overhang beside the garage was occupied by Maureen's Micra. Now that was presumably inside the garage. Hard to believe I wasn't back in the long-established routine. The lawn and the front of the house were just the way they had always been. A plastic bottle was rolling in the gutter, its twitches accompanied by a flimsy supermarket bag dancing on a swirl of wind like a condom enjoying a frolic. The tree in next door's front garden leaned over our low hedge and shed leaves on to our grass just the way it had always done. Everything had its place in the pattern. A walk to the station in the morning, on to the train, back in the evening, maybe a pint in the pub by the station, and then back along this quiet avenue and up this drive to the side door. Weekends in the garden or going out to lunch with Maureen's friends in The Coach and Horses in the woods. A pattern of life as predictable as the patterns of the flock wallpaper in our village pub and the Chinese takeaway opposite the church. You got used to it, ceased to notice any of it. It was a painless way of life. Numbing.

Had I really prodded myself into disrupting it all?

Maureen opened the door and waved me through. 'Make yourself at home.' The little laugh that followed had been meticulously rehearsed.

I sat down in what had been my usual armchair, though this did now feel quite strange. Facing me from the mantelpiece was a photograph of Mike. It had never been there in my day, but there was no reason why Maureen should not have dug out a photograph of her first husband and got nostalgic over the good times he represented.

I nodded towards a play script carefully, casually, placed on the arm of the sofa. 'A new production?'

'Oh, that.' She made a pretence of being confused, sweeping it under the table on to the magazine ledge. 'Sorry, I wasn't thinking.'

'They're still going strong?'

'Of course. Though some things are getting

a sight too strong. That man Cowan, for instance.'

'Dear old Reggie? I thought you were great buddies.'

'That slimy little lounge lizard? Now I'm on my own, he thinks . . . well, because I've been abandoned' — she savoured the word and gallantly choked back a tiny sob — 'I ought to be . . . available.'

Available. Where had I heard that word before?

'I have to fight him off at rehearsals,' she cried. 'Just can't keep his hands to himself. He's insufferable.'

Reggie Cowan was a local estate agent and a key figure in the Tithebarn Players. He always managed to claim romantic leading roles for himself, even though he was in his late fifties. He could still present a distinguished presence on stage, though seedy and spattered with dandruff if you met him in his office. Maureen hadn't always found him insufferable. They had been great thespians together, always the ones to embrace each other at final curtain call, pretending to look amazed and flattered when the curtain went up for a final dribble of applause, and waving their arms extravagantly in the bar after a show. Now it appeared that Reggie was a cad. I waited for her to use the word, but even

Maureen couldn't bring herself to utter anything so outdated.

'And you?' she said. 'Your current girlfriend — everything satisfactory in that direction? Not that Lisa female after all. Frances something, isn't it?'

'So you still enjoy a gossip with Barry.'

'I need *someone* to keep me in touch with what's going on.' She glanced at the mantelpiece clock which the Corps had given us as a wedding present. 'He should be along any minute. The three of us have got a lot to decide.'

'Just three of us? You're not flying Walter down by helicopter, landing on the lawn?'

'May as well face it: Walter's not going to be much help from now on, is he?'

Before I could broach my own reason for coming here today, Barry arrived. He slapped me on the shoulder, kissed Maureen extravagantly, and sprawled on the couch, making sure we were looking at him before he issued his command.

'Right, then. Let battle commence. We're surrounded by competitors. Good or bad? Do we go on competing, or gracefully bow to superior forces and take the goodies they're prepared to offer?'

'I don't want to finish up with nothing,' said Maureen. 'And I don't believe false pride should stand in the way of a settlement.'

'And you, Craig, old lad? Still determined to fight on until the last defender lies dead on the field?'

'I'm in favour of staying alive,' I said. 'And I see no reason why we shouldn't.'

I could have predicted every line of the argument. All too obviously Barry had been offered any number of sly inducements. Maureen said very earnestly that it would be good for all of us to work within a really powerful group, relieving us of all financial and administrative worries. Not that I had ever noticed her being very attentive to financial and administrative matters.

Barry had marshalled a few brisk arguments. 'The main thing we have to keep in mind is that if Pop decides he hasn't got the stamina to carry on — '

'When I last saw him,' I said, 'he was very determined to continue.'

'So until he's well enough to see sense, we're just stuck? Just struggling to keep the Craig & Hebden flag flying in spite of being surrounded?'

'Until he's too sick to see what you call sense,' I corrected him, 'yes.'

And I could see that all Barry's efforts now would be to persuade Walter that he really was too sick to carry on. Why not take the money and spend it on soothing treatment in his retirement?

It went on for nearly an hour. Barry grew very sullen. Maureen crossed her legs, uncrossed them, made us a pot of tea, and pouted whenever I said I wasn't going to give in to a greedy octopus with too many tentacles and too little brain.

As he was leaving, Barry said: 'Well, I'd better have another word with Pop and tell him what we've discussed today. And sound him out about what he really thinks.'

Or tell him what he really ought to be thinking. Whatever other pains he might have, poor Walter was in for a bout of arm-twisting. And I had no doubt that Barry would be reporting back personally to Foster Keating.

Maureen, I could see, was wondering why I wasn't getting ready to leave as well.

I said: 'As well as sorting out all these business matters, isn't it about time we sorted out personal ones as well?'

'Such as?'

'Let's say regularizing the situation.' I remembered how Fran had laughed at that word. 'It seems sensible.'

'Sensible? Who for?' She was clearing away the cups and saucers, but abruptly she stopped, and her head lunged forward accusingly. 'Your floozy's in the club. Is that it?'

Just for once her know-all act had some substance to it.

'As it happens, yes, she's expecting a baby.'

I might have guessed that spitefulness would be her first weapon. 'How d'you know it's yours?'

'Let's just say that I'm sure.'

'But she's got a husband, hasn't she? Or so Barry says.'

'For once Barry is right.'

'How d'you know it's not his?'

I certainly was not going to feed her any tasty bits of material for gossip.

'I'm sure,' I said again.

'And how's he going to take this?'

That was something I couldn't answer until Fran told me how she had broken the news to him. If she had got round to it yet.

'And just because you're the one who's got her pregnant, *if* it *is* you,' Maureen rasped on, 'you think you've got to marry her? The way you felt you had to marry me as an obligation to an old comrade. Pathetic.'

'Not an obligation,' I said. 'Not like that at all.'

Her lips puckered into a snarl. 'You're not going to talk about love? For Christ's sake spare me that.'

No, I wasn't going to talk to her about love.

'You're so pleased with yourself, aren't you? Bloody smug. Just what you've always wanted. When I think what I had to go through because of that.' She drew a deep, shuddering breath. 'Well, anyway, you can whistle for your divorce.'

'Maureen, let's not quarrel about it. It had to come to this. I'm not making any excuses, and I don't want to hurt you — '

'Do you not, now? A bit more of that gallant gentleman stuff, what what?' Her indignation was impressive. She was really enjoying herself. 'That hasn't worried you in the past.'

'Let's just talk about it,' I said. 'Without getting too bitter about things.'

'You heard what I said. Nothing doing.'

'Sooner or later' — I was keeping my voice as level as possible — 'it's possible to get one nowadays even if it's contested.'

'It'll be a whole lot later.' She was enjoying herself now, really into her dramatic stride. 'You can bloody well wait. You'll have to wait quite a time. Your bastard could be a couple of years old before you get what you want. And maybe by then you won't want it anyway.'

★   ★   ★

When I got back to the flat that evening I wanted Fran desperately, but it seemed wrong to demand comfort from her so soon after feeling the bitterness which Maureen was so good at conveying. For the next two days I was on the move again, finishing with a visit to Hesketh-le-Street.

Walter was in bad shape. He was back home, but unable to move around at his usual rate, cooking for himself and striding out every day to the office. Instead he had a home help, a sturdy middle-aged widow who might have designs on him but seemed much more likely to quarrel with him in his cantankerous moods and eventually walk out. I had a hell of a row with Barry, declined an invitation to lunch with Rhona, and got home with an urge that I wasn't going to talk myself out of this time.

I rang Fran's number. Her voice was on the answering machine, as impersonal as the voices you get exhorting you to press button C if you want to make a booking, or D if you want to record a financial entry.

I left a message imploring her to ring me back as soon as possible.

On the Friday evening I caught the tail-end of the TV news with Toby finishing an interview in which he was explaining the need for an expanded military presence in his constituency. As a spokesman for the Government's commitment to co-operation with the United States in their missile defence system, he also advocated a policy of intervention and pre-emptive strikes overseas with all the fervour of one who had never himself had to wear a uniform.

The interviewer asked: 'Isn't this just pandering to American imperialism and the greed of the Pentagon for more and more cash?'

Toby looked righteously indignant and acquired a petulant throb in his voice as he went on to expound his vision of democracy and freedom and traditional British values, and also the value to his constituents of the new construction work and new commercial facilities which would inevitably be part of the programme.

Fran was not by his side this time.

Again I rang, and again I drove round to Marylebone. Still nothing.

I felt a deathly chill in my guts. Fran had disappeared in order to have an abortion. *I'm going to sort this out. It should never have got this far . . .*

But she had also said she loved me. How could she love me and go off so callously to destroy our child?

On the Sunday morning there was a ring at

my door. I pressed the buzzer immediately without any question through the entry-phone, so desperately anxious for Fran to walk in. But when I stepped out into the hall, a tall man's silhouette was framed against the sunlight through the open front door.

He said: 'Where is she?'

For a second I couldn't grasp who he was and what he was talking about. Then he took a pace forward and I could see his face. It was the face I had seen on television.

Toby Leith said: 'Where is she? Where's my wife?'

'I'm sorry,' I stalled. 'I don't understand what — '

'Oh, come off it. I've always known where she'd be, and I knew about you and where you live. And I know she wouldn't willingly have let me down over this.' His fists were clenched, his knuckles gleaming white as if they had been polished as assiduously as his fingernails. 'A constituency meeting . . . she *knows* how important it is to me. For God's sake, man, where is she?'

I felt sick that this man knew about Fran and me, knew where I lived — and how much else? How could she have let him in on it: as a joke between husband and wife, a perverse game they enjoyed playing?

I forced it out: 'Have you checked on her flat?'

'I don't have a key. We agreed she needn't let me have one. Saved embarrassment.' He managed a resentful sneer. 'I suppose you've got one?'

'No,' I said, 'I haven't.'

Toby Leith had started out peevish, and was finishing up plaintive. I was reminded of one of those jumped-up middle-ranking officers who could never acquire the baritone bellow of a sergeant-major on the parade ground but produced only a shrill bark of supposed command, growing shriller and less commanding as it went on.

'Where *is* she?' he bleated again.

Two days later the police arrived and asked me a similar question and went on asking a lot more.

And then there were the videos.

PART TWO

IN BOND

1

The plain-clothes officer who arrived at our office with a sergeant in tow might be at as much of a loss as Toby Leith, but it was not his professional style to show it. He flourished his warrant card at Diana, grinning dourly at her attempt to ask if he had an appointment. She looked beseechingly at me through the window, but I nodded for the lock to be triggered. I had been expecting a visit like this sooner or later. Expecting questions to which I still didn't know the answers.

The two of them marched on into my office, showing their warrant cards again.

'Detective Chief Inspector Plant of the Missing Persons Unit. And this is Sergeant Welbeck. I wonder if you can help us, Mr Craig?'

I waved him towards the seat facing my desk. His sergeant stationed himself by the door, as if to make sure I didn't do a runner.

'Help you?' I made it as vague as his opening remark, but of course we both knew what it was about.

'It's a matter concerning a missing person, sir. What can you tell us about the whereabouts of Mrs Toby Leigh?'

He looked awkward yet menacing as he hunched forward on the chair. It was probably an acquired mannerism, not contrived, rather an unease in unfamiliar surroundings which made him instinctively aggressive. The vertical lines in his cheeks were as deeply etched as a washboard. His yellow-tinged eyes were tired. Some other task before he reached me had perhaps taken up too many hours? But he looked about the room sharply enough, maybe hoping to spot a large bloodstain on the filing cabinet or to frighten me into pointing out a dismembered corpse under my desk.

'Why should you suppose I know anything about Mrs Leith's movements?' I stalled.

'The lady has been reported as missing by her husband. Our inquiries have led us to you in the belief, sir, that you might be able to throw some light on her disappearance.'

'Why should she be considered as missing? If she has some private concerns to attend to, or simply wants a break, why assume there's anything suspicious about her movements?'

Plant's podgy lips made a weary twitch. 'I'd have thought it was clear enough, sir. Mrs Leith failed to attend a constituency meeting which was very important to her husband, with an election coming up. He assures us that this is quite uncharacteristic of his wife. Now, I gather that you are very friendly with the lady.'

'And where did you gather that?'

'It would save us all time, sir, if you would simply answer my questions. You do know Mrs Leith?'

'I do.'

'On what terms, sir?'

'As a business associate and a friend.'

'A close enough friend for you to be able to tell us her present whereabouts?'

'I've no idea where she is. I wish I did.'

Plant brooded on this for a few long moments. Then he said: 'And you can't think of any reason why she should have disappeared from her pied-à-terre' — it came out slurred and somehow obscene — 'without notifying her husband? Or a friend as close as yourself?'

I said: 'Have you any specific reason for supposing there's anything unusual in Mrs Leith's absence? She does have a busy professional life, you know, as an image consultant to various companies. Not just our own.'

'An image consultant. Yes, Mr Craig, we're aware of that.' The concept of image consultant was obviously something he had trouble taking in. 'But it's still unlikely she'd have gone off to an appointment at a time when Mr Leith had made it clear that he needed her at his side for a much more important engagement.'

He waited. In the background the sergeant cleared his throat as if to emphasize his threatening presence.

How could I tell them, any more than I could have told Toby Leith, that I was pretty sure she had gone off to have an abortion?

When I wasn't forthcoming, Plant also cleared his throat, more hoarse and impatient than his sergeant. 'As a matter of interest, Mr Craig, can you tell me what make of car Mrs Leith drove?'

It seemed pointless. If it was relevant, surely Toby Leith would already have told them?

I said: 'I haven't the faintest idea. I assumed she had one, but we never used it. We always used mine.'

'*Used* it, sir?' A meaning, know-all smirk.

'For visiting my company warehouse at Deben Head. And for driving to a few other places.'

'Purely on business, that is?'

'As I've told you, we're also good friends.'

'So Mr Leith informed us. But you weren't worried enough, as a friend or a business acquaintance, to be like one of those other companies you've mentioned? One in Leeds, anyway, found it so unlike her to be late delivering some report to them that they were concerned enough to get in touch with her husband.'

'I'm quite sure that this is a personal matter which Mrs Leith will explain when she gets back. I don't see where I come into it. It's entirely up to her.'

'Quite so. But in the meantime, we can't just sit around, in case she *doesn't* oblige us by showing up of her own accord. We have to carry out an investigation according to the usual routine in the case of a misper — a person reported missing by a close relative.'

They would probably put Fran through some irritable questioning when she did show up again. She would have to come up with some explanations: one to me, a different one to her husband, and maybe another one to the police?

I said: 'Inspector, I can't help you. I wish to God I could. I'm just as worried as . . . well . . . '

'As her husband, sir?'

She would come back. She had to. We would pick up where we had left off. Somehow, with or without our child.

Only it couldn't be quite the same.

Where the hell was she?

151

After another twenty minutes reshuffling fruitless questions, Plant and his sidekick left reluctantly, with what sounded like a stock warning that they would probably need to interview me again.

I waited for a phone call from Fran. Went on waiting. And tried to concentrate on routine work. I decided, just to get away and do something, *anything*, to go down to Deben Head and check on things there, just to make somebody else miserable.

Work at Heathwaters was proceeding at one hell of a pace. It looked way out of place. I was used to seeing half-finished shapes of concrete and glass all over London, with cranes forever lurching across the sky above labyrinths of scaffolding and fencing, and hoardings announcing some grandiose new project. Nothing unusual about the dimensions of this, then. Except that you didn't expect to see anything quite so large and sprawling out here in the countryside.

No attention had been paid to a campaign of protest organized by local shopkeepers and residents, involving two large public meetings and a stream of letters to the local paper which George Goffin had saved for me. The promoters of the theme park and its accompanying supermarket contented themselves with stating bluntly that the new complex would get the town out of a financial hole, bringing in labouring jobs on the building sites and full-time employment in the theme park and supermarket. Protesters predicted that the resort would get its materials from large suppliers, cutting prices to do small local shops out of business, and visitors to the theme park would be transported to and fro by a tourist company, who would get a rakeoff on all supposedly historic souvenirs, most of which would probably be made in China.

'Good for local construction jobs, they did promise,' George grunted. 'Only there's precious few of them so far. All contractors' men brought in from outside. And great loads of prefab panels and shelving and metal counters carted in from God knows where.' He was unusually voluble, getting more and more grumpy. 'Though they dew be danglin' promises in front of a few.'

'Such as?'

'Folks as'll never get to top jobs are hoping for good pay just for tiffling about. Waitin' to give their notice when that supermarket dew be ready to need staff. Tiffling about,' he repeated scornfully.

'You don't mean some of our own men are aiming to quit?'

'Likely. More money, they say.'

I tackled two of them, men who we'd always thought of as fond of the firm and its pay and working conditions. But I was in the wrong mood for tactful questioning. Their sullen expressions reminded me of those on the faces of squaddies up on a charge back in my Logistic Corps days. In the event, you could put on a man on a charge simply for dumb insolence. But the way things were at the moment, we didn't want industrial unrest here. Better to get out and calm down while I drove north to check on Walter's state of health.

Even in the short time since Fran and I were last here, two roads had been sealed off to allow new water supplies and drains to be laid, and I had to drive a long way round to reach the main road. There did seem to be an unreasonably large number of men about with *Security* flashes on their jackets.

On the way to Hesketh-le-Street I called on a number of regular customers on the way. One of them asked, a bit sheepishly, if we were hoping to stay in business, what with all these take-overs he'd been reading about. And Walter, hunched uncomfortably in a chair at home with a pot of painkillers on the

154

table beside him, asked the same. 'You think we can hold out, Craig, man?'

'Provided we stick together.'

Neither of us mentioned Barry by name, but his unreliable shadow drifted between us. And, more solidly, when I got back to London he wasted no time showing up at the flat, eager to find out what I had to tell him, if anything. The police had been to see him, asking about my movements and what he knew about my relationship with Mrs Leith.

'Of course I played it as cool as I could, old lad.'

'Of course.'

'But I did warn you she could turn out dangerous, didn't I?'

★　★　★

DCI Plant lived up to his promise. Or threat. He was back, not in the office but on the phone. He sounded very pleased with himself.

'You'll be interested to know, Mr Craig, that we have found Mrs Leith's car.'

I wanted to say something, but my throat was gripped in a sort of stranglehold, tightening each time I tried to speak. I wanted to ask everything, to know all the answers all at once; but I could only mumble helplessly.

'I wonder if you would care to come round to the local station, sir? I think you know where it is.'

I managed a few croaking syllables. 'Of course I know. We've provided that nick with enough drinks and snacks . . . for leaving parties, one time and another.'

'I don't think we're contemplating a party this time, sir. But we can always offer a cup of hot tea if you find you need it.'

'Can't you . . . tell me . . . on the phone?'

'I'd prefer that you assist us with our inquiries in a properly equipped interview room, sir.'

'Equipped with what?' My voice was coming back. 'Racks and bull whips?'

'Something much more interesting than that, sir.'

I could have argued, but he was probably well prepared to make a formal charge of some kind and insist that someone came to collect me by force. So I went along. They couldn't have found anything incriminating, since there was nothing incriminating to find.

We settled into a dismal grey interview room with a battleship grey table and four steel chairs, while a uniformed officer pressed a button and solemnly intoned the time and the names of those present.

'Right,' I said. 'Where did you find the car? And you're quite sure it's Fr — Mrs Leith's?'

'It was a Fiat hatchback, registered owner Mrs Toby Leith. It was spotted half hidden in a large clump of scrub and bushes on the fringe of woodland near Westleton in Suffolk.' Plant had fallen into the characteristic sing-song of a policeman giving evidence in a witness-box. 'The doors were locked and there were no keys in the driver's door or inside. However, once our SOCOs had opened it up, we did find some interesting things.' Like a conjuror spacing his tricks for dramatic effect, Plant reached down for a plastic bag propped against a leg of the table. He opened it slowly and drew out a dark green sweater.

'Ever seen this before, sir?'

'Yes, of course. It's mine. I must have left it at the flat.'

'Mrs Leith's flat?'

'You know perfectly well I mean Mrs Leith's flat. I remembered when I got home, and meant to pick it up next time I was round there.'

'Yet we found it in the vehicle near Westleton.'

'She must have meant to give it to me next time we met.'

'Even though you say you never used that car together.'

'Obviously she used it herself. She may have been on her way to see me but — '

'But didn't reach you? Or did she, Mr Craig? Arranged to meet you out in the country, near the hotel where you'd had a previous assignation?'

'What's that hotel got to do with anything?'

'Well, now . . . ' There was something quite new in Plant's voice now, something gloating. 'As it happens, there were also three videos in the Fiat.'

'Some of Mrs Leith's promotional material, I suppose.'

'Perhaps you can tell us, then, what she was promoting.'

At a sign from Plant, the constable wheeled a trolley with a video deck on it into a position facing me, and inserted a tape.

It was taken by a camera which must have been angled from the top of a corner cupboard — the tall cupboard for cups and glasses I remembered well. It showed Fran and myself on her capacious sofa, our two naked bodies moving slowly at first and then writhing out of focus, off the edge of the frame and then back in again. Her face turned upwards suddenly. In ecstasy? No. She had a wry, distant expression, as if calculating something — a specific degree of pleasure, hoping it was going to get better . . . or simply something as banal as trying to remember the date her library book was due back.

Then as her legs flailed and her body was wrenched almost off the couch on to the floor, my shoulders and face reared up. I could still feel that wonderful climax. And then the screen went blank.

Someone flicked the light switch near the door. Plant was staring at me, waiting for a reaction. I wasn't going to give him the pleasure of showing any. Not that I could even assess my own reaction yet. I was winded. Shivering inside.

Plant said: 'Your relationship with Mrs Leith would seem to have been rather more than the friendly business association you spoke of earlier. Unless, of course, you were merely helping her professionally in some image consultancy campaign.'

I said nothing because there was nothing to say.

Another video was slotted into the machine; the light went off again; and the screen came alive again.

This second scene was in a hotel room. It was the bedroom in the Old Manor House Hotel. This time the pace was slower yet more sensuous. It was almost like watching a film in slow motion, waiting for it to speed up. And when it did, Fran's expression was no longer half rueful, half calculating. She looked so happy, laughing with joy, utterly obsessed. I felt a deep wrench of love and terror at the same time.

When it stopped, I tried to keep very calm. 'These were in Mrs Leith's car?'

'They were. Along with what you admit was your discarded pullover. She'd been showing you these stimulating records of your — ah — pleasant times together, and they got left in the car after you'd watched them?'

'No. I've never seen those before. I can't imagine — '

'Don't leave all that much to the imagination, do they, sir? Potential use as blackmail, maybe?'

'That's really grotesque. She'd got nothing to blackmail me *for*.'

'Not going to use them somehow or other, and you wanted her out of the way?'

'Rubbish. Look, who took those films? Who's been spying on us — on me?'

'Just on you, sir?'

If I hadn't been prepared for those two exhibits, I was even less so with a third. And here Plant was more and more obviously gloating.

The setting was the same as the first one. Fran's naked body was the same, threshing rhythmically to and fro on the same couch, and her face was wearing that original detached, coolly appraising expression, not the flare of delight she had shown in the hotel room. But the face of the man heaving into view above her, thrusting and grimacing . . .

It came bursting out: 'That's not me.'

'Well, now,' said Plant with relish, 'it's not, is it?' He watched me watching those tortuous movements on the screen, then said: 'You know who it is?'

'No, I don't.'

'But you were aware there was *someone*?'

'No.' I was unable to look away from the screen.

'Come now, Mr Craig, you must have guessed there was someone.' This time it wasn't a question but an accusation. 'And that meant that this woman had been cheating on you all along. You weren't happy. Very unhappy indeed to find you hadn't got a monopoly. She didn't deserve to go on living, two-timing you like that. Made you sick to the guts, I imagine.' Again he was relying on a brief silence to do some of his work for him before adopting his most world-weary voice. 'When did you decide you'd had enough?'

161

'It wasn't like that.'

'Then what was it like? Have I been barking up the wrong tree, Mr Craig? Was this whole business simply a commercial arrangement between you, Mrs Leith, and others? Making porn movies to be sold on through — '

'I don't have to listen to filth like this.' I was driven to my feet, leaning across the table with my arm raised.

'Assaulting a police officer isn't going to help you, Mr Craig.'

The video came to an end. I slumped back on to my chair.

I had to say something. Had to struggle out of this nightmare. 'Look, that car — was there any sign of . . . anything?'

'Such as?'

'Anything. Anything at all to suggest where she went after leaving it?'

'Are you worried about any traces you might have left, Mr Craig?'

'This is outrageous. Why on earth should you suppose — '

'I take it you'll have no objections, Mr Craig, to submitting to DNA and other tests so that we may eliminate you from our inquiries . . . or pursue them?'

'What are you going to compare them with?'

'Traces in the car. A thorough examination of the lady's flat.'

'So you're going to break your way in there as well as into her car?'

'No need for that. As it happens, we've already been into the flat without any need to force an entry. We were provided with a key by the company administering the block — Hilary Holdings of Baker Street.'

Hilary . . .

'Look' — I was getting desperate — 'if anything else has cropped up, it's your duty to tell me straight out.'

'As I explained earlier, sir, it's my duty to find a missing person — a lady who has gone missing under very peculiar circumstances. And whom you might by now have wanted out of the way.'

'Why should I ever have wanted her . . . for crying out loud . . . 'out of the way'?'

'You'd found out.'

'Found out what?'

He gestured towards the blank screen. 'That she'd been stringing you along. She was threatening to blackmail you with those films of your — mm — performances, and you were desperate to see the back of her.'

'You're just floundering, man. One crackpot theory after another.'

'Or maybe you'd found out that your own

starring role wasn't the only one. She may have had quite a team of different . . . well, what we might call male leads, like that one in what you'd been supposing was your own personal love nest. Not surprising if you got into a jealous rage, tackled her in that car of hers, and . . . well, exactly how *did* it happen, Mr Craig?'

It was grotesque, almost laughable if it hadn't been so threatening. I was getting to feel sick deep down inside. I came out with the stock remark in such cases. 'Before I say anything else, I think I'd like to consult my solicitor.'

'By all means, sir.' Plant looked pleased that things were now falling into a familiar pattern, and obliged with another well-worn incantation. 'Craig Spencer Craig, I am arresting you on suspicion of the abduction of Mrs Toby Leith . . . '

'Abduction? For Christ's sake, man, what am I supposed to have done with her? Why should I — '

'That's what I intend to find out, sir. Now, if I may continue.' The recital was like music he sang in the same key, at the same level, whenever he had the opportunity. 'You do not have to say anything, but it may harm your defence if you do not mention, when questioned, something which you later rely on in court. Anything you do say may be given in evidence.'

My solicitor was as reassuring as ever. But there's a difference between being briskly professional about local property deals, conveyancing, analysing distribution contracts and approaches to the small claims court, and being equally confident about rebutting a criminal charge. Poor old Donald Carmichael was way out of his depth; but he assured me most earnestly that he would seek the best advice on the subject and find me the best barrister.

'At least it's not a murder charge.'

'Thanks a lot, Willie. Very cheering, I'm sure.'

Not a murder charge. In case they couldn't make that stick first go off, and wanted it in reserve for later.

What fools they would look when Fran showed up. But then, what excuses would she give them?

Or me?

If she could even be bothered with excuses.

2

My barrister turned out to be a woman. Claudia Jeake was in her early thirties, but dressed austerely as if to add a weight of years and gravitas to her appearance. She wore a white blouse and dark green jacket and skirt, and her earrings were deeply glowing garnets which echoed a dark hazel tinge in her eyes. She had nice skin, surprisingly long fingers, and long, rather thin legs. Sensible shoes, of course.

I had spent two nights in a police cell before being brought before a magistrate and formally charged. I pleaded not guilty to the charge, and was committed to the Crown Court for trial. Willie Carmichael asked that I should be released on bail to await this appearance, but the police raised serious objections. I was remanded in custody, and sent to a prison some miles out in one of the draughtier bits of Essex.

If I had been a policeman, with the suspicions which they now held, I think I'd have gone for the release on bail, in the hope that the accused would lead us to the supposed kidnap victim — or the corpse we were really, basically hoping for. But I wasn't a policeman; and I knew, which they didn't, that there had been no abduction, and no corpse.

Or was there? I had long sleepless nights with waking nightmares. Had Frances fallen foul of one of those other men over whom DCI Plant had so suggestively licked his lips? Or had she made a mess of the abortion, and was lying somewhere . . .

The cell was bleak but tolerably comfortable. I could watch TV, or read. But I couldn't concentrate on anything. Only pursue wild suppositions, all of them slithering through my grasp and swirling away, mocking me as they went.

Now my appearance at the Magistrate's Court had been reported in the press, surely Fran would come forward with some sort of explanation?

Unless she was no longer capable because . . . oh, Christ, here come those torments again.

Miss Jeake's voice was solemn and methodical, suppressing what I detected could be an intrinsic musical quality.

'Now, Mr Craig. I've gone through the deposition prepared by Mr Carmichael, but I hope you'll be prepared to answer some questions. Anything which can give me a

167

clearer idea as to how we should proceed. I would like to emphasize that I am not here to pass judgment on any personal matters, or to express my own views. I merely want you to provide the basic facts so that I may clarify the legal position to you.'

Having delivered that little speech, as formal as DCI Plant's recital of the caution, she relaxed her shoulders and smiled, inviting me to take her into my confidence.

'Exactly what do they hope to pin on me?' I asked.

'The charge is one of abduction. My own impression is that they'd like to go for a murder charge, but there is presumably no evidence of that. And no corpse,' she said, 'as yet.'

I didn't like the way she said that. It was like a potential verdict on my nightmares.

'I had no reason to abduct her,' I said. 'Or kill her.'

'You *had* been having an affair? I'd be grateful if you could be quite frank about that, one way or the other, so that I know where I stand.'

'You could call it that, only it's not the way I think of it. It was more important than that.' Why was I talking in the past tense? 'It still is,' I said.

She nodded, looked at me intently for a

moment, then looked down at her notes. I wondered what she was wondering. Sizing me up as a contemptible womanizer, or a poor fool who had got involved in something beyond him?

She said: 'What exactly went wrong? At some stage, there was a misunderstanding? These things do happen,' she added forgivingly.

'They want to go for murder.' It burst out of me like a belated echo of what she had said. 'But, as you put it, there's no corpse. So they stay with abduction for the time being, and if that falls through they can always try for murder later — which they couldn't if they'd tried me on that charge and lost *that* one, and couldn't bring it again, and — '

'Mr Craig, please. I know you must be upset, but don't get too involved in twisted theories. Let's view it exactly as it stands at the moment. Had you and Mrs Leith quarrelled over anything?'

'No.'

'There was no reason why she should disappear of her own free will?'

Sooner or later maybe I was going to have to tell her about the abortion. Or what I suspected about it. But the words stuck in my throat.

She was looking at me now with a staid

expression, like a schoolmistress wanting me to confess to a minor misdemeanour and throw myself on her mercy.

'There's no way I'd have harmed Fran,' I said. 'And any idea I might have murdered her just doesn't make sense. I loved her.'

'That wouldn't be much of a defence, I'm afraid. There've been so many murders where a lover has turned killer.'

'Not in this case.'

'Mr Craig, with regard to those — ah — revealing videos.' Her pale cheeks had gone faintly pink.

'You know about those? You've . . . seen them?'

'The police disclosed them on my request.'

'They had no right to do that without my permission.'

'Mr Craig, I'm on your side, remember? Would you have refused to give permission?'

'I suppose not. But . . . '

'There's the possibility of part of the prosecution case suggesting that you and Mrs Leith collaborated on pornographic videos for profit, or for personal stimulus, but in the end quarrelled about them. About selling copies, or about your demanding too much of her, or — '

'Or what? Any more repulsive ideas to come up with?'

'Mr Craig, please. I'd like you to understand that the relationship between us is confidential. It's in your interest to advance whatever defence you can stand by, but also to tell me anything which might impede our case, and leave it to me to give you an honest appraisal on points of law. If there *is* anything relevant that you're holding back, please let's have it out in the open.'

Tell her that Fran was expecting my child and had probably gone off for an abortion? *I'm going to sort this out. It should never have got this far.* It might simplify matters — or give the prosecution something else to twist to their own ends.

'And,' said Miss Jeake with a steadiness which might conceal laughter or disgust, 'have you any idea who the other man in those — ah — scenes might be?'

'I don't know,' I said, 'and I don't want to know.'

I doubted if she believed me. And I didn't blame her. I hated the bastard, but I'd have liked to know who the hell he was and why he had been there.

The newspapers had by now got the beginnings of a story. You had to admire the professionals doing their job, straightforwardly reporting the charges against me at the Magistrates' Court and the date for

171

appearance at Crown Court, yet contriving to phrase the bare facts in such a way as to suggest an undercurrent of perversity. Television managed a skilful blend of two different yet perhaps related stories. There had been more protest demonstrations near the revived air base at Skelmerby, with the usual scenes of young people climbing a perimeter fence while mounted police tried to drag them down. Three young women had been charged under the Protection from Harassment Act as persons pursuing a course of conduct which caused someone to fear that violence would be used against them. Three young women causing those delicate Americans alarm and distress! The story continued into an interview with Toby Leith, the constituency MP. After a brisk skim through the usual platitudes, the interviewer asked in an admirably sympathetic tone whether Mr Leith had yet had any new information about his wife's disappearance and the charges laid against a businessman who was thought to have been involved in some way with Mrs Leith — 'Which must be very distressing for you on top of all these other problems.'

Toby played up skillfully, converting his usual slack pout into a stiff upper lip as he agreed that it was a terrible strain, and that he himself felt to some extent guilty. His devotion to his constituents and his intensive parliamentary work had perhaps made him neglect his wife. He was devastated by what had happened, but still wanted his wife back at his side, desperately wanted her found — if she was still alive.

In my confused half-waking dreams I reached out to grasp Fran. Or, when I had sunk back helplessly, I was suddenly aware of the scent in the corner of her neck, heard the rustle of her contented laugh . . .

We were together in Tours.

In Saumur.

In the Old Manor House Hotel. Only that had gone suddenly sour. I was aware, as I hadn't been before, of a secret camera watching, recording, contaminating us.

★   ★   ★

Maureen came to see me. She was dressed in a new, figure-hugging twopiece suit in electric pink, and had had her hair done in a style which might have advertised itself as bouffant but above her narrow face looked like a top-heavy spray of icing sugar.

She held her arms out as if to embrace me, but touched me only briefly with her fingertips. 'What a journey! But poor Craig, I simply had to come.'

'I can't offer you much in the way of a drink.'

'It's so utterly wretched, seeing you in a place like this. But you look as if you're being decently treated.' She half turned her head away, making sure that her voice carried, less for my benefit than for the watchful officer discreetly positioned three or four yards away.

'I've no complaints,' I said, 'apart from the fact that there's no earthly reason for my being here in the first place.'

She sat down and edged her chair a couple of inches closer. I could tell from her forbearing smile that on the way here she had chosen to play the part of the loyal little woman in spite of all I had done to her. She lowered her voice. 'I have to be honest, Craig. Whatever difficulties we may have had, you know me well enough to know that's the way I am.' She allowed herself a nicely calculated pause, and took my silence as implying assent. 'And honestly, I wouldn't blame you — truly I wouldn't — for getting rid of that woman. I never thought it would last.'

'I didn't get rid of her, as you put it.'

'Oh, but Craig . . . ' Her smile became even more understanding. 'People don't just disappear. What *did* happen? In the end she was demanding too much — was that it? I know you've never been all that . . . well,

174

passionate. Did you blow your top and kill her just to shut her up, or something?'

I wondered for a moment if she had been put up to this, offered some sort of dispensation or reward by the police if she could worm something out of me. But I didn't go for that, and I didn't think the police were quite that unscrupulous. Maureen was just being Maureen.

I said: 'It's nice of you to come, but I don't really have anything to confess.'

'Was it to get rid of the baby?' It came out very low and dramatic, but I must have looked indifferent, which was something she could never tolerate. 'Are you going to use that in your defence?' Her voice rose to its normal pitch. 'She didn't want to be responsible for all the trouble the child was going to cause her and her husband, so you fixed an abortion, only it went wrong. And you had to get rid of *her* as well, but it wasn't murder, it was just trying to tidy up after an accident.'

'Maureen, you don't know what you're talking about. That's all out of some cheap thriller.'

'One that you're going to find expensive. And what about the rest of us?'

'The rest?'

'Walter and Barry. And me. The firm. All

this bad publicity. We'll have to consider selling out before it's too late. Barry wants to, and Walter will come round.'

'I wouldn't bank on that. Anyway, what's that got to do with this situation here?'

'If the three of us want to sell, I don't think a convicted criminal would be allowed to override those three directors.'

'I'm not convicted yet,' I pointed out.

As she got up, ready to leave, she said: 'You're hopeless, you know. You and all those women — bound to get you into a mess sooner or later.'

'*All* those women?'

'Oh, this Frances Leith. And that Lisa — all that pathetic cover-up stuff about Customs and Excise. Always grabbing at whoever's on offer because you couldn't ever be faithful to a decent wife.'

Her shoulders sagged in a touching despondency as she reached the door and turned to give me a sad, forgiving wave.

When it all came to court, would she be called for the defence or the prosecution? Which side had she already chosen in her mind, offering her the most dramatic possibilities in the witness box?

A painstakingly typed letter arrived from George Goffin. I could almost visualize him pecking away at it, key by key.

Don't know whether this wull get thru to you but we all just want to say we don't believe one word of this rubbish about you. Pennington's girl friend has had a baby. Maybe they're going to get wed. Fred Johnson nearly lost a hand the other night. Going home from the Queen's as usual on all fours but keeping his right hand along the kerb to make sure he was heading the right way got hit by a woman on a bike. Got home all right, just havin to cross the rud at the end. God knows how he'll find his way home if the family ever moves.

Hoping you are in good spirits and look forward to seeing you back.

I turned the TV on to a drivelling sitcom because I didn't want to sink back into self-pity, and had no appetite for any serious programme. I hardly bothered to follow the plot, but found my attention grabbed by a name which had become all too familiar in recent months. Two of the women characters came back from a shopping spree with Buywise bags. Bottles of beer passing to and fro between men playing cribbage had the proprietary brand label stocked only by Buywise. Product placement, it's called. And during the commercial breaks, the advantages of placing orders with the local branch on line were hymned against a background of jaunty pop music.

★ ★ ★

Miss Jeake showed up again. She looked even more in her critical, schoolmarmy mood, eager to reprimand me.

'You didn't tell me that the missing woman was pregnant.'

'Where did you get that?'

'The police disclosed it. They got the information from your wife.'

That was what I'd been most afraid of. Not just sniggers about those videos, but the whole story of Fran and myself being bandied about. People totting up the juicy bits. Maureen must have been in her element.

'And you and Mrs Leith had a quarrel over the matter?'

'I've told you. We didn't quarrel. About anything.'

'The prosecution may be minded to suggest that you were horrified at the idea of her having a child, and — '

'I *wanted* her to have the child. I loved her.' How many times did I have to say that?

'Then why didn't you mention this earlier?'

'I'm sorry. It was something I wanted . . . well, kept to ourselves. Fran wouldn't

178

want it bandied about.'

'And there's no question of something going wrong? Of you arranging for Mrs Leith to have an abortion, and then things going badly?'

'I wanted her to have the baby,' I insisted.

She looked not at me but at her notes, as if ticking off each little point she had planned to raise. 'So you believe that the child would be yours, not her husband's?'

'I'm quite sure of it,' I said.

For a moment I thought she was going to ask how I could be sure that, as a married woman, she wasn't having normal relations with her husband. But there was the flicker of a knowing smile which suggested she had already sized Toby Leith up. Then the smile faded and she looked even more earnestly at her notes. 'And it couldn't have been . . . anyone else's?'

'No. I'm sure of that. The way Fran told me . . . '

Of course I was sure. Wasn't I? I tried not to dwell on the picture of that other man in the flat. Miss Jeake was probably less ready to turn a blind eye to his performance.

'Were you and Mrs Leith aware at any stage that you were being filmed?'

'No.'

'It wasn't something you would — ah

179

— willingly have taken part in?' Again she had gone that quite fetching pink.

'Certainly not.'

'I have to ask this sort of thing, Mr Craig, to be quite sure of my ground.'

'Of course.' I wondered what her own sexual pastimes might be, and whether she was in fact quite hooked by the idea of being filmed in the act.

'In which case,' she went on hurriedly, 'it must mean that somebody placed cameras in position with the foreknowledge of where you were going to be indulging in your — ah — private activities. Mr Craig, can you think of anyone who has a grudge against you?'

I thought of Maureen; but even Maureen's sometimes fevered imagination could never have dreamt up anything on those lines, or had the know-how to set it up.

Various competitors? Toby Leith, more devious and angry than I had suspected?

I said: 'It makes no sense.'

'During your army service, were you ever seconded to some special group? Something you weren't supposed to talk about? An assignment to MI5 or MI6? And for some reason fell out with them — or they fell out with you?'

'Nothing of that kind, no.'

Quite untrue. But I was still bound by the

180

old rules and regs. I wasn't even in a mood to blame those dilemmas in the past. If I hadn't turned down the position offered, Mike wouldn't have gone in my place and got killed; I would never have married Maureen; and probably would never have met Fran.

And wouldn't be here now, with this distorted cloud hanging over me.

'Some sort of commercial espionage, then?' Miss Jeake was saying.

'You want me to see Fran as a corporation Mata Hari? It wasn't like that. Not Fran.'

'It wouldn't have occurred to you at the time, but can you be sure — '

'Of course I can be sure.'

I said it with more conviction than I was beginning to feel. And afterwards, alone in my cell, my dreams got more and more tangled. I kept reaching out, waiting for Fran to appear in them. But there was no sign of her. I found myself looking for a parking space for the car, and then finding that I hadn't got the car with me anyway. Suddenly I was in a plane over Bosnia, checking on roads that were still viable, and then coming down to earth to get behind the wheel of a truck that wouldn't start. But I was bloody well going to make it start. It was my responsibility, and I had never shirked responsibility, had I? Now, sleeping or waking, I felt myself enmeshed in a web whose strands were tightening in a sticky embrace. All irrational . . . or was there a real, calculating spider at the centre of it? I was used to there being a logical explanation to everything, a logical way of solving problems. If it had given me nothing else, that was what training in the Logistic Corps had confirmed.

But trapped like this, how could I do any precise calculations to defeat those being made for me by whoever had devised this web?

I was determined not to become paranoid; yet more and more I was worrying, wondering about the pattern of this snare. All an unfortunate set of circumstances; or something calculated — and if so, for what reason?

The hours, the days, the weeks dragged on.

Until suddenly it was all over, just as nonsensically as it had started.

3

A week before I was due to appear in court, Willie Carmichael came in with two matters to discuss. With one of them he felt reasonably at home. With the other he was still in foreign territory, impressed by the magnitude of what I was facing but not equipped to make authoritative statements on the matter.

'Mr Quirke's been wondering how long you'll be . . . well, out of action.'

'He's not the only one.'

'I mean, if you're not in a position to — ah — take full part in the everyday running of the firm — '

'So dear old Barry is assuming I'm guilty. Nice and loyal of him.'

'Mr Craig, he does assure me that he's only concerned with the welfare of the firm. As painless a transition as possible.'

'Transition to what?'

'A firm offer has come in from Buywise. Their Mr Keating has sent me a formal offer of amalgamation which he wants put to the next meeting of the board. Whenever that can be arranged,' added Willie awkwardly.

'We're not selling out to Buywise or any other greedy conglomerate.'

'The document makes it plain that senior administrative positions will be guaranteed for yourself and Mr Quirke, with a possible non-executive directorship for Mr Hebden. In my view, taking all current market conditions into consideration, the terms are very favourable.'

'The answer is still no.'

'It does need discussing, though.' Willie sparked into a sudden brightness. 'But one good thing. Mustn't be too wildly optimistic, but chances are that you *will* soon be able to attend meetings and all that.'

'They are?'

'I've had a word from Miss Jeake, who says she thinks maybe things are going to be all right. And of course these other matters will have to wait until we know what the court's decision is next Wednesday.'

'You mean everything depends on the length of my sentence?'

'With a bit of luck your next appearance may be the end of it.'

'How can it be the end of it, when I still don't know — '

'I mean, there's a possibility they're maybe going to drop the charge against you.'

'So that they can concentrate on bringing

an even worse one?'

'Look, Mr Craig, I know how you must be feeling. But this is important. Miss Jeake doesn't know the full details, but it's been leaked to her that two prosecution witnesses have changed their story.'

'What witnesses? Considering there was nothing to witness.'

Except those videos. Who had set those up, and how many people had witnessed them — and why?

★ ★ ★

It was a sunny morning outside. Inside there was the institutional gloom inherited from long months and years of fear, sullenness, and droning argument. But Miss Jeake was in cheerful mood. Perhaps she was always like this at this stage. No point in making the condemned man even more depressed. Face your fate with a smile.

'Two witnesses have withdrawn. The proprietor and his assistant at the Old Manor House Hotel.'

'But I've never denied we were at the hotel a couple of times.'

'Not in the first week in September, though?'

I thought back. I had lost track of time. Was

that week in September the time we were in France, or . . . no, that was when I had been trying to get in touch with her, and . . .'

'No.' I was groping. 'How did that get dreamed up in the first place?'

Miss Jeake looked slightly resentful. 'You're sure you haven't got somebody working against you?'

'Only some business rivals, I'd imagine. But not that subtle, I'd think.'

'Somebody pretty knowledgeable must have known how to feed misleading information into wherever it was. Planting false dates into the hotel computer. I mean, the skill needed — '

'Easy nowadays,' I assured her, 'if you've got powerful enough equipment and someone with the expertise to handle it.'

Buywise, I thought suddenly. The financial pages of various papers had already written admiringly of the company's database that tracked not just the spending habits but the lifestyle of a vast number of folk in the country, taking in information from a variety of sources. With easy access to electoral rolls, credit agencies, store cards, hotel booking records, and even local or national government bodies, it was by now a master of intelligent profiling. And with resources like that, enabling them to listen in on anyone they hoped to find useful, they would not be beyond implanting information or misinformation wherever they chose.

But why should a purely commerical organization go to such lengths concerning just one human being? Or even to win a commercial battle over one small firm such as Craig & Hebden?

The matter of the falsified hotel records would, Miss Jeake assured me, be one she proposed to raise in court, along with all the other factors we had agreed on.

In the end it proved unnecessary. The prosecution presented no case. It was all over in a dizzying few minutes. A few formalities to go through, a few murmured consultations, the court rising, and the accused was free to go.

Without a stain on his character?

As we approached the door leading to the open air and freedom, with Willie Carmichael trotting happily behind, Miss Jeake said: 'You looked rather splendid in court, while you were waiting. You've been used to staying calm under fire, I suppose.'

'They haven't done any firing at all. Kept me hanging about all this time, and then simply called off the campaign. What sort of bungling bloodymindedness got everybody into this tangle?'

'That wasn't just a climb-down because of lack of evidence, you know. There really has been something odd behind this whole thing.'

'Meaning someone still has doubts, including yourself?'

Miss Jeake brushed against me as I held the heavy door open for her. Her head turned as I followed her out. 'I've often had to defend people while doubting their innocence. Matter of principle, it's my job. But you . . . ' She had gone quite pink again. 'You're quite different.'

As we shook hands, I thanked her and was trying to find a phrase to round off the whole business so that I could get back home and start to reassemble my life. But she was still holding my hand. 'If you should ever need any advice — I mean, business advice, or if you ever need to call on anyone to . . . well, I'm not a specialist in commercial law, but I've done my homework.'

She was hinting, and I wryly wondered what she was hinting at. A dinner for two to start with; a relaxed, non-professional chat; and then, gradually, since I was alone and without a woman now . . .

How could I let her down gently without offending her? Did she still not understand what Fran had meant to me? Or was I flattering myself, off balance after being kept locked away for so long?

Abruptly I said: 'How would you recommend I set about finding who that other man in those bloody videos is?'

Her hand slid away. 'You're not planning to do anything silly? I mean, having got out of this bit of trouble, you're not going to stir up trouble somewhere else? Jealousy's too dangerous, Craig . . . Mr Craig.'

But supposing, I thought, that that other man was the jealous kind? And knew about the videos, or at any rate somehow knew about me, about my existence? Enraged enough to do away with Fran — and maybe with the resources to plant suspicion on his rival?

We went out of the shade into the sunshine, and into the lascivious gaze of cameras and reporters.

A taxi edged close to the kerb. 'For you,' said Willie Carmichael proudly. 'I fixed it the moment we knew.'

I'm a free man, I said to myself as I sank back into the seat, while eager faces pressed close to the window and then floated away again. Free to concentrate on finding out who had been playing a malicious, bizarre game with me, and what the next moves might be.

4

Barry threw his newspaper towards the coffee table, and like a conjurer produced a bottle from one of our Craig & Hebden chiller bags dangling from his left hand. 'Thought the occasion warranted some of our best bubbly, eh? And don't tell me you've been away so long you've forgotten where the glasses are kept?'

Reluctantly I fetched two glasses. Barry exaggerated each gesture as he thumbed the cork out of the bottle, shouted as it ricocheted off the bookcase, and splashed champagne into the glasses.

'Well, here's to us.' He sprawled back in one of the two armchairs I had picked up to supplement the spindly little bits of furniture provided with the lease. 'Great to see you again, old lad. I mean, I'd have dropped in to visit you when you were . . . well, when the bloody idiots had shut you away . . . but, well, you know how it is.'

'Bad for your image?'

'I don't think like that. Just that I felt it made better sense for me to concentrate on keeping the business ticking over. I mean, with both you and old Walter out of action, *someone* had to grapple with the everyday problems.'

I felt I ought to be contributing something to the conversation, but I really had nothing to say. Barry was in his usual form, presenting the picture of himself he had always believed in, and there was nothing anyone else could add to that or subtract from it.

'Of course they came to see me,' he went on. 'And I had to tell them what I knew, old lad. About Fran, that is. I did warn you she could turn out dangerous, didn't I? All the same, I knew that crazy accusation would never stick, of course. But you do see that I couldn't very well pretend not to know — '

'Or guess,' I said. The champagne tasted flat. I would have preferred a good malt. 'And say what a blow it was to the firm you'd worked so hard to build up.'

'Well, damn it, so it has been. One hell of a blow. And like I said, the old man thinks we'd better get together and sort things out just as quickly as possible. Only we can't expect him to travel down here. In his condition he's really not up to it.'

'I agree.'

Barry's mobile suddenly emitted a few bars of a Sousa march. Switching his allegiance already? He rammed it to his ear, nodded and grimaced approval as if he could be seen at the other end. 'Yes, I'm sorting it out right now. We'll be back to you. Fast. *Ciao*.' He beamed at me. 'That's it, then. I'll go up and have a chat with Pop, and come back as a sort of proxy on his behalf, right?'

'No. We'll all three of us go up there — you, me and Maureen. And later we get Willie Carmichael in to check our decisions are on the level and legal.'

'But there's no need for all of us — '

'I think there's every need. All decisions should be open and above board.'

'I don't like the way you're putting that.'

'A meeting in Hesketh-le-Street next week, to suit Walter. Shall we try for next Tuesday? I'll make the arrangements.'

Barry was as bouncily quick as ever to switch his attitude. 'All right, old lad, all right. If you insist. Anything to cheer you up. And I tell you what. On the way back' — he drained his glass — 'maybe we might drop in, you and me, at York. Big steam rally there, all next week. Just like old times, eh?'

Nothing would ever be just like old times.

When Barry had left, I reached for my laptop to sketch out arrangements and notes for the meeting, anxious to jerk myself back into present reality after the nightmare. But my fingers were trying to type in a desperate

Where are you. Fran, where are you?

When I phoned Maureen a couple of days later to tell her of the plans for the Hesketh-le-Street meeting, she gushed how happy she was that I had been let out, and agreed with Barry that it was time we had this meeting, and could she ask me for a lift? Silly for each of us to take a car for a long drive like that. It would make good sense for us to travel together and talk on the way.

★ ★ ★

Maureen did most of the talking. Not about the actual running of the business, but using it as a peg on which to hang a subject that interested her far more.

'Are you going to sue them for wrongful arrest? Can you afford it? You do realize you'll have to pay for it yourself? Can't expect the firm to stand it, you know.'

'Willie Carmichael's had a word with my barrister, but she doubts if we'd get very far. If I'd been imprisoned and then set free on appeal, all right, we might have got damages. But as things stand . . . '

'Oh, yes. Your lady barrister. Barry says he thinks she took quite a shine to you.'

'Typical of Barry. And what the hell would he know about it anyway? He managed never to come too close during the entire proceedings.'

'Craig, I'd have thought that silly affair would have been a lesson to you. You're not at it again already, are you?'

'No, I'm not at it, whatever it may be. Not at anything.'

I stared straight ahead, trying to cut out her voice by concentrating on the traffic coming in at its usual frenzied pace from slip roads, cutting in and out of the two lanes while the Saab seemed to urge itself on, hungry for the three lanes a few miles ahead.

'Honestly, Craig, you're hopeless. Really hopeless. You and all those women — bound to get you into a mess sooner or later.'

It was like an old-fashioned gramophone record, jammed and repeating itself.

'All those terribly confidential meetings with heaven knows who. And thinking I never noticed.'

She let out a little gasp as a huge artic came up on the inside and made the car judder with a blast of air. 'Don't you realize' — she raised her voice over the dying echoes — 'you're going to have to be honest with us? Your partners, I mean. I mean, in a business like ours there does have to be mutual trust.'

'How trustworthy have you and Barry been behind my back, while I've been away?'

'Craig, I'm willing to make allowances. Obviously that fling of yours was just a temporary thing. You needed a change. But now that it's out of your system, I think I can face up to the challenge.'

It's not out of my system, I wanted to say. Never will be.

She was going on, dropping her voice half an octave to infuse it with the appropriate gravity. 'Both Barry and I have known for some time now that your mind hasn't been on the job. My psychiatrist says that some of your war experiences out there in Bosnia probably resulted in stress without you realizing it, and when you began losing your grip on business out here in the real world, you reacted according to the way you'd been trained. Faced with a problem, you were used to destroying things in your way, blowing them up, and this was symbolized in our personal relationship as well, so . . . '

I turned on the radio, very loud. The pop music wasn't to my taste, but neither was Maureen's voice.

We had driven for another half hour when the programme was interrupted by a news summary. A large demonstration was taking place outside Lakenheath airfield, the US strike-jet base in Suffolk, after the revelation that the Americans had accumulated three

195

times the number of nuclear warheads there than they had previously admitted. The news-reader went on to report similar attacks on the controversial new developments at Skelmerby. Attempts had been made to contact the local MP for his comments, but Mr Toby Leith was unavailable. News was coming through that at an Alderthorpe constituency meeting the previous evening he had been de-selected as their member. Doubtless he would be issuing a statement in due course. It was understood that a majority of voters wanted somebody more powerful to represent them in the general election six months from now: not one who, like the present Prime Minister and his closest allies, was too much under the thumb of the United States and allowing them too much freedom in expanding their bases on British soil.

Maureen asserted herself through the broadcast. 'Isn't that the husband of that woman of yours?'

'He's Fran's husband, yes.'

'Must be a bit of a weirdo, letting all these things happen in his private life as well as mucking up his public image.'

The pop music came blasting back.

By the time we reached Hesketh-le-Street, there had been a later bulletin reporting assaults on other early warning installations

and airfields, including Fairford in Gloucestershire and Mildenhall on the Suffolk/
Cambridgeshire border.

'Bloody fools,' grunted Walter. 'Where's
any of it going to get them? The lot of them,'
he added, to make it clear that he had no
time for either side.

He ought by now to be well settled back at
home, in these surroundings I had always
associated with him. But he looked shrunken
and no longer in full possession of the place
or clearly aware of what might be going on
outside. Rhona had insisted on coming
round to provide tea and home-made
scones, and made a great affectionate show
of kissing and hugging me. 'Lovely to see
you again, pet.' But once she had neatly laid
out the cups, saucers and plates, and we
were settled round the table, Barry looked
hard at her and said: 'This is a meeting
exclusively for directors of the company.'
Rhona's eyes widened pathetically behind
her glasses, and she slunk away.

'No reason why she shouldn't have stayed,'
Walter grumbled.

'She'd only have kept interrupting. Believe
me, I know what she's like.'

Walter's shoulders slumped, and he looked
at the door as if trying to send an apology
through it to his daughter. But he didn't

make the sort of protest I would have expected of him in the past.

'Now.' Barry had arbitrarily appointed himself chairman of the meeting. 'Let's be quite frank about the whole set-up. No holds barred. We've got to thrash this out before it's too late.' He stared a challenge at me. 'In your . . . er, absence . . . we've had a firm offer from Foster Keating of Buywise.'

'So Willie told me.'

'He's been perfectly frank about things. Very helpful. Patterns of shopping are changing, and we have to get into the swing of it. The big chains have a financial and purchasing clout that individual suppliers or even medium-sized groups can't hope to compete with. The one-stop shopping mall is the answer to twenty-first century appetites. Let's face it: the idea of the bits and pieces of our own loose organization, with a few suppliers in France, a tinpot little brewery here in a northern backend of England — '

'Since when was our brewery tinpot? Or this a back-end of anywhere?' Walter was attempting his old roar, but it came out as a throaty splutter. 'Even those Buywise bastards don't think it's a backwater. They've bought that land at top of town that's been talked about for years now as maybe a kids' playground. Not enough, that development of theirs over at High Rigg. They've put in for planning permission for another of their hypermarkets right here. And with this bent council of oors, they'll know where to shove the money to get their way.'

'Exactly,' said Barry. 'But it's not just the local council. Buywise is being approved by the government in lots of places. Needed as a competitor in a market too much dominated by one national chain. And wouldn't it be better to amalgamate with this up-and-coming combine and share in their profits rather than watch our own small-time set-up drift into loss? Consolidation is everything today.'

'Consolidation? Doesn't that just mean letting the big buggers in everywhere?' Walter grunted. 'Handing 'em everything on a plate. Look what's happening to the pubs. Land-lords being offered new furniture, bloody machines, running rooms into one great barn, slashing prices on fancy beers and alcopops. And then finding out they've sold their freedom.'

'What it basically means,' I added, 'as well as supposedly freeing pubs from tied house status and then gobbling them up, they're squeezing out the original suppliers — buying up all the premises they can, and putting enough weight into the competition for shelf space to drive every independent supplier out of the supermarket chains.'

'All right, so that's the way it's heading.' Barry looked pleased rather than regretful. 'So let's see what we can make out of it. The last time I saw Foster, he had some very sound creative ideas to offer. And for keeping you and me, Craig, on in an executive capacity. Seems very impressed by your distinguished military career, old lad.'

'Wants me to run a private army to gun down competitors?'

'He was talking about using your know-how as head of security for the whole group. Makes good sense to me. And Pop here can retire on a hefty pension.'

Maureen chipped in: 'Or if you didn't want to do that, there'd still be enough money from the sell-out for you not to have to work at all. We could travel. We never did go anywhere much, did we? Now things could be different.' She smiled shyly at me. 'A chance to sort things out. A fresh start.'

I tried to shake myself out of a feeling of chilly detachment. I was sitting next to Walter, and had always been close to him. But Walter, too, seemed to be drifting away. I couldn't reach out and grasp him. All the old man's tenacity, reliability, were ebbing away. Old Walter — really an old man now.

But damn it, someone had to put up a fight.

I said: 'We've got a flexibility the big boys can never manage. There'll always be room for small, efficient groups with good local contacts. And nobody can match our facilities at Deben Head.'

'That's one of our best selling points.' Barry was rattling on. 'Buywise will be taking that into account — in a big way, believe me — in the offering price.' Barry looked at me with a coy smile, oddly like Maureen's. 'They seem to know a lot about the layout of the buildings, the quay, and the rest of it. Seem to have done their homework. Or' — the smile became even more knowing — 'had somebody do it for them.'

Walter's head turned slowly and unhappily towards me.

Maureen shed her coaxing tone and was abruptly snapping out shrill questions. 'Did you show that woman round the place? And talk about it afterwards? In bed? You must have talked about *something* . . . afterwards.'

Barry shifted impatiently in his chair. 'I told Foster we'd be ready to meet him a week from now, after this meeting of ours.'

'Did you, now?' I was tired in a quite different way from Walter's tiredness. These last weeks had been more of a strain than I had realized at the time. I had come through, but now was drained by an enervating disillusionment with everything: with the blunderings of the law, with the threats to the firm we had worked so hard to build up, and with Barry's eager greed. But I just wasn't capable of working miracles: one which would bring Fran back, and one which might drive the firm clear of the predators closing in on it. 'We don't give up,' I persisted, 'until I've sounded out some of our key customers. I'll do a spot check on my drive back.'

'No need for that, old lad. I've been in contact with most of them. That's my job, isn't it? And they're fully aware of what's going on in the marketplace. We don't need to consult them any further. It's up to us to make the crucial decisions.'

'Quite agree,' I said. 'But we need to have a proper basis for such decisions. To see which supports are strong enough, and which are likely to crumble. Sound them out before we're panicked into any wrong conclusions.'

Barry lowered his voice as if to soften the implications in what he was saying. 'I think you'd do better to keep a low profile for a while, old lad. I know you'll want the world to see you're neither bloody nor bowed, but there's bound to be a bit of . . . well, uncertainty. Awkwardness.'

'No smoke without fire?'

Maureen fidgeted. 'Anyway, if you think I'm going to trail around for hour after hour while you — '

'I expect Barry will be happy to drive you home,' I said.

★　★　★

First stop was at the head office of a restaurant chain on the outskirts of Carlisle.

'Good to see you again, Mr Craig.' It sounded sincere enough; but within ten minutes it became clear that things had happened while I was cooped up, out of action. 'We'd like to keep on taking things from you, Mr Craig, but to be quite frank, we've had some very competitive offers from an expanding group.'

'By the name of Buywise?'

'Well, no. Not exactly. I believe there's a link-up, but these are purely on the direct supply side. Nothing to do with their retail operations.'

'You honestly think you'll get better service from these new boys than you've had from us over the last few years?'

'Well, my fellow directors have been doing their sums, and, well' — he was becoming defensively aggressive — 'you can't blame us

203

for looking for the best deal going, can you?'

It was the same in smaller places. One shopkeeper in Lancaster looked uncomfortable the moment I came in. Behind the counter with its spread of newspapers and magazines, the shelves had usually carried a range of wines, spirits, and bottled beers supplied by Craig & Hebden. Today a few of these remained, but there were glossy new displays from other sources.

'I thought we'd seen someone from your place only recently, Mr Craig. Mr Quirke, wasn't it?'

'I'm sure he wouldn't have neglected you.'

'Like I told him, we'd like to keep taking your stuff. Stop those big-booted bastards taking over everything.'

'But?'

The owner edged towards one end of the counter and began inconsequentially shuffling some packets of chocolate biscuits to one side and then back again. 'They're hinting at cutting off our daily paper supplies and the Sundays if we don't sign up for an overall deal on . . . well, *everything*. From one wholesaler. They say it makes economic sense.'

'For them it does, yes.'

The man turned away towards the shelves. 'You see how it is, Mr Craig.'

'Yes, I see how it is.'

As I drove off, a Vauxhall Vectra pulled away from a parking meter and stayed behind me for several miles before turning away at a crossroads. Yet ten minutes later I was almost sure the same car was there again, this time three slots back and keeping that distance for another twenty miles.

Imagining things? Imagining the still dissatisfied Plant setting his bloodhounds on the trail, still hoping to sniff something out — preferably a dead body?

At lunchtime I slewed into the car park of a large pub outside Shrewsbury which drew its main supplies from our Wolverhampton depot. The landlord had been a hail-fellow-well-met type, almost as brash as Barry Quirke, but a lot more straightforward. It was a blow to find that he was no longer there. 'Taken early retirement,' said his successor brusquely. This new landlord was in his early thirties, with the sort of moustache that had gone out of fashion after the demise of black-and-white movies. He offered me less than half his attention, devoting the rest of it to snarling at a cowering girl polishing the pump handles and then at an elderly man who stumbled up from the cellar, recognized me, but got only half a welcome out before it was sliced short.

'A major re-think?' I said, looking along the bar through the door at the end to the newly redecorated restaurant.

'You can say that again. High time too. Get rid of some of those scruffy old layabouts who clutter the bar up for hours on end. Make this a bistro bar, and a proper high quality menu next door there.'

'You'll have seen our wine list.'

'Your Mr Quirke went on about it. He did say you'd probably be amalgamating with a larger group in the near future, though, so he might have more to offer. Look' — he glared over my shoulder at something going on beyond the kitchen door — 'you've called at a bad time. I'll get in touch with you when I'm good and ready, OK?'

It was surely the same silver Vectra that crept out of a layby as I passed it, and slid into third place behind two widely spaced trucks. When the trucks turned off towards the motorway round Birmingham, it increased speed and raced past me. I swung into a filling station a few miles on, and there it was beside a pump to my left. The driver stooped over the filler nozzle, never looking round. I got a brief glimpse of his profile, and thought for a moment that I had seen it somewhere before, and was tempted to walk across and challenge the man face to face. But if they weren't following me, I could be making a complete fool of myself. And if they were, they were wasting their time, since I could lead them to nothing.

I headed for the Craig & Hebden clearing house in Wolverhampton. On the outskirts I decided to spend a few minutes in a snack bar, preferring to call itself a bistro, which took only small orders from us, but took them regularly, paid regularly, and had always offered an unfussy welcome.

Above the door, the name of the licensees was given in gilt lettering as Tom and Olive Leggett. Tom greeted me with a surprised twitch of his bushy eyebrows, but after a moment's hesitation held out his hand.

'Back to the old grind, then, Mr Craig?'

'And glad to be so.'

Olive Leggett was a brawny woman with a sloping, apparently onepiece bosom which thrust its way ahead of her through the curtain from the kitchen, setting its strands of beads rattling and tinkling together.

'Got away with it, then, did you?'

Her husband shook his head and flapped his left hand at her in a vaguely reproachful gesture.

'My name was cleared.' Even in my own ears it sounded stiff and inadequate.

'Even so, you know what folk are. We'd as

soon you were off these premises. Maybe some ghouls would like to see you in here and have a gossip about it all, but that's not our sort of trade.' She drew a shivering breath, and didn't seem to mind a touch of ghoulishness herself. 'Where d'you suppose that poor woman is, then?'

'Look, love,' Tom Leggett attempted, 'it's none of our business.'

As I left after confirming that they were in no immediate need of any supplies, I heard the woman raise her voice, making it clear that Craig & Hebden, too, were from now on none of her and her husband's business either.

I was halfway across the gritty car park when my mobile chimed its six notes. The caller was Diana from London office. 'Thought you'd want to know, boss, that we've just had a message from Deben Head. Georgie Goffin has been arrested.'

'Georgie? What on earth for?'

'It all sounds very weird. Charged with drug smuggling and maybe helping to smuggle illegal immigrants into the country.'

'Who the hell dreamt up something as crazy as that?'

'At the moment he's being held in Debenbridge police station. Do you want me to contact Mr Carmichael and get him to — '

'Leave it to me. I'll head across there straight away.'

I hurried towards the car and was stooping to open the car door when hands closed round my throat from behind. I was shoved sideways, and then my head was banged on to the side of the Saab's roof. It nearly knocked me out, but somehow some old instincts came surging back. I let the attacker's weight carry us in the direction he had started, scraping my right cheek and temple painfully along the metal, then I sagged limply down on one knee. He came off balance against my shoulder, and went sprawling. But I was too dazed and out of practice to follow through and get on top of him. He wriggled round and got a grip on my head again, and was shouting, 'You bastard, you dirty murderous bastard,' and then my head was slammed against the door and I blacked out.

5

When I came round I had no idea where I was. But I couldn't fail to recognize the face of DCI Plant staring down at me, looking as pleased as that crumpled face could ever manage to look.

'Some member of the public disgusted with you getting off so easily?'

I tried to sit up. 'Who the hell . . . ?' Something banged a drumbeat in my head, and I slumped back.

'You were lucky, Mr Craig, that one of our patrol cars happened to be passing.'

' 'Happened?' ' Even through the haze of pain I was pretty clear on one thing. 'You mean you've been keeping tags on me. Hoping to be led to . . . '

No, I couldn't bring myself to say it: *a corpse.*

'Just as well, Mr Craig. Otherwise you might have come off a lot worse.'

It took a few minutes for me to get my immediate bearings and discover that we were in a local hospital ward — what would once have been called a cottage hospital, though God (or some governmental consultant in nomenclature) knows what the name is nowadays. A nurse hovering in the background looked sympathetically at me and disapprovingly at Plant.

He said: 'Can you identify your assailant?'

'I got only a glimpse of him. No time to do anything but fight him off.'

'Obviously someone with a bit of a grudge. Unless it was like I said, just a member of the public who disapproved of you being let off without a stain on your character.'

I closed my eyes and tried to force the throbbing to slow down. And a face came into focus, drifted off into a haze, and re-shaped itself.

'Just a minute . . . '

When I opened my eyes, Plant's face was unpleasantly close to mine. 'Yes, sir? You do remember? Somebody?'

'I can't be sure. I think there was someone outside on the street when I came out of the court. But no. I'm not so sure. Maybe it was that TV news report about the Skelmerby demo. He was in the crowd.' I closed my eyes again. This time the face was brazenly clear. On a screen. But not the TV screen. 'It was *him*,' I shouted. The nurse came hurrying towards us. 'The man on that bloody video of yours. That sod with . . . with Frances.'

Plant looked interested, almost sympathetic; but it was hard to tell who his sympathies were directed at.

'Well, sir. An angry rival, eh? But who exactly was he?'

'One of us had better find out. And quickly.'

'Take it easy, sir. Don't go looking for trouble on your own. We'll start looking.' Plant nodded impatient acknowledgment of the nurse's reproving noises, and heaved himself to his feet. 'Just take it easy for a few days, Mr Craig. Right?'

By no means was it right. As well as the pounding in my head there was the pounding question of what had happened to George Goffin.

I asked for my mobile, and rang the office.

Diana was twittering on about what had happened to me, and how awful, and did I need someone to drive up and see me, or transfer me somewhere more comfortable, when I interrupted and demanded what the news was about Georgie.

'Oh, Mr Carmichael has been down to see him, but can't make any sense out of it all. And he was worried about not hearing from you, after you'd told us you'd be — '

'I'll be there,' I said, and rang off before she could twitter any more well-meaning inquiries into my own welfare.

The hospital asked if I was quite sure I was capable of driving, but on the whole were glad for me to discharge myself, so no longer blocking a bed.

I headed for Debenbridge.

Without thinking, instead of taking the direct route to Debenbridge beyond Ipswich, I found myself automatically taking the road which I had travelled with Fran, not jolting into consciousness of what I was doing until I saw the roadside hoarding advertising the turn-off for the Old Manor House Hotel a quarter of a mile ahead.

I was tempted to call in and demand an explanation of the lies they had supplied to the police about that last supposed date we were there together, only to withdraw them at the last minute. But that would have to wait. The plight of George Goffin came first.

The closer I got to Debenbridge, the more problems obstructed the usually tranquil rural roads. At one stage I was held up for ten minutes at temporary traffic lights controlling the way past a battalion of machines, one laying tar over a widened stretch of the road, others hauling into place a section of what looked like main water or sewer pipes. But who needed new pipelines of that calibre here?

As I waited, above the noise I could faintly

hear the honking of a skein of geese on their flight path towards Minsmere nature reserve — a flight path resembling that of Cold War American planes on their way to the Heathwaters runways, landing, taking off again, manoeuvring . . .

Scanning the English countryside for future reference? The puzzling thought came out of nowhere, yet sank in alongside other suspicions that had been taking shape over the last few weeks.

When at last I got the green light, I drove slowly past the inferno of boiling tar, steam, and a swirling black cloud which forced the stench of bitumen into the car. Half a mile further on, a new roundabout was under construction, with a wide new road leading off across the fields towards the perimeter fence of the old airfield. The old road had been flanked by a string of sycamore and beech, with one huge chestnut at a minor crossroads. Today they had been replaced by a phalanx of speed cameras. Only I didn't recognize the model. Something new, more sophisticated, no doubt. More like complicated CCTV installations than the ordinary speed cameras. But why so many watchful eyes? They stood like sentinels all the way into the town, as domineering as a sequence of speed bumps to slow traffic down. And set well back into the fields, a group of what looked like mobile phone masts. Covering what sort of expected traffic, along this unimportant road?

I was slowed again by a convoy of lorries turning into a side entrance to the new Heathwaters complex, presumably feeding the rapacious appetite of the expanding development. As I moved off, my attention was snatched away from the road ahead by the sudden mad swinging up and down of the car's speedo, slamming over to 150 and then dropping back to stick at zero. At the same time the dashboard clock lit up for a moment and then stopped.

The engine stalled. I coasted a few yards, switched off, switched on again, and revved furiously. After a couple of hiccups the Saab purred forward, though after five minutes the clock was still dead.

I'd experienced this sort of trouble before, though not in this part of the world. The freakish misbehaviour of the electrics was characteristic of exposure to micro-wave radiation, such as that found near secret radar installations. But why here? None of the old World War II and Cold War hardware should still be functioning.

At last I was in Debenbridge, edging through a congestion of cars and vans unusual in this sleepy town except on market day. The public car park was full, and it took fifteen minutes to find a space in a back street a few hundred yards from the police station.

I braced myself and climbed the three steps to the main door.

'My name's Craig. From Craig & Hebden, of Deben Head. I'm here to ask about my employee, George Goffin.'

The desk sergeant gulped, said 'Just a moment, sir,' and reached for a phone at the end of the counter. He stayed there, not coming back to make any kind of explanation. Two minutes later, an inspector hurried down the stairs beyond a side door, and introduced himself. 'Inspector Matthews, Mr Craig. I wonder if you could come with me.' He led the way into a small interview room, as bleak as every such room in every such police station, and indicated one of the drab steel chairs at a grey-surfaced table.

'Now, sir . . . '

'I've been told that George Goffin, one of my most trusted employees, has been arrested. Assuming he's on these premises, I'd like to see him.'

'I'm afraid that won't be possible, sir.' Inspector Matthews sounded as hoarse as if he had a bad cold.

'Why not? I don't know any of the details,

216

but I've been told by my office that he's been arrested on some absurd charge of smuggling. I would like to know how this came about, and I'd like to see him.'

'Unfortunately, Mr Craig, that's not possible.'

'In that case I shall have my solicitor down here again, and between us we shall be — '

'Sir . . . ' Matthews seemed reluctant to look directly at me. 'It's all very distressing. I assure you we are all deeply disturbed by events.'

'What events?'

'The prisoner was . . . um . . . we had no reason to suppose he was likely to . . . I mean, if we'd had any idea . . . '

'Stop blathering, man. The whole idea's ridiculous. What grounds have you got for all this? And what are you trying not to tell me?'

'I'm sorry, Mr Craig.' The inspector sounded more aggressive, as if the whole thing had suddenly become my fault. 'It was a pretty stupid thing to do. Absolutely no need.' He was becoming more and more aggrieved. 'But your Mr Goffin . . . well, he hanged himself in his cell last night.'

Georgie Goffin . . . hanging himself? I felt a wave of nausea bubbling up inside. Yet I understood at once; understood something this policeman could never have grasped.

Poor Georgie. We all used to laugh at his boasts of yanking his own teeth out with a piece of string. And now it had been string or something tougher round his neck, yanking the life out of him. Unable to face the shame of it — of being arrested, of the sneers and the murmurs and what everyone in the warehouse and in the town would be saying about him.

Of course it was pathetic. Unnecessary. But that accusation had been too huge and appalling. And knowing Georgie Goffin as I did . . .

Yes, it was all too predictable that he would have hanged himself.

I wanted to cry. Or shout. Or smash a fist into somebody's face.

With an effort I said: 'There's going to be an inquiry into this. That I can promise you.'

Behind me the door opened.

'Well, what a delightful surprise. Craig, after all this time.'

I recognized that voice at once. And knew from the timbre of it that my appearance here had in fact come as no surprise.

I turned.

It was Lisa.

6

She was as slim and steely as ever, in a black trouser suit and crisp white shirt, with a platinum brooch at the throat. The pale, smooth skin of that throat and over her high cheekbones still showed no wrinkles. Maureen had been the pale, porcelain doll type. Lisa was paler, almost dead white — hair, skin, even the whites of her eyes looking bleached. But this was no ashen pallor but a fierce, supernatural whiteness. Those eyes were chill and lethal. Lethal: that was a word I had associated with her in the past, though not to her face; and here at this moment it rang just as true. Of course she had not changed. Lisa Maitland was unchangeable, implacable.

'Aren't you going to say anything, Craig? Still the strong, silent type?'

'I'm going to have plenty to say, don't worry. For starters — '

'Inspector, perhaps you'll let me take over.'

Inspector Matthews looked as if he might protest at this trespass on his authority; but only for a second or two. It was all too obvious what the pecking order here was. He got up and with stiff politeness turned the chair towards her.

When the door had closed behind him, Lisa said: 'Well, now. A long time since we were alone together, Craig.'

'And just what the hell is all this nonsense about George Goffin? And where do you come into it?'

'Pretty obviously Revenue and Customs business, I'd have thought. Especially when it comes to possible misuse of import facilities and bonded premises.'

'Still in the old firm? Somehow I'd have expected you to have moved on to dizzier heights by now.'

'I'm at a level which suits me. Since the pooling of anti-terrorist resources, including the formation of the Littoral Protection Agency and SOCA, there's been a drive to share specialist knowledge. 'A drive to globalize the fight against organized crime'.' She was obviously quoting, with a touch of derision, from some official handout. 'Various sections have been working independently for years, but now they're being dragged under one umbrella.'

'And when they're not snooping on potential enemies, they practise snooping on one another?'

She nodded approval, as if welcoming me

back into a mutually supportive team. 'There are individual cells within MI5 and Special Branch that need watching. To see they don't succumb to temptation when they've made a haul, or been travelling to and from foreign parts.'

'While looking back over your shoulders all the time to see what our American friends are up to.'

'Recent developments in the NSA require constant surveillance from well-meaning allies.' She was making it sound more and more like a chorus in which we were both in imperfect harmony. 'There was an attempt to recruit you into something similar, way back,' she said silkily. 'But you chickened out.'

'I sussed what was being asked. Surreptitious killing. Not warfare out in the open. Liaison with a so-called security group — one of the private armies getting rates of pay four and five times the rate for one of Her Majesty's loyal servants. Mercenaries operating under their own rules, including torture and dirty tricks forbidden the regulars. Subtle assassinations. Including one's own associates as often as not. I wouldn't have to soil my own hands with the actual dirty work, of course. Just the logistics man, the facilities provider. I didn't like the smell of it.'

'So you let your mate Mike Heriot take

your place. And get killed.'

'Nobody could have foreseen that. I've no idea what mission he went on, but he never came back.'

'And you felt honour bound to console his widow.' Her deadpan voice was as cold as an outright sneer. 'And all the time you could have played things the way I do. Tell the top brass what they want to hear, and then get on with playing one's own little games. Let the puffed-up idiots get away with their ego-boosting games, learn their jargon, and use their own jargon to promote your own self-interest. And now and then interfere in their inquiries just to amuse oneself.'

'And you're amused with this disgusting cock-up?'

'At least it's brought us together again.'

She couldn't really be that flagrant, could she? Still so intense behind that light-hearted flirtatiousness?

'Tormenting an innocent bloke like George Goffin?' I kept it as level as I could. 'If you're so good at organizing things the way it suits you, how come you involved a harmless, decent little man in such a blunder?'

'Is it a blunder? That's what we want to find out.'

'The idea of little Georgie ever getting himself involved in anything as complicated as drug smuggling or the illegal immigrant trade is too ludicrous. And if you're going to come out with some crap about acting on intelligence received, it makes a nonsense of the idea of intelligence.'

'Simply copy-catting, maybe. Not long before you took over the Deben Head complex, there was a smartass who set up a scheme for importing high-grade cannabis in a Dutch lorry carrying loads of sports shoes through Felixstowe. We had him monitored from the word go. Came in here, drove off to London, and right into our loving arms.'

'Even if he'd heard of that, George would never have dreamt of organizing anything similar.'

'Acting under orders, then?' She tilted back so that the chair squealed against the floor. 'Maybe you're right. A nonentity like Goffin could hardly have devised a scheme like that. But if we'd had the chance of holding him, he might have spilled the beans about who did.'

'He wouldn't have had a clue what you were on about.'

'After a while he might have found things to say. You must know the scope of the recent anti-terrorist laws. We could have held him for quite a time without charge. And gone on applying for extensions.'

'And tortured him into telling any lies you

wanted him to tell?'

'Or the truth. He might have steered us in your direction, Craig. After all, you're the boss. You give all the orders on those premises.'

'Not recently. You may not know it, but I've been out of action for quite a time.'

'Oh, yes, I do know that.' Her smile managed to be both cold and gleeful. 'But before that, had you set this whole operation up? Or was it going on right under your nose without you knowing it, because you were occupied with . . . well, something else, something very interesting? More pleasurable things on your mind — and not just your mind?'

'Either way this really is a load of crap, and you know it.'

'What was it like in custody, Craig, brooding over your sins?'

'It's been accepted that I didn't commit the sins attributed to me.'

'Not exactly. Just not proven that you did commit them.'

'Any more than you're able to prove that anyone at Deben Head had any hand in smuggling — drugs or asylum seekers.'

Lisa scraped her chair back a few more inches and seemed to relax, like a friend in casual conversation idly looking for another topic to bring up. When she had found it, it came out almost as a challenge. 'You've left that second-hand wife of yours, then?'

'So you know about that as well.'

'I've always followed your career with interest. That bit came out in the press at the time of that fascinating story about you and Mrs Leith.'

I sensed that she knew the whole story without needing to read about it in the papers. I knew more about Lisa than I had let myself remember over these past few years. We had once worked closely together, and there had been a danger — oh, danger was there all right — of us getting much closer. I was the one who had drawn back.

'What went wrong with the marriage, then?'

'In the end it didn't work.'

'That's all you have to say about it?'

'Yes.'

'Still the stiff upper lip. The perfect officer and gentleman. Not a word of reproach?'

'None.'

'So,' she said, 'no commitments any more.'

'I'm still committed to Frances Leith. And I want to know what's been going on. And where do *you* come into it?'

'I come into it only in the course of my duties. You can't have forgotten how very conscientious I always was in that field.'

No, I hadn't forgotten.

* * *

Towards the end of the Balkans conflict, awaiting my own discharge, I was returned to be put in charge of a supply depot in Kent. That was where Lisa Maitland had come into my life; and into the lives of a lot of grumbling, resentful soldiers. With Customs and Excise, as it then was, it was her task to check on things brought back by returning troops. There had been rumours of looting and acquiring what were known in the ranks as 'souvenirs'. I was awe-struck by the young woman's killer instinct. She was so quiet, lean, but tense. Like a beautiful, languid cat calculating just how and when to pounce.

Those men who whistled at first sight of her soon learned to detest her. They had been fighting a war which they had been assured was in a noble cause, and here was a bureaucratic bitch trying to find them guilty of something even more heinous than killing their fellow human beings. 'Christ, we've been risking our bloody necks out there, and we get home not as bloody heroes but under suspicion as bloody small-time smugglers.'

She knew instinctively where the 'liberated'

tobacco and drugs would be. She could estimate at once the difference between a local trinket and a stolen artefact.

Yet it was at this time, in this depot, that Lisa showed an unexpected awkwardness. She had been invited by the adjutant to a mess dinner and dance, and arrived in a clinging white satin dress which prompted an immediate whisper from a young lieutenant of 'Phew . . . the Snow Queen'. It was a phrase I never forgot.

Her hosts took it in turns to try and thaw her out.

Maureen was not present at that party. She was still only three weeks into being a widow. Lisa, with no scruples about mixing business with other people's pleasure, confronted me. 'Captain Craig, an unfortunate matter has arisen. The widow of your late colleague, Captain Heriot, has returned to this country with a silver narghile which she claims was given to her by her late husband and which she cherishes as a memento of him. It has quite obviously been obtained quite improperly, whether by the officer himself or by Mrs Heriot. This puts me in an embarrassing position.'

'After what she's gone through, you're not going to persecute the poor woman?'

'I don't regard my duties as persecution.'

I found myself dancing with her two or three times. Some of the other men fancied doing the same, but somehow she subtly brushed them off and unobtrusively drifted back towards me.

Late in the evening, very close in a slow number more intimate than the intermittent pop numbers blasting out of the disco, she said: 'We really ought to find somewhere to talk. About this situation with Mrs Heriot, I mean.'

Was she suggesting I might take the heat off the situation by sleeping with her? With the name of Maureen Heriot slipped in to offer room for retreat if challenged.

I let it pass.

A month later I proposed to Maureen, to the approval of my seniors, if not to Lisa Maitland.

'How are you intending to fill in the time until her status as a widow is confirmed?'

'Damn it, it's all authenticated. We know where and how Mike died. The corps records confirm it officially.'

'Of course. But there are always formalities to be gone through. Giving you both time to think,' said Lisa. 'And for you to polish up your skills for your new bride.'

It was flagrant, yet spoken in such a dry, half-mocking tone. Like that earlier remark, to be followed up or ignored without awkwardness. Anyway, that was how I had interpreted it at the time. And I had not followed it up. I had supposed that that was the end of it and we were unlikely to meet again.

★ ★ ★

We did meet again when she unexpectedly showed up to inspect the Deben Head premises taken over by my father on behalf of Craig's Vaults. And then again when I took over after my father's death. Everything was so straightforward and accounted for that it hardly seemed necessary for her to go through the whole inspection again. But she stayed two nights at the Old Manor House Hotel and invited Maureen and myself to dinner, though I could see no way she would be able to justify that on her expenses claim.

'I'm afraid Maureen's not with me.'

'She couldn't dash down for the evening?'

'She's appearing in one of the local drama company's plays.'

'And you're not there to lead the applause?'

'I'll be there for the last night. That's tomorrow.'

But she was insistent that I come anyway,

on my own. We talked around a number of subjects. It was more like a genial sparring match than a conversation. But I suspected that something else was going to be said.

It came over the coffee and brandy. 'You really need to rest up tonight before driving home for the drama? Or to freshen up? After all, you won't be expected to play the passionate husband at home after the show, will you? All too exhausting for the star of the show. Or if she does expect an additional performance, you could do with some rehearsal. Here and now?'

You couldn't say that Lisa was unsure of herself. She would not only not show it, but wouldn't ever admit it to herself. Yet there was a tension in every syllable this evening.

'It's a very comfortable hotel. Very restful.' This was her last attempt, if it really was an attempt. 'Ever been shown round it?'

'Can't say there's ever been any occasion,' I said. 'We've put up some visiting clients here, but I've never inspected the facilities personally.'

She wouldn't demean herself by asking outright for something, or allow herself anything so childish as disappointment. Our talk petered out into commonplaces, until the time came for me to thank her for the meal and hope she'd let me know if any queries about the Deben Head premises cropped up later.

★ ★ ★

Now here she was again, suddenly sharp and impatient in the way I remembered well.

'I think it's time you accompanied me round these premises of yours.'

'Is that necessary? You've always had such a good memory.'

She took a surprisingly long time to answer. Then, very still and not looking at me, she said: 'Yes, there are things I've kept in my mind for a long, long while. But one does need memories refreshing from time to time.' Her shoulders twitched for a moment and now she was looking brisk and matter-of-fact. 'Besides, we need to have one of my colleagues along to put him in the picture.'

'You won't find anything.'

'Too well hidden?'

'There's just nothing to find.'

We were met at the gate by a man who had been waiting in an electric-blue Jaguar.

'Nice to see you again, Captain Craig.'

So many things had happened since Martin Agnew was last here, hinting that he would appreciate a conducted tour of the premises. Now it seemed he was to be part of just that.

I glanced a query at Lisa.

She said: 'As I told you, Craig, liaison between essential security groups has been tightened up. We pool our resources at every stage nowadays.'

Agnew's sallow features and bleak eyes would never be the sort to brighten up, but he managed a smug little grin. 'Shall we be on our way?'

I treated them as if it were a routine customer's tour, pointing out the facilities and pretending not to notice the restrictions that had been slapped on the place by some faceless authorities. Two warehouses had been sealed off. Our staff were trying to carry out their usual jobs under severe constraints.

Lisa interrupted me now and then to point out where drugs could have been smuggled in. She related the story of one drug baron in jail in the Netherlands who had still managed to organize everything from a fairly comfortable cell. And then she was jabbing her forefinger at an overhang at water level where illegal immigrants could have been hidden.

'You're not expecting to find a couple of dozen immigrants cowering under a shelf of Pinot Grigio, are you? Or like Nelson, shipped in from abroad in a cask of brandy? Or was it rum?'

Agnew cleared his throat fussily, anxious to

assert his authority. 'You do realize that once this little awkwardness is sorted out, Captain . . . er . . . Mr Craig, this place of yours could play a very profitable part as a supply base for the theme park and the supermarket. I'm sure the planners could fit you into a very good deal.'

'So that's what I'm being set up for?'

'Let's be frank, Mr Craig. I did suggest when we first met — '

'You didn't suggest that a nice steady drip of misinformation and bad publicity would wear us down so that you could dictate your own terms. And what' — I swung towards Lisa — 'has all this got to do with antiterrorist activity, and liaison between Tweedle-MI5 and Tweedle-CIA? Oh, and where's the other puppet?'

'Sorry?'

'Foster Keating from Buywise. Don't tell me he isn't in on this somehow?'

'Can't imagine why you should suppose that.'

'No, neither can I. But somehow I do. And what cluster of initials does *he* come with?'

'To set your mind at rest, Mr Craig, I think we may come to the conclusion' — Agnew wasn't quite winking at Lisa, but he might as well have done — 'that our own investigation will be suspended, without any prejudice towards the conduct of Craig & Hebden. And since there's no call for a major inquiry, the verdict on the unfortunate Mr Goffin will be that he took his own life while the balance of his mind was disturbed.'

'And Craig & Hebden will undoubtedly look after the widowed mother of their late employee,' said Lisa. 'You're that sort of old-fashioned employer, aren't you, Craig?'

She led us back to the Jaguar. 'Satisfied, Mr Agnew?'

'I think there are one or two points we need to discuss before finalizing our report.'

'Quite so. We can sit down together sometime tomorrow. I've got one or two points to sort out with Mr Craig first. Leave it to me. I'll authorize that freeing of restraints on the loading bay and the bonded storage. But with one of the SOCA guards to keep a watching brief, and offer the company any reassurance they need.'

Whatever questions I might have had about her present level of authority, it was pretty clear which of these two gave the orders.

After we had walked a couple of hundred yards along the water's edge, with some strands of sour green weed lapping against the quay, speckled with the red and orange of some soft drink cans, Lisa said: 'Not a very romantic setting, this. I think we both need a drink. There's a tolerable pub in the town.'

'I wasn't anticipating an interview like this becoming romantic.'

'No, you never did anticipate that sort of thing, did you, Craig?'

How could someone so icy be so full of suppressed passion?

Lisa glanced back at Agnew, still standing beside his car and watching us, and led me towards her own silver-grey Mazda.

Sliding into the seat beside her, I was aware of a subtle perfume which must have been very expensive stuff, but off-putting beside the musky memory of the scent that came off Fran's skin. I wondered whether to steer the conversation into my own control by suggesting it came from a seizure of contraband. But even as a joke it wasn't worth making. She would have been far too self-righteous for that sort of thing.

★　★　★

I remembered the cosy bar of The Paddler Inn in happier times, when Barry and I had spent an hour or two with men from Deben Head at Christmas or when an especially prosperous couple of months had meant overtime and hard work. Including George Goffin.

I might almost have named him out loud. Lisa said: 'Just for the record, this was where your Mr Goffin was arrested.'

Sadistic bitch.

I said: 'I don't think they can whip up your favourite cocktail here.'

'Vodka and tonic will do.'

When I had brought her glass and my own pint of Hebden's to the corner table in the window, I saw that I hadn't been quite right about her being unchanged. There were wrinkles after all. Or not so much wrinkles as little creases beside her eyes and the corners of her mouth. And not creases of laughter. It had always been bewildering that such an almost classically beautiful face should have been so stark and unrelenting.

I said: 'Just how deeply is that Agnew character involved in all this?'

'In all what?'

'All this wheeling and dealing over the rebuilding of the old airfield and that thumping great supermarket. Why the hell did he need a tour of our premises? Just an excuse to size things up and report back. Who to?'

'Talking about tours, that woman of yours had a conducted one, didn't she? Sizing things up and maybe reporting back . . . to somebody?'

A young man was making his way towards us from the far end of the bar. He stopped behind Lisa and looked at me over her shoulder in a half bumptious, half ingratiating way.

'You'll remember me, Mr Craig.'

Vaguely I did remember the face, but couldn't place it. 'I'm afraid I — '

'Steve Palmer. Editor of *The Debenbridge & Heathwaters Gazette*. We've often given favourable coverage of Craig & Hebden's activities in the region,' he added reproachfully.

'Of course. And we've contributed a fair amount of advertising to your pages.'

'I was thinking, Mr Craig, we ought to have some idea of your views on this unfortunate business of George Goffin's death. And some light on your own recent experiences.'

'When I can sort out just what is going on, I'll think about confiding in other people. Not necessarily the Press.'

'The sooner the better, Mr Craig. Otherwise some less friendly newspapers will be making up stories. You know the way some of them have.'

'I've every reason to know that, yes.'

Palmer shifted his weight from one foot to the other, said 'Well, then,' and turned back to the bar.

Lisa said: 'On the subject of less friendly newspapers, he won't be long in that job. He's due to be made redundant when the takeover's completed.'

'Takeover?'

'Their whole sheaf of papers has been acquired by a French group. Or, to be absolutely accurate, a distinguished French name backed by an American consortium.' Her cool gaze followed the unsuspecting editor. 'He'll have no difficulty getting a job stacking shelves in Buywise.'

'And what do you have in mind for Craig & Hebden?' I demanded. 'You've seen over the premises, you've made vague accusations against me and members of my staff, and then backed down. And driven a hardworking man to his death.'

'Sad, but very silly of him. Let's call it collateral damage. That's a phrase you've heard before, I'm sure.'

'What he must have suffered those few hours in that cell. And all you can say it's like so many others trampled on, torn to pieces inside and out. Call it 'collateral damage', and somehow it's pathetic rather than tragic.'

'Come to that, I've had my own bit of suffering. All my advances to you over the years, all spurned, rejected, mm?' She was laughing, but there was no laughter in her eyes. 'I don't know why I've bothered, really.'

'Neither do I.' I tried to keep it as light as she was pretending it to be.

'You know, Craig, there are some women who might build up quite a nasty complex about being given the cold shoulder quite so often.'

'You're above that sort of thing,' I said. 'In your job, you have to be way above anything as petty as that.'

'Courteous as ever, Craig.'

'And after all, we've been out of touch for a long while. Things have moved on.'

'But this time,' she said, 'I fancy we'll stay in touch. We've still got a lot of unfinished business on our hands.'

7

Jean-Pierre tilted the bottle and poured reverently into the glass, his face in a shaft of sunlight like that of a weather-beaten rustic from some pastoral oil painting. A faint breeze through the vines interlaced across the ceiling of his cosy little cave might almost have been a sigh of appreciation to accompany the gentle glug-glug of the liquid dropping into the glass.

'The first *écoulage* of juice run from the vat,' he said. 'It is to be a fine vintage, yes?'

I dipped my nose into the glass, inhaled, and sipped. 'Yes. Oh, yes indeed. This'll be a beauty.'

'At first I am worried. It was too cold a start. Then there was a drought, and heat . . . *et aussi*, it is a small crop. But then — eh, *bonté du ciel!* — *les pluies*. Just enough rain. And the hang time all it must be. And so there is this.'

We both drank and sat in silence for a few minutes.

The whole atmosphere was as soothing as it had always been. Yet behind me was the memory of the calls I had fitted in just before coming here. The repetitiveness that had once been enjoyable, visiting friends and colleagues in the same business. Only now there was unease, or downright coldness: a once profitable shop with a FOR SALE board above its empty window; a formal notification of planning permission being sought for development of a pre-purchased site; a once hospitable retailer refusing to open the door.

I tried to drive the sour taste away with another mouthful of Jean-Pierre's nectar. 'This is your fine Mourvèdre once more. There'll never be another to touch it.'

'That may be too true, *mon vieux.*' Jean-Pierre stared into the rich blackcurrant hue of the wine, fidgeting uncomfortably. 'I must . . . well, whatever happens, at least I have that slope to cultivate for myself.'

I had been right to sense that cloud waiting to thicken behind us and over our head, along with a suspicion that threatened to turn the wine to vinegar. 'What do you mean, 'whatever happens'?'

Jean-Pierre twisted the stem of the glass between his gnarled fingers. 'While you are away, they come to see me again. To buy me out, yes? But they agree I may use — keep for myself — one slope of this Mourvèdre.'

'And you've given in?'

'*Hélas*, what is one to do, Craig? In France,

changes come too fast in the vineyards. Not just the Australians, but now the Americans. They lay down the law, as you say. *Their* law. The big combines, their wine writers, the dealers, they work together to produce . . . how shall one say it . . . ?'

'Identikit wines.'

'Just so. Between them they treat wine as if . . . they are like . . . if at sea, we say *le chalutier* . . . '

'A trawler.'

'Ah, *oui*. The trawler, it scoops up everything from the sea bed without choosing. And these men, they reduce food to pap, their beer is consistent wherever you find it, and now they wish our wine to be all of a . . . a sameness.'

Jean-Pierre reached for the bottle, poured again, and raised his glass high as if to offer a last grand toast, a last taste of the real thing before it became just an ingredient in a bland drink sold in multinational supermarkets in bogus half-price deals, conning the customer and crippling the grower.

I ventured: 'But last time we met we agreed that was so, and you weren't in favour of giving up. What's changed?'

'They persuade me who is the stronger. I did not want to see it is true, but I see it is true. And they tell me you and your partners are preparing to sell out.'

'Do they, indeed? And you believe them?'

Unexpectedly sharp, Jean-Pierre said: 'That woman. Very beautiful, your friend. But she ask a lot of questions. She was very interested.'

'You mean interesting?'

'No. I mean interested. She ask those questions.'

'Out of politeness, naturally.'

'I think perhaps you find out, yes?'

'Find out what?'

'Oh, I . . . *eh bien*, I think perhaps you find she was not a true friend. She was perhaps working for somebody else? And that is why you . . . *qu'est-ce qu'on dit?* . . . ended the relationship?'

'Now just a minute, Jean-Pierre. I didn't murder her, whatever your newspapers may have said.'

'It is not for me to criticize. You and I, we are friends. But I think we reach the parting of the ways. I sell out, but I keep the one little slope for myself. They had to agree to that.' It was a sad, ironic little smile. 'Even in the Communist times, I had friends in the Moravian vineyards who worked for the state winery but were allowed each his own little patch and his little cellar. Attempt to dismiss them or send them where they do not wish to

243

go, *et voilà*, the grapes they go sour. Mysterious, yes? The commissars, they sneer at such superstition . . . yet were afraid to challenge it. So it is today also. I keep my one personal tract because I refuse to sell the rest without that agreement.' The smile grew more contemptuous. 'These Australians and Californians, they concentrate on marketing rather than learning the . . . the *characteristics*, yes? of individual vineyards and true winemaking. But' — he ventured another wicked little grin — 'I still plant the poisonous little bit of such superstition in the minds of them.'

There was really little else to say. I thought dismally of the similarity between Jean-Pierre and George Goffin. Both of them brought up in the simple tradition of a straightforward way of life, expecting to go on doing their chosen job in the accustomed way. Do your best, collect your wages or the profits you've earned from conscientious work, and expect steady employment for the rest of your adult life. No mad ambitions. Loyal, straightforward, undemanding.

I looked down the slope, reeling away to the winding road below. Beyond, there was a blue haze on the shallow hills, the colour of grapes themselves. Homer's wine-dark sea had become a wine-dark landscape.

Incongruous in such a setting, my mobile tinkled into life.

'Craig, old lad.' It was Barry. 'Thought I'd better let you know. They've found Fran's body. Don't know whether you want to come back and face the music all over again, or whether you'd be better off staying where you are.'

PART THREE

HEMLOCK

1

Detective Chief Inspector Plant's wizened face was as hard and implacable as a stone carving of some vengeful Aztec god. He led me at a steady, funereal pace towards the shrouded shape on the mortuary trolley.

'Good of you to get here so quickly, sir. Especially as you had to cut short your holiday abroad.'

'No holiday,' I said. 'Purely business.'

'Like Mr Leith. Only he was in America, at some international conference. Couldn't quit halfway through. Especially,' said Plant, unexpectedly shrewd in political matters, 'when his seat's in danger at the next election and he needs all the clout he can get. Fortunately for us, you've been much keener on this matter in hand.'

I said: 'There's no closer relative to do the identification?'

'Not that we can trace, sir. And I knew you'd want to come. And I was all in favour of your doing so.'

Hoping I would break down and confess?

The mortuary attendant stood with latex-gloved fingers curled under the edge of the plastic shroud. Plant looked at him and at me, relishing every second of it. Then he nodded, and the top of the sheet was zipped back to show the head. A head so hideously battered that all her features had been squashed into a slimy, bloody pulp.

Plant was enjoying every moment of watching my face. 'You're standing up to this pretty well, sir, I'll give you that. But I suppose those years in the army pretty well hardened you to this sort of thing?'

I wanted to throw up. I'd seen worse — far, far worse, to both men and women — in Kosovo and in the aftermath of Srebenice. Only those things hadn't been done to this woman, the woman I loved.

'Where was she found?'

For a moment it looked as if he wasn't going to answer. Then he tried a question of his own.

'You wouldn't be knowing, Mr Craig?'

'No, I bloody wouldn't. *Where?* In that car of hers, or near it? Or . . . ?'

'She was dumped in the reeds by one of the meres along the edge of the bird sanctuary. Not all that far from that hotel you were both so keen on,' he added pointedly. 'And incidentally, Mr Craig, it doesn't seem like she was pregnant, so where did your wife get that story she reported to us?'

I reached for the zip and, before he or the attendant could stop me, I dragged it down and pulled one side clear away. And then I started to laugh. I couldn't help it. it just came out in a great burst of joy. I stood above this wretched sight, and I was laughing uncontrollably.

'You callous bastard.' Plant's right fist was clenched, and for a moment I thought he was going to have a go at me. But his training had been too good for that. 'Really enjoying the sight of what you've done, aren't you? You — '

'That's not Fran.' I was almost weeping now. Weeping with joy.

'What the hell are you talking about?'

'What made you think this was Mrs Leith? Whatever she was wearing — '

'The corpse was found naked. Maybe she'd been caught in flagrante, as they say. Up to her old tricks. With somebody. You wouldn't know who, sir?' That last snarl lashed out like a whip across my face.

'No, I would not. And anyway, I'm telling you, it's not Fran.'

'And how can you be so sure, Mr Craig?' As I leaned forward, pointing towards the pallid skin over her haunch, he yelled: 'Don't touch, you bloody pervert!'

'The hip,' I said. 'Her left hip. It was slightly deformed in her teens. And this one isn't.' When Plant stared, at a loss, I said: '*Is it?*'

Having made sure he had had a good look, I let the attendant reclaim the edge of the body bag.

Plant pulled himself together. 'If that's not her, then who the hell is it?'

I was in such an ecstatic mood that I could almost feel sorry for the poor man's bewilderment. But then he turned on me again. 'Look, is this some kinky game of yours, Craig?' He had dropped the 'Mr' but was certainly not using my Christian name in any friendly fashion. 'What d'you hope to gain by dreaming up a cock-and-bull story like that?'

'And what do *you* hope to gain by trying to foist an unidentifiable corpse on me?' When he could find no answer, I said: 'While you get down to doing your job properly and finding out who that woman really is — or was — would you have any objections to my leaving now?'

'Yes, I would,' snapped Plant. 'Right now I'd like you to come along to the local station with me.'

'If you're going to trump up any more ludicrous charges against me — '

'It's for your own benefit.' He sounded reluctant at the idea of bringing me good tidings. 'We think we've got the man who attacked you. Once I knew you'd be coming here I got one of the Debenbridge sergeants to fix an identity parade. It won't take a minute.'

Morose, he uttered not another word on our way into Debenbridge

★   ★   ★

I had been sitting in a bleak little room for less than five minutes when there was a shout in the passage outside, a thump against the door, and two louder shouts and a thudding of feet. The door burst open, and a young man threw himself into the room, heading straight at me. The face was unmistakable: this was the man from that scene in Fran's flat. Two uniformed constables behind him caught up just as I was thrusting myself to my feet.

'You bastard! You murderous bastard. Satisfied now, are you?'

It was a wild, flailing attack. Unlike last time, I'd had enough warning, with a few seconds to take all his weight against my right shoulder and stoop a few inches, enough to get leverage and heave him past me, then swinging to pin him against the wall.

'Not much of a peacenik, is he, Mr Craig?' Plant was sounding not just formally polite again but almost respectful.

The two officers edged in to either side and relieved me of the burden.

'Dominic Viney,' Plant intoned, 'you've already been cautioned, but I think I need to remind you — '

'Sod the identity parade. Sod the lot of you. All right, so I did attack this murderous bastard here. And I'm not ashamed of it.' He wriggled between the grip of the two policemen and spewed a torrent of words at the DCI. 'It doesn't matter what you do to me, I've got nothing to be ashamed of. Trying to get my hands on that hunk of filth there, killing the woman I loved, a woman I could have saved. Saved from herself. Redeemed. Godalmighty, when'll you get round to charging that swine and making it stick this time? You've found her, haven't you? When are you going to — '

'Mr Craig assures us the body we discovered is not Mrs Leith's.'

'And you believe him? You're going to let him get away with that?' All at once the aggressiveness drained away, and he sounded deflated, almost apprehensive. 'If it's not her, then who've you found?'

'We shall be investigating the matter thoroughly. I can assure you of that,' said Plant fervently. 'In the meantime, you'll be returned to your cell until we can arrange a magistrate's hearing. Won't keep you long, I promise.'

The two officers led Viney away, trying to make it firm but sympathetic, although there was a moment at the door when he tried to wrench himself round as if to have another go at me, beginning to gasp a sentence then losing the will to complete it.

When he had gone, Plant said: 'We shall need you to give evidence, of course, sir. I'll notify you as soon as we have a date.'

'Do we have to go through with all that? I'd rather he was just chucked out with a caution.'

'So that he could come back and have another go at you, sir?'

All I could think of, and wanted time to think more about, was the fact that the poor dead woman wasn't Fran. I wanted to make sense of it. And wanted to believe that Fran was alive, somewhere. But could this Dominic Viney offer anything in that direction? 'Given time to cool his heels and see sense,' I suggested, 'he might give us a lead on how he became involved with Mrs Leith. I mean, what's his background?'

'That we do know. He makes no attempt to conceal it. Proud of it, in fact. A mad keen believer in world peace. Though you wouldn't think so, the way he went for you, would you? Or the way he and his mates tear away at fences and smash office windows and official noticeboards. Hates nuclear weapons, hates poisonous chemical research, above all hates the Americans. One of the top organizers of demos all over the country whenever there's a whisper of any of their resources being built up on supposedly RAF airfields, or British airports being used by the Yanks as staging posts for this 'extraordinary rendition' business. But as to how Mrs Leith got involved in all that . . . or maybe it was nothing to do with that. Any more, I suppose, than it was with you, sir. Just something purely personal.' He glanced at me slyly as if inviting a helpful confession of some kind. 'Odd, though. Both of you involved with the lady, and then finding out about each other. What's the connection, Mr Craig? Or what separate games was she playing?'

'I don't know what the hell you mean.'

'Neither do I, unfortunately.' As he escorted me past the desk sergeant to the outer door, there was a hint of a grudging apology. 'I'm beginning to wonder. That is, I don't quite see where you fit in.'

'Fit in?'

'I shouldn't be saying this, sir, but I'm beginning to get a weird hunch you've been deliberately put in a difficult position. And I'm also beginning to think you didn't kill Mrs Leith. Or that woman up there, whoever she is.'

'Many thanks. So you're quite sure, at last, that I've not been up to something?'

'What I do think, sir, is that someone's got it in for you. Trying to plant things on you, I might say.' He emphasized the word to show that he was unbending far enough to share a joke on his name with me. 'I think you'd better watch your back.'

And as I drove away I thought it was time I sat down and, like the cool-headed logistics man I'd been trained to be, sorted out what so many apparently disconnected things added up to. All right, Captain Craig Spencer Craig, sit yourself down and draw up a fact sheet, and an organigram, and place this character here, that one over there. And see where the link is.

What specific orders have been given? Who has been calling the tune?

And what's the actual tune?

Who, precisely, is up to what? And where do I come into it?

I'd had enough of being pushed around like a pawn in a vicious, blundering game. Time a pushy little pawn set out to retrieve a lost queen.

Better watch your back . . .

2

For clearing the mind while at the same time filling the veins with a tingle of enthusiasm, there are few stimulants to compare with old Jo Seb's great G-minor organ fugue. I selected the CD track, poured myself an equally encouraging Coal Ila, and pressed the button. When it was finished I resisted the temptation to play it through again, and settled down to disentangle the counterpoint of themes, inversions and counter-subjects from the confusions which had plagued me for so many months.

In the first place, stay calm and objective. Just as, in the old days, when there had been a complete cock-up — the big cheeses stomping around the place, shifting the blame wherever they could find an unwary back, all panic stations and loud barking — someone had to stay put and untangle the threads. Give me the facts, the movement orders, bills of lading, whatever, and leave me to it.

Trouble is, there's always the personal element which can dangerously distort the cold clear figures.

Surely I would never have got snarled up in

this business if I had never met Frances Leith.

Shouldn't have drifted into marrying Maureen. Shouldn't have got involved with Fran. Would she still be alive if I hadn't? But she *was* still alive. Had to be. But who was keeping her quiet?

Walking with her along a river bank, hardly even needing to look at one another. Not needing to talk. They could video our physical ecstasies, but could never comprehend our silences.

Stop it. We want facts, not daydreams. How the hell did all these things happen, and why did somebody, somewhere, start pulling strings to drag me into it all? There was no way I could be that important to so many other people.

All right, I had seen a lot of things in the military set-up best not revealed to a world content with the skilful propaganda fed to it. But I hadn't written a whistle-blowing book about any of it. Northern Ireland, Bosnia, Kosovo, a few incidents in the first Gulf War: I kept my opinions to myself. I hadn't been the most dedicated officer, and once I had mastered the jargon and knew the requisite motions, I wanted to get out before I was tempted to start playing their insidious little games.

Item. Not sure it has anything to do with the main questions I'm asking, but it sticks in my memory, the way the most absurd things stick. For many months in the Logistic Corps I served under a brigadier whose favourite order was 'Action this day', barked out with what he imagined was Churchillian authority. Everything had to be done at a second's notice, at the double. He was not happy when I took my time over largescale deployment of material, sitting still at my desk, making phone calls until I was quite sure transport was available in the right numbers at the right times and could be sent in the right directions. 'A whole bloody war could have been started and finished before you'd even signed the despatch chits, Craig.' But after two occasions when he had overridden my dispositions and snapped out 'get cracking *now*', with the result in one case that bridge pontoons for a major training exercise at Otterburn finished up in Oulton Broad and in the other that a convoy of trucks destined for the Stranraer-Belfast ferry were rushed, despite the drivers' well-founded protests, to Liverpool, he tended to leave me alone, though still honking and grumbling in the background.

Not that they were all like that character. Some were much more sinister. Not kicking up a fuss but operating quietly, watching you, deciding whether you were worth some kind of promotion, or a sideways shift, or something which would flatter you enough to keep you from using too much of your existing knowledge in the wrong way and stirring up mischief.

There had once been a hint that I should attend an interview for a post in the army's Joint Interrogation School. And then, even vaguer but somehow of great significance, an attachment to Psyops, the psychological warfare HQ at Old Sarum. That one did sound fascinating, but it was just around the time when I got a whiff that Psyops was changing from its concentration on a foreign enemy and in danger of being used by the CIA against our own countrymen.

Then, in the middle of the chaos in Kosovo, some bright spark recommended me for transfer to SIB, the Special Investigation Branch. I was told that it would involve a change of identity. 'Not as if you're married, so there's nobody to worry about the new name. And we can probably find something less weird than Craig Craig.'

I preferred to stay the way I was. By now I was tired of army life and all its blunderings, and my reluctance made it clear that I would be unsuitable for such a job. So they moved

Mike Heriot instead; and he got killed.

Due for demob and making it clear I wasn't going to apply for any remustering, I was approached by a smartly dressed city executive type whose crisp, barking manner gave him away as a poorly camouflaged military man. He offered good money — a very fat salary — to recruit me into a PMF, one of the Private Military Forces working alongside regular troops in what he described as 'A bit of a scuffle that's going to take place in Iraq any time now, believe me.' I had just the sort of know-how these chaps would need. PMFs were the future of modern warfare. And more profitable than regular service.

In the end I committed myself instead to Craig & Hebden. But still they came: Agnew and Keating, picking up where the spooks had left off, suggesting jobs in Buywise if I would be a party to their takeover of Craig & Hebden.

Why had there been this continuing concentration on me? I couldn't possibly be that important.

And — the thought jabbed viciously out of the back of my mind — just what part had Fran been playing . . . watching me, playing the commercial spy, reporting to somebody . . . And what had they done with her?

263

No. I was suddenly back again with a different Fran. The real Fran. Remembering the smell of her shoulder, hearing her clipped, awkward little laugh, the sound of her reluctant voice on the phone, and the sigh as she succumbed and we walked and talked and made love, and sank into those infinitely rewarding silences. There had been so few months of her, yet it was as if I'd had no other life. None worth mentioning, anyway.

Yet there was this uneasy gut feeling that all the time the happiness had been a fantasy: a sour suspicion that, not just during the hours with Fran, somebody had been monitoring me all along.

Back to the questions I had scribbled on a pad and maybe ought now to feed into the computer. The whole idea was to stay cold and analytical. Stay with it. No distractions. Least of all about Fran.

Start, because I had to start somewhere, with Buywise.

Why should they be so keen to have us?

Of course the big supermarket chains liked to gobble up competitors rather than compete with them. But we were suppliers rather than retailers. The exploiters had never specifically offered to buy wines and spirits from us as a free entity. They simply wanted to own us.

Or our premises, anyway. Direct deliveries to our Deben Head wharf and a short distance up the road to the Buywise store. All too easy. European produce, wines, fruit, packaged meat — the whole operation had been virtually blueprinted by Craig & Hebden for the benefit of the takeover boys.

Pause for coffee. The aroma awoke an immediate memory of Fran and myself drinking coffee . . . And a sudden, even clearer memory of her asking me . . . *You've got some plans to fight off the predators . . .* and *Doesn't your wife hold some shares?*

No, that wasn't how I wanted to remember her. Force myself back to the real crux of the matter. All that stuff about a theme park, a virtual military museum, linked with a restaurant and a supermarket drawing some of their supplies through our Deben Head wharf and warehouse: supposing those same facilities of ours could be used for more than commercial requirements? Not groceries but armaments. And men at arms. Shock troops, swiftly landed, with all the necessary military installations and supplies waiting for them in rejuvenated bunkers and food stores around the old airfield which in the past had held so many mysteries, and might find these being renewed. But of course they needed to get their hands on the wharf and warehouse without drawing attention to their motives: make it seem like a Buywise business takeover, not a political/military development.

A crazy idea. But no crazier than some of the things I had lived through in recent years. And things I had studied before actually becoming involved.

During World War II, cunning movements of men and vehicles, and leaked radio messages, suggested that the coming Allied invasion of Nazi Europe would be launched through the Pas de Calais. All this to conceal what was really being planned.

I began some forays across the internet.

There was a time when you had to plough through the financial pages of newspapers and try to relate them to the political pages, and even keep an eye on the top job vacancies, to find out what was going on in the commercial world. Now it was simply a matter of surfing the internet, picking up a hint here and there, and then narrowing the search down and letting the machine do your collating for you.

The Pentagon had long ago built up databases of all its supposed enemies within the US and elsewhere. Our own country had more quietly but clumsily been doing the same thing, amassing information on people not to be trusted — or to be available when scapegoats were needed. Gradually it was becoming more and more comprehensive as the Civil Service merged all its databases into one network with a single entry point, so that someone with the right access could, for example, surf between the Revenue and Customs database, criminal records, and health and education records in search for information on any group or any individual. And there were enough Buywise hits to build up a virtual encyclopedia of commerce. They too were devoted to amassing personal details, all in the name of commerce — but available to anyone who knew the road in. Customers filling in questionnaires, not realizing that these might also be handed on to governmental snoopers. And there was the steady encroachment of RFID — radio frequency identification, microchips embedded in tags on every item on the shelves, which could be read by a central control. Deducing from the statistics where everybody was, what their appetites were, virtually who could be relied on to exist without causing trouble, accepting advertisers' assurances as truth, and accepting political propaganda as gospel. With MI5 or Special Branch able to check up in a matter of seconds.

Funnily enough it was an earlier American President, Eisenhower, who had long ago warned against the dangers of 'the military-industrial complex'. He might have been predicting the day when a handful of American businessmen wanted the Iraq war and the huge contracts for rebuilding, while equally top-rank criminals set about looting the great Babylonian museums to sell on to their wealthy contacts.

Like the military, supermarket chains tried softening up the enemy rather than starting with a clumsy all-out offensive which might cause too many casualties on your own side. You didn't brutally blow up small shops in a town: the butcher, the baker, the greengrocer, the hardware store. You worked to undermine them gradually, then leave them to wither away of their own accord. 'Collateral damage' — such a bland excuse, in business or military campaigns. I soon saw it as highly probable that Buywise was in on things the way big American construction companies were in on the 2003 Iraq invasion before it even started: part of the whole rationale behind it, even, was that of co-ordinating those rebuilding plans with the destruction of specified targets by the invading forces. Today, Buywise was finding it suspiciously easy to get round planning regulations and setting up new outlets close to old or newly refurbished airstrips. And then there were their nudging suggestions about buying what had once been a well-equipped wartime bunker — converted into our Deben Head warehouse. Securing this neck of land while antiwar protestors didn't notice, being engaged in demonstrations up north.

It began to make disturbing sense. The American neocons wanted to consolidate their 'Star Wars' defences surreptitiously, knowing that even their allies were growing doubtful about that alliance. The Polish government was blowing cold at the suggestion that they should surrender sovereignty over a huge site which would be the main European base for the 'Star Wars' missile defence programme. Sites in Britain, including Mildenhall and Lakenheath in Suffolk and Skelmerby in Lincolnshire, had been warily ceded to the Americans. But they needed yet more in their defensive wall, already strong in Suffolk. Deben Head would be an ideal addition, like one in the sequence of forts and milecastles along Hadrian's Wall in Roman days. Supplies of any kind could be shipped in without drawing attention to too many convoys on the roads, too many aircraft landings. A lot more accessible than those installations in Yorkshire and Lincolnshire. Here was one of their old airfields in prime condition, with things underneath it which nobody had ever been notified of. By the time the public and demonstrators awoke to the reality of their use, it would be too late. They would still need Menwith and Fylingdales and Skelmerby as part of their network, but the key stuff could be better positioned and more efficiently supplied right here where it had been equipped for World War Two.

Conspiracy theories, to be sneered at? But from the end of the 20th Century onwards it had become obvious that a large number of conspiracy theories were too close to the mark to be dismissed with the CIA's favourite mantra when in a dicey situation — 'plausible deniability'.

I spread the search wider. Wherever one of these new Buywise supermarkets was planned, there was a boom in road construction or adaptation. In the north, some of those roads were provided at intervals with barriers so that they could be cut off during spells of heavy snow. Yet a lot of them were in areas which did not have a great deal of snow, and had never before installed barriers. Another supermarket in the Buywise chain was opening in the Scottish Borders near an old experimental rocket site which had supposedly been dismantled. But had it? I searched . . . and came up against a firewall. Somebody wanted this left undisturbed. While locals were getting angry in a provincial sort of way about the supermarket, and getting up petitions to keep the local Post Office open and not incorporated in the supermarket, they weren't noticing what was really going on behind all the scaffolding.

Any more than the Debenbridge locals, protesting about the threat to their local shops, knew what part the old Heathwaters airfield was being prepared to play in a new military complex.

Shortly to be designated, like two supposedly RAF airfields in the West Midlands, as US territory, not subject to UK laws? 'Use of deadly force authorized.' That's what the perimeter fence notices said. And we all knew of the CIA's snappy little order when some undesirables had to be removed from the scene: 'Terminate with extreme prejudice.'

Suddenly I was with Fran again. They wouldn't have done that, would they? Why should they?

I dragged myself back to dull, verifiable facts.

Propaganda had been telling us over recent years that some Middle East villains threatened our freedom, and we must brace ourselves to resist, with the aid of our good friends and protectors from across the Atlantic. So the American military and the American megastores were taking over ever so quietly, with their main weapon of money. All of it agreed to by our own government for our own good, though without our actually being asked.

There was an old contact I might risk. Walt Lomborg had been an 'embedded' news reporter with the US forces early in the Iraq shambles, but after copping a minor injury in the left leg had escaped to a job with the American Press Bureau at Canary Wharf. Our paths had crossed a number of times, most fruitfully when I organized wine tastings for London pressmen. After a few glasses he had sometimes hinted at grisly Pentagon secrets and of scandals in certain corners of the White House. Coming from the realities of his countrymen's experiences in a war zone, his contempt for the manipulators behind that war had been fairly impolitic. Nowadays he might not want to risk telling me anything; but he might let just a few useful little hints drop.

I decided to approach him in the old-fashioned way, by telephone. Not that there was much security there. They must already be well aware that I had been searching. Mobile phone voice mails could be intercepted as easily as watching a semaphore signal; keyloggers could record every keystroke made on a target computer; and phone messages nowadays were almost automatically recorded. Still, I might draw some fire. I had gone too far to bother about covering my tracks.

'Great to hear from you, Craggy. You aiming to offer us a consignment of your best claret at a knockdown price?'

'I might run to that in exchange for some information. Or enlightened guesswork on your part.'

'Uh-oh. What am I supposed to be enlightened about?'

'Does the name of Heathwaters mean anything to you?'

'That theme park stuff near your warehouses. Yeah. All going ahead at one hell of a speed. You do know what it used to be in the old Cold War days?'

'An airfield, yes. So-called RAF, but actually run by your compatriots.'

'All buddies on the surface, sure. But underneath that surface?'

'Rocket launchers? I've always supposed so.'

'Much more spacious than that, feller. It was the regional headquarters for the select few if nuclear war broke out. One of a country-wide network for the benefit of key local councillors who'd eased themselves on to the list, plus a few senior law enforcers, and a selection of military men. Very plush facilities, believe you me. They'd have been crazy to demolish that cosy little labyrinth. And what d'you suppose has been added now, under your glossy façade of nostalgic museum and burger bars and supermarket?'

'Would we be talking about an outpost of the US Contingent Defence Outwork?'

'Man, you've been doing your homework, haven't you? Only not so much of the outpost. This is key stuff, Craggy. Along with what they call the secondment of business-men in a 'commercial advisory capacity' ' — you could hear the inverted commas in his voice — 'to liaise with their opposite numbers here. Several of those guys are planted in the US Embassy here in London. And some of them, would you believe, have ties with Buywise, all on the grounds of ensuring feeding the troops in a time of crisis.'

'All working in perfect harmony,' I said bitterly.

'Well, no. No way are they all buddies. Everything's in one hell of a mess right now. The White House and the CIA are hardly on speaking terms. The spooks are refusing to tell the President the rubbish he wants to hear about further dangers in the Middle East, so the White House has set up its own Office of Special Plans, more for trashing the CIA than for providing verifiable information. And at the same time someone in the background is finding some nasty cracks in the basic business. Coping right now with what the stock phrase has it as a 'smoking gun'. Just wait till you see next weekend's financial pages. In the meantime, get yourself hunting the web until you reach the name Dreghorn.'

'Another shady construction company contributing to the President's election campaign?'

'Goes further back than the construction companies. It's the money jugglers who really count. But when they let some of the balls slip . . . Believe me, that Enron scandal way back will have nothing on this. If you're going to risk tackling this . . . '

He had gone. Somebody somewhere, one of those Personal Digital Operatives dominating modern telecommunications worldwide, had intercepted and flicked the switch on him.

Five minutes later, Diana phoned from the office to tell me about an invitation to the formal opening of the Debenbridge Allied

Forces Museum and Leisure Park.

'Opening? But it's nowhere near complete.'

'According to the accompanying letter from a Mr Foster Keating' — she slipped into recital mode — ' 'although there is still a great deal to be done, it is felt work is sufficiently advanced for influential local representatives to be invited to a meeting in the lecture hall, which *is* complete, at which progress will be explained and questions will be welcomed.' '

Barry, she reported in a different, slightly edgy tone of voice, had taken the actual invitation cards. The sponsors were putting him up at the Old Manor House Hotel.

'You know where that is, don't you?'

'Oh yes,' I said, 'I know where it is.'

3

Barry came down the staircase that I remembered Fran going up with that slight twist of her hip, pausing at the landing to smile back at me. Luring me on . . . calculating?

Halfway down Barry stopped, maybe doing his own bit of calculation, needing a few seconds to summon up a convincing line of his usual brash, great-to-see-you chat. I let him wait as long as he needed while I finished my conversation with the man behind the reception desk.

'If I stayed here on that date you reported to the police, then I must have paid the account. And my name should be in the register. May I see your record of it?'

'Look, we admitted there'd been a mistake. It was all in the computer, only then it disappeared. Don't ask me why.'

'I think I do have the right to ask you why, considering the trouble you caused me.'

He was a tall man, but not an impressive one. Perhaps he could be professionally suave and dignified when everything was going smoothly; but evidently things had not been going smoothly for quite some time. 'That damned woman. She was supposed to be sorting things out, switching everything to the computer, but she hadn't got a clue.'

I recalled a gaunt woman, almost as tall as he was, with tightly cropped grey hair and a grey complexion. 'Your wife?'

'Partner.' He ground it out as if it were an obscenity. 'Only not any longer.'

'So what did happen to that particular entry in the computer? The dates I'm talking about . . . '

I was about to recite them for him when he burst out again. 'Bloody useless bitch. She let things get stuffed in there from outside somehow — don't ask me, I've got no use for the blasted thing — and then the police came, and when they came again it wasn't there and . . . look, I've read about computer hackers breaking into big business and military secrets and all that. It's in the papers all the time. But I didn't know anyone could just open the door, sort of, into an ordinary little machine like ours and cock up entries to suit whatever it is they're up to.'

'Easy,' I assured him.

Hacked into, I suspected, by some distant but powerful expert and planted in order to frame me. And then for some reason removed.

'But who'd want to?' he bleated.

'That's what I'd dearly like to know.'

'Well, I can't help you. If that woman was in on it . . . well, anyway, I've chucked her out, right?'

I was about to ask him whether he'd had a hand in installing hidden film equipment in a certain room when Barry made up his mind. He came down quickly, with a sprightly step, beaming as if he had only just recognized me.

'Didn't expect to see you here, old lad. Thought you might be staying put in France until things settled a bit.' His hand gripped mine and took its time to let go. 'It must have been one hell of an ordeal.'

'How did you learn about it?'

'That dismal little copper. Wanted to get in touch with you. Of course I played dumb — hadn't a clue where you were, but I said I'd try to contact you.' He shook his head in fulsome admiration. 'So you decided to come and face the music?'

'It's not her,' I said.

'Sorry, I don't get you.'

'The corpse,' I said. 'It's not Fran.'

He stared. 'Not Fran? Then what the hell is this all about? Who *was* it?'

'That's Plant's business. And getting on to Fran's trail is going to be mine. But in the meantime, what's the programme here? Di told me about our visit here and our invitation to the grand opening.' I added some emphasis to the 'our'.

'Dead loyal, that girl. To you, anyway,' Barry added with an edge to his voice.

'What time do the festivities commence?'

'Look, old lad. I didn't think you'd be up to it, with the shock you must have had.' He squeezed my arm. A great one for physical contact, Barry. 'Obviously Walter wouldn't be up to it, and I didn't think Maureen would be all that helpful, eh? I thought I could cope on my own. After all, it's only a bit of PR. Just as well for one of us to show up and hear what they have to say.'

'Two of us,' I said.

'Well, of course, if you think you're up to it — '

'Yes,' I said, 'I think I'm up to it.'

'If you say so, old lad.' He glanced at his watch. 'Well, see you there.'

'Since I assume you've got the official invitation with you, maybe we'd better go together. I wouldn't want to be turned back at the gate because I had no official chitty to show.'

Barry always had a selection of grins from which to choose. This was one of the more reluctant ones. 'Right, I'll give you a lift, then. I suppose your old banger will be safe here for an hour or two.'

I was having doubts whether around here was safe, but I had been used to living dangerously and it looked as if I had been recalled to that kind of duty.

The sides of the road to Heathwaters had sprouted even more features since I was last here, and when I glanced over my shoulder, there was another arc of those unusually hefty masts closer to the shore.

'A bit of a blind spot here.' Barry, observant as ever, had noticed my reaction. 'I'm told some of the locals objected to these things going up so fast. One of the most persistent of them was bought out. Got a packet from the sale of his house, and moved away to live with relatives somewhere over towards Bury St Edmunds. You've got to hand it to these guys, you know. I mean, the way they get over obstacles — all so smooth, and so little real fuss.'

Yes, they could rely on Barry being an admirer. An adaptable man with a talent for making the right noises at the right time, and with a nose to smell which way the favourable wind was blowing.

But what about when that wind began to smell so badly that it was time to change direction and find a more favourable breath?

We were slowed down a few hundred yards

from the entrance to the complex, tacking on to the end of a queue that moved slowly forward, undergoing inspection by a couple of broad-shouldered men in dark blue uniforms with white shoulder flashes saying SECURITY. The entrance was unexpectedly wide: enough for the largest delivery artic you could imagine. Or for a tank, or a fleet of rocket launchers. Was that just me, indulging in cynical exaggeration?

Inside, strutting traffic marshals waved us imperiously towards a car park, formed by an enclosure of moveable metal fencing at the end of the old runway.

Only it wasn't the old runway any more. It had been illustrated in some handouts and in a couple of weekend colour supplements as a display base for various aircraft and weaponry of World War I, World War II, and the Cold War. But did it need all this widening and re-laying simply for static artefacts?

We were waved into a space beside a butcher's van from Debenbridge. There was a mixture of vehicles: some other tradesmen's vans, including two builders and decorators, an electrician, and a sanitary engineer; and some contrasting Jaguars, hefty 4x4s, and rusted runabouts.

Suddenly, out of the haze at the far end came a shattering blast of pop music. It tore into my eardrums as if to punch great holes in them. Testing speakers for a forthcoming festival? More like Psyops at Fort Meade directing decibels at prisoners as part of a torture programme. But then, to most rational folk a modern pop festival is torture anyway.

Abruptly it was turned down, but there remained a steady thudding, a threat always ready to be intensified again.

'Blundering idiots!' As we followed signs and the peremptory waves of the marshals towards the lecture hall, a familiar figure appeared. I might almost have expected this. It was not the first time Barry's presence had seemed to be the cue for Foster Keating to show up. 'Sorry about that racket.'

'Hi there, Foster,' gushed Barry. 'As you can see, Craig has been able to make it after all.'

'Glad you're here.' But there was a suspicion of a peevish query in his glance at Barry.

'Wouldn't have missed it for the world,' I said.

'At the end of the presentation, I hope we can have a word.'

'On what subject?'

Keating waved at two of the Security types who appeared to be hassling a middle-aged man getting out of a local butcher's van which had taken a wrong turning. 'Need pulling together. We aim to get that all sorted out before we open. Ever heard of Security Risk Management, Mr Craig?'

'It's the flashy new name for a corps of bouncers.'

Keating forced a smile. 'Straight to the point, as usual. But you do realize that with your distinguished military record, and your CV after that, you could be just the man to get down to the real nitty-gritty?'

'I've got other plans.'

'Aren't they a bit under threat right now?'

'From whom?'

He shrugged. 'I'd still like to make it a date after the show.'

Barry hurried us into the lecture hall, with murals of bombers and the flags of all nations, with the Stars and Stripes predominating. At each door stood a heavy, trying to look as benevolent and unthreatening as a St John's Ambulance man, handing out a printed questionnaire to each entrant. Hoping to accumulate more snippets of information for their database, no doubt.

We found that our seats were three and four in from the end of a row, three rows up from one of the side doors. I estimated the time it would take to make a dash for that door in case of trouble.

What trouble? Let's just say this was force of habit. Always check on the most practical getaway when you're ushered into a confined space.

The rows of seats were packed with men from various jobs and professions in the town, some in their best suit, some in sports shirts and jeans. Most of their womenfolk had thought the occasion a good excuse for a new hairdo. Closer to the platform I could see the back of a head I thought I recognized. When he turned to his neighbour I saw that it was Steve Palmer, from the local rag. Still functioning, then, in spite of Lisa's hints.

Why had I half expected Lisa to be here?

On the platform, four chairs had been set with mathematical exactness behind a long mahogany table, overlooked by a huge cinema screen on the back wall. When the hall appeared to be quite full, four men marched on stage from the left. A few people clapped half-heartedly, like an audience not sure whether to expect a comedy act or a solemn opening speech.

Foster Keating was one of the platform party. Another, sallow-faced and looking now like some dour official censor ready to pounce on anything out of order, was the MoD character I had seen way back at the beginning of these developments — Martin Agnew. A third had a face so everyday and nondescript that it was hard to believe anything could possibly motivate him enough to produce a smile or a glare. But I'd met plenty like that in my time. Second-level executives who had been programmed to act ruthlessly when necessary, without the slightest change of expression or, inside, the slightest feeling of remorse for what it might be necessary to do to underlings — or even to competitive equals.

The fourth man was the first to speak. He came round the table and stood plumb centre on the stage.

He wore a three-piece charcoal grey suit and blue-striped shirt with a buttoned-down shirt collar. Lots of London types with holiday homes in East Anglia wore that kind of thing during the week in the city, but in Suffolk at weekends they usually favoured open-necked shirts with some fashionable logo on the pocket, and Armani slacks. This one looked like a *Christian Science Monitor* journalist among the sybarites of the east coast.

He introduced himself as Harrison Sumner. His relaxed manner suggested that even uttering the name was in itself a relaxing, amiable exercise. He went on to say how very honoured he was to be here today among this truly representative gathering of local folk.

'And what would *you* be representing, then?' A broad-shouldered man stood up, asked the question, and sat down without waiting for the answer, satisfied with the faint sputter of amusement from his neighbours.

'I like to think I represent the future.' Sumner stared out far above the heads of his audience. 'A really prosperous, *sharing* future for everyone in this hall. Everyone in this beautiful region.'

His voice was measured, leisurely, and persuasive. His accent was not so much American as smooth, practised English with an occasional faint tang to add crispness. Not pushy but inviting a compliant smile.

'We old friends from both sides of the Atlantic share so many memories,' he said. 'My countrymen were privileged to be your guests here for many crucial years. That relationship is still very much alive for us. But together we must also work for a mutually assured future. On a solid foundation of our days as comrades in arms' — his right arm lifted slowly to make a solemn, sweeping gesture along the mural to his right — 'we must consolidate that special relationship and allow no enemies, large or small, jealous rivals or outright terrorists, to shake our faith.'

As the clichés rolled out there were a few shuffles and murmurs in the audience, wondering why they should have been invited here to undergo a PR exercise that differed little from the handouts already given to the Press. I might have wondered about the air of urgency, too, if it had not been for the tips given me by Walt Lomborg.

'And now, let us beg fifteen minutes of your time to show you a brief film of our progress so far. And then we'll be very happy to answer any questions you may have.'

The house lights were dimmed, the screen behind the platform party blazed into life with what at first looked like a mathematical puzzle. Then the outlines resolved themselves into a metallic network of cranes, with accompanying music suggesting they were about to separate and dance. Gradually the viewpoint widened, the cranes backed away to a stately gavotte, and the screen filled gradually with a planner's daydream of graceful buildings and spacious courtyards displaying historic aircraft, tanks, and artillery, glowing with an intensifying colour as the reconditioned runway raced towards the bright blue horizon, while the music changed to a stirring march.

Some of the audience muttered awestruck approval. A few shuffled. One man shouted,

'That's all a commercial, that's what,' and waved an accusing arm until his wife nudged him back into surly watchfulness.

The film concluded with a long shot of a supermarket frontage dazzling with lights and topped by the name of Buywise.

The questions that followed were as predictable as Sumner's platitudes. How were they going to cope with the extra traffic that would clog the roads once the whole complex was open to the public? Just who was providing the money for the whole thing, and who was going to reap the profits?

Most of these questions had already been asked — or, rather, flung like missiles at intruders — in the press, on local TV, and in Community Council meetings. But they were more enjoyable here, when the questioner could see himself more than lifesize on the screen behind the platform. Other members of the audience peered into their mobiles like disciples waiting for assurance from a soothsayer. Beside me, Barry kept consulting a new model the size of a paperback novel.

'Why have you suddenly decided to have this meeting, when the place is only half finished?' came an aggressive question from the back of the hall.

'A very good question, sir. Let's just say that we've reached a stage when we felt it was time to draw the community closer about us. There have been some complaints, in the press and, I believe, in certain social gatherings in the town' — his smile managed to be companionable rather than patronising — 'that work here has gone too fast and without local consultation. Maybe we have been so keen to get ahead that that is true. I apologize for that. Truly. And that is why we thought we would open the doors, and show you that we have nothing to hide. When we've finished here, I hope you'll wander round the installations, as far as they have gone. In the room across the reconstructed parade ground, opposite this hall, is what will eventually be the main information centre, fully equipped with video displays and every facility for calling up historical records and current events. Right now it's displaying plans and mockups of the various features as they will be, including the supermarket, designed to supplement facilities in the community rather than compete with amenities already in existence.'

Barry was nudging me to draw attention to the fact that he was about to get to his feet.

'Since, Mr Speaker, you have made it clear that so many historic elements are to be incorporated into this ambitious exposition, is there any possibility of restoring the old railway line? Early in the twentieth century and well into the fifties there was a regular steam train service to Debenbridge, and a branch line into Heathwaters. It proved an invaluable supply route during the Second World War, and if the displays here are to be even halfway authentic it should be restored just as it was.'

He beamed down at me, inviting my approval of this revival of our old shared interest, and managed a self-approving wink. From the platform, Foster Keating nodded benignly. It seemed probable that Barry might be accorded a little sweetener, a concession in return for his loyal support.

I got up.

'Isn't it time you came out with the full story? That just as US construction companies helped prod Bush into the Iraq fiasco so that they could profit from rebuilding, right now the condominium of Buywise and a shifty finance company are in league with the Pentagon to establish 'Star Wars' outposts throughout the British Isles, in the guise of — '

'I don't think we have come here to listen to way-out conspiracy theories, Mr Craig.'

'Some of it is certainly way out. Even our muzzled Press has been allowed to report that the US has been negotiating with Poland and the Czech Republic over setting up advanced radar stations as part of their missile shield project — '

'We're in no way concerned with — '

'*And* missile interceptor sites. All to be declared extraterritorial and sovereign US bases. Australia's also getting drawn in. That's for the near future. But it's already happening here in our own country, right here and now. Is that what we want? Cameras spying on our every move, nuclear weapons rolling through the streets.'

'Good for you, sir,' somebody shouted from the back of the hall.

'And isn't this hurried get-together largely triggered by a need to get support before a certain venture capital company whose CEO is one Elmer Dreghorn, brother of the General Dreghorn in charge of the Theatre Missile Defence wing of the NMD, withdraws its backing because both men are about to be charged with corruption by a federal investigation?'

Barry, whimpering, was plucking at my sleeve. 'For Christ's sake, Craig, what are you up to?'

The two heavies from the nearest door were heading up the aisle, ready to shove their way along towards me. But two local farmers stood up to block their way.

'Hands off him. Let him speak.'

'Aye, you go right ahead, Mr Craig.'

'If these folk have their way, every day from now on your every move's going to be followed by those spy cameras — round here, in the town, at your workplace. The checkout clerks at Buywise will want to see our loyalty cards. The police are steadily collecting your DNA, whether you've ever been convicted of anything or not. And under an agreement never discussed in Parliament or announced to the public, all personal database information is fed without question to any US security agency which asks for it. Are you happy with that?'

Two other heavies came shoving their way towards me from the other end of the row.

Suddenly there was an explosion somewhere in the distance, outside, and the volume of the speakers by the runway screamed hideously upwards. At the same time a variety of mobile ringtones sprang into life like the quarrelsome chirping of any number of birds. Barry fished his latest acquisition from his pocket, stabbed at various buttons, like a child reacting to a sudden upset by reaching for his comforter, and stared into the flickering colours on his expanded screen. 'Good God, what's going on out there?'

On the platform Keating, red-faced, had turned to shout something at Sumner. Whatever was happening, it was not a part of the official programme. I heard myself laughing for a brief, instinctive moment. Everything this evening had been so interlocked, carefully planned, all under one meticulously calculated control. But somebody had pressed the wrong button — or the right button at the wrong time.

The first of the two doormen had elbowed his way past six protesting men and women. I braced myself, vaulted up on to the shoulders of a couple immediately in front of me, sprawled over their neighbours, grunted the best I could offer in the way of an apology, and blundered my way towards the now unguarded door.

Outside in the dusk, the blare of the speakers was overpowering. Headlights stabbed along the perimeter road, and floodlights were suddenly blazing down from tall standards like those around a football pitch.

I tried squinting through the hellish glare, but couldn't make out any features that would tell me which way to go.

Then there were two of them, grabbing my arms and manhandling me towards what solidified out of the dazzle as a high brick wall. I was pushed through a door into utter darkness for a few moments. By the time my eyes could cope again, another door had been opened and I was hustled into a small room with a bright light trained on me.

Lisa said: 'Hello again, Craig.'

I was not too dizzy to be unable to rise to the occasion. 'Ill met by floodlight,' I said.

4

She was seated in a large revolving armchair, swinging it a few degrees to and fro behind a heavy desk with a VDU tilted towards her from one corner. A panel with an impressive array of buttons was sunk into the desktop. Her light grey jacket and slacks were almost a camouflage in this grey-walled room; but her high, glacial cheeks shone out of that greyness like a light ready to be adjusted. There were other lights: above her head, one on the end of a flexible stem; behind her, a battery of them poised at different angles.

The men who had hustled me in shoved me down on to an upright steel chair a lot more spartan than Lisa's.

She said: 'Make yourself comfortable.'

It wasn't the sort of place where you would ever feel comfortable. Very much the opposite.

'An interrogation room?' I said. 'With some nasty fitments?'

'You fancy doing the interrogating?'

'Actually, I think I'm getting the hang of the answers. I imagine all you need do is confirm them. This room, now. And maybe some others along the corridor. Equipped to deal with awkward characters who just don't want to talk. Here to cut out the long haul. That airstrip out there could serve as a staging post on one of those 'extraordinary rendition' flights from the US. Only with the right facilities here on the premises, maybe there's no further need to refuel and press on to some useful country where torture is an everyday practice. All the equipment's right on hand, ready and waiting. Right?'

'Jumping to conclusions, Craig.'

'The right conclusions. Really comprehensive, this set-up, isn't it?'

She was still smiling. It was the sort of smile she would produce, I guessed, when after months of hard work she had exposed a drug smuggler or a financial fiddler — a smile almost of admiration at the trickster's impertinence but touched with enjoyment at her own skill in outwitting him.

She looked past me. 'All right, you two can go.'

There was a mumbled protest. 'I don't know, ma'am. Not sure the Commander'd be keen on — '

'Right here and now, I'm in command. And I don't think I'm in any danger from this old acquaintance.' When they had gone, she raised one thin flaxen eyebrow. 'Am I, Craig?'

The room was unnaturally quiet. Whatever noise might still be going on outside, this place was soundproof. To stop any screams being heard outside?

I said: 'What was all that melodrama out there? Trying to put the wind up the entire local population?'

'There seems to have been a minor slip-up. It'll be looked into.'

'A military cock-up? A dummy run that went wrong?'

Just the faintest flicker in her would-be imperturbable eyes showed I had registered a direct hit.

'Nothing's gone wrong that I know of. Except some people getting on their hind legs and speaking out of turn. When it comes to putting the wind up the locals — '

'All right,' I said. 'Let's stop arsing about. Where's Fran?'

'Not still obsessed by that trollop? She was only using you. Under orders. That must have dawned on you by now.'

'A lot of things have dawned on me. But not where you fit in. Or where Fran fits in. But that's not the point. Where is she *now*?'

'Tell me where you got all those stories you started peddling out there in the hall — '

'And then you'll tell me what you've done with Fran?'

She had always enjoyed feeling herself in charge of a situation. That I remembered well. Yet here there was something taut and angry tugging at the lines in that too-flawless face as she leaned towards me.

'You first.'

It was essential to keep it light and along lines that suited me. 'And you'll confirm each point as we go?' I said.

'Try me.'

★ ★ ★

I took up where I had been abruptly cut off in the hall. After just a few words I was tempted to stop and refuse to go on playing this grotesque game. What possible sense could there be in reciting a string of dangerous facts or suppositions in this room with this one woman, while God knows what was going on outside? My speculating about things, no matter how accurately, wasn't going to alter any of them. Not until I was out of here and free to speak and do something about it.

If I ever was. Trying to treat it as a game of wits for two was all very well. But who was going to award points at the end of the match?

Still, maybe like some poor wretch in this room waiting for the real torture to begin, I had to go on talking.

'Basically,' I said, 'we've already handed over Diego Garcia and Ascension Island to the US, and now it's time to hand over bits of our own country as 'Son of Star Wars' outstations. Making sure they're under NMD control from the States. And these things have to be in place fast, because folk over there are no longer sure we Brits can be relied on as allies. The old special relationship ain't what it used to be. And on top of that, the coming presidential election isn't in the bag. Nor the next general election in this country. The real powers behind the throne — or behind the White House, or the Pentagon, or whoever's running the Theatre Missile Defence side-show and calling the tune right now — they want things consolidated.'

Lisa was expressionless. 'Interesting.'

'And the boys who provide the cash want their cut of the profits. All those secret slush funds have to come up with a worthwhile dividend. Buywise, now, not just getting prime sites in the UK for their ordinary retail business, but acting as a supply chain for all the reconditioned military bases.'

'Isn't that rather a melodramatic way of putting it? Of course there's some truth in the idea of a contemporary overall pattern. But it's a healthy one. It's the reality of our world today. Globalization. Not just individual companies linked up for shareholders' financial benefit, but whole worldwide projects. We're all bits of one big happy monopoly now. Governments, armies, transport, food supplies, scientific projects, drugs and therapies and the media all geared to keep everyday life going smoothly. Food chains and hardware suppliers to feed the populace and feed the troops defending us, and protect them from wind, weather, and enemies. Come on now, Craig — I don't have to lecture *you* on logistics, do I? We're just one great global family concern now.'

'With a tight little band of neocons in the United States as paterfamilias, laying down the do's and don'ts for the entire household.'

'Would you prefer them to be laid down by Afghanistan, or Iran, or Syria?'

'I'd prefer it all to be openly discussed,' I said, 'rather than imposed by a clique of pre-conditioned goons in a ring of armoured watchtowers. Especially those labelled 'use of deadly force authorized'.'

A light in the corner of the desk panel began flashing a rhythmic signal. Impatiently Lisa pressed a button and turned her head to watch the VDU glow into life.

'Idiots!' It was rare to see her puzzled.

'They weren't supposed to … not until I …'

I stood up and leaned over in an attempt to see what was on her screen. She immediately shut it off, and looked capable of closing me down as well. 'Sit down, Craig.'

'It's a bit unsociable. Like watching your favourite sitcom when you've got a distinguished guest in your sitting-room.'

'Sit down,' she said, 'or I'll have you fastened down. Painfully.'

'How to win friends and influence people.' But I sat down, studying her face, with its arrogant mask of invulnerability. 'Things going just a bit pear-shaped? Just like those awkward questions being asked in Congress right now.'

'Everything's under control.' She was making an involuntary movement to ease the tightness out of her shoulders. 'Now, where were we? What's next on your fantasy tour?'

I wondered again what would happen if I did simply get up and walk out of that door. Probably get manhandled back in again by her two bruisers. Anyway, now that I was here, until I could appraise the situation a lot more positively it was worth while using this interrogation room for just that: interrogation, only with me doing the questioning. Something was going on outside. It must all have something to do with what we were talking about, here inside.

I said: 'All right, I'm getting the general picture. But where do *you* fit into it? I don't see Revenue and Customs being involved in covert military shenanigans. You seem to carry a lot more clout than a mere VAT snooper.'

'So gracefully put, Craig. But all right, you're not so far out when you sniff a hook-up between US global defences and an international supply chain. But there's nothing sinister about that. Makes perfect sense, I'd say. You don't send troops into battle or spread them out as a worldwide defence force without being able to fill their stomachs. And pay for it from the profits of trading with the general public as well. What's your problem?'

'Another of my problems is, where do *I* come into all this? I mean, I can see your Buywise connections would want to drive Craig & Hebden out of business, just to consolidate their own wider game. But there's been more to it than that, hasn't there? That crazy business about the law chasing me, and keeping me out of circulation for a useful time, and then dropping the whole thing. I couldn't ever have been regarded as all that important.'

She was staring not at me but at the panel

in the desk, as if preparing to reach out and conjure up some instructions with her fingers rather than speak directly to me.

'You're wrong, Craig.' When it came, it was a fierce whisper. 'So wrong. And so unobservant. I thought I'd made it clear last time we talked.' She was forcing the words out as if every syllable was meant as a lethal stab. 'You were important to *me*.'

Before I could sort this out in my own mind, the door was flung open. Agnew and Keating stamped towards the table, looming over me as they glared down on Lisa. 'Do you know it's all coming apart out there?' All trace of Keating's glib, soft-sell accent was gone. 'They're all flooding out of the hall and wandering about like a lot of cattle. And the TV cameras taking every blundering bit of it in.'

'A few slight hitches,' said Lisa, freezingly calm. 'But remember, the programme's not going out live. We do have editorial control over the end product — a documentary with some chosen extracts to use for commercials in due course.'

'With half the damned population of the region right in the middle of it, getting the kind of impression we were specifically planning to avoid?' Agnew was trying but failing to keep that stiff upper lip image he must have practised throughout his career. 'There are bound to be independent TV and Press scavengers muscling in any minute now, without us having any editorial control. And the women are running ragged, trying to find the ladies' lavatories.'

It was too much. I burst out laughing, and was rewarded with a glare quite different from the suave matiness he had tried on me all those months ago.

'Perhaps we'd better open the restaurant doors a bit earlier than we had planned,' said Lisa. 'It's all running ahead of schedule, unfortunately, thanks to our friend here and his outburst in the lecture hall.'

'You can say that again.' Agnew jabbed a petulant forefinger at me. 'And just where *does* he come into it?'

Lisa was on her feet. 'I think we'd better continue this outside.'

The two men hesitated, but she was coming round the desk and forcing them out — not with a gun in her hand, or strong-arm guards to manhandle them, but simply by the determination in her eyes. They went out.

I got up, ready to follow and find out what new bizarre situation was brewing; but the door had locked automatically. It took only a few minutes for Lisa to come back in, with the door clicking shut again behind her.

For once there was colour in her cheeks — a pink glow high on the cheekbones. 'That settles that little matter.' She was jubilant. But where had she acquired the authority to dispose so summarily with men like Agnew and Keating?

I said: 'I think I'm the one who ought to be asking that question.'

'What question?'

'The one Agnew was asking. And what I was asking you when he came in. Where *do* I come into all this?'

Lisa settled back into her chair. The bristling confrontation with Agnew and Keating appeared to have relaxed rather than ruffled her. She had the air of a hostess waiting to dispense drinks and catch up with the latest gossip rather than that of a tough career woman with a taste for gruelling inquisitions.

'I think it's time I told you a few things,' she said. 'It'll pass the time while those clodhoppers sort themselves out.'

'And the ladies find their way in and out of the loo?'

★　★　★

It was a narrative with details and places I recognized, but whose basic thread grew more and more incredible as she spun it out.

One thing which I could find credible was that she had indeed moved on into higher things from that job in what became Revenue & Customs. It had simply provided a useful entrée into so many other powerful enclaves. Even as she was telling me her matter-of-fact story, with a self-deprecating twist of the lips every now and then, her cool, fey eyes told another, less modest story. Behind them was the determination never to let go until she had won. She reminded me of a store detective I had known in a supermarket we used to supply in Peterborough. That inconspicuous little woman would saunter from counter to counter like a dithery customer unable to make up her mind about what she wanted to buy. Once in a while she would dig out a shopping list from her bag and frown over it. Until she spotted a shoplifter. She knew how to stalk her prey without being noticed; and then, suddenly feral, when and how to pounce.

Somebody must have recognized those qualities in Lisa. I got the gist of her progress as much from what she was not telling me as from her actual words. Without naming MI5, MI6, GCHQ, NSA, DIA or any of the other groups of spooks, she admitted having been recruited into a department liaising with a

US electronic surveillance team, loosely referred to as Integrated Support Intelligence or Tactical Co-ordination.

'A whole tangle of different webs,' she said, 'with resident spiders always keener on scoring off one another than on cooperating in the national interest.'

'And one special spider going from one web to another, snatching the best bits from what others have patiently constructed?'

Lisa would have been incapable of anything so crude as a smirk; but at least an increasing complacency crept into her tone. 'Let's just say I worked to specific guidelines with an overview of several groups. *Quis custodiet ipsos Custodes*, as they say. I became a sort of watcher over the supposed watchers. But,' she said, 'they made one mistake. Each one of them, as I moved along — or moved upwards — thought they were using me. While all the time, as I think I told you a little while ago, I was using them. You think all those MI5 and MI6 types are somehow subtler and more knowledgeable than mere mortals? Look at their dismal record. They rarely *know* anything, so they're only too happy to *believe* what somebody slides into their In tray. Intelligence? They're the most credulous people in the world. The easiest to manipulate.' Lisa sounded dreamy with satisfaction.

'I love pulling strings, Craig. Watching the puppets dance.'

A light sparked rhythmically on her desk. She tapped a button, and lifted an earpiece.

'All right. All right, don't panic. Put an announcement out on the speakers about the restaurant being open. Free buffet for all our visitors. And then some music on the speakers. We'll time an announcement explaining the dummy run for . . . what time is it now? . . . right, thirty minutes from now.'

'Dummy run?' I echoed. 'So I was right. All part of a military exercise, displaying this stronghold's potential to overawe the public?'

'Not so much military as civil defence. To show folk how prepared we are against terrorists, illegal immigrants, the lot. How all our precautions swing into action at a moment's notice. Heathwaters still protecting the community from invasion, the way it did over the latter part of the last century.'

'Only somebody jumped the gun? Pressed the button too soon?'

'Craig, did you ever know any local pageant, firework display, tattoo . . . or, for that matter, any military manoeuvre go ahead without *some* hiccup?' She leaned back as if content simply to be here, in charge. And with me as an audience.

After what seemed an interminable minute

and more, I prompted her: 'And no hiccups in your career of pulling strings and making the puppets dance?'

'Very few. Except a personal one. Repetitive.' She was staring straight at me, no longer complacent. 'And damned offensive.'

'Must be irritating when the puppet refuses to dance.'

'Oh, but you did, Craig. Most of the time. And that was worth watching. After what you did to me. Or didn't do to me.'

There were no torture implements in this room. Or none that I could see. Yet the oppressiveness of this enclosed space was becoming worse. Lisa was too close, too intense. Her easygoing boasting had become something else. Like an inquisitor timing each move before increasing the pressure, she was waiting for my next reaction.

I said: 'Sorry, but I still don't understand what part I was allocated in all this melodrama. Or why I got shoved around.'

'One of my perks, Craig. I've followed your career every inch of the way. Once I'd picked up the scent, I kept getting a recurrence. Once you've been in the frame, as it were, you're never deleted. Long before the current clamour for ID cards, your every move would anyway be on our database. And whenever I saw a chance of intervening, I did.'

Lisa went on spelling it out with slow relish. Their whole organization had to get rid of a lot of petty nuisances so that they could get their installations into place. Preferably without violence. As I'd already sussed, financial experts knew where to buy up land to block other developers, and where to get a neat juxtaposition of Buywise with designated defence outstations. Craig & Hebden were just one of the small nuisances, like a fly that needed swatting. If the worst came to the worst, arrangements could have been forced through for a compulsory purchase order to be slapped on Deben Head, reclaiming it for official defence purposes. But that would have drawn too much attention to what was planned. The media would almost certainly get a sniff of what was really behind it all. It would be possible to sit on a few of them and throw official secrets warnings and talk of commercial confidentiality at them, but that would only hot up the chase. Much better to destroy our firm's credibility in the market-place bit by bit, making room for the Buywise link. Starting by infiltrating our operations and tracking down all our contacts — suppliers, outlets, credit rating, the lot.

Infiltration? Everything around me, everything in my body, was getting colder. 'Fran?' I said wretchedly.

'That wasn't my idea. I told them it wouldn't work. Told them you'd never fall for anything that crude. You were too puritanical to hop into bed with anyone just because it's offered.'

'Thanks for the testimonial.'

'But I was wrong, wasn't I? Not only that. She'd always been just the right sort of operative. She enjoyed sex every now and then — on *her* terms, nobody else's. Satisfying a passing hunger, but never committing herself to anything long-term. Enjoying the sheer skill of wheedling facts out of men for our benefit. But I was wrong — you did fall for her, and gave her everything we wanted. Starting with the trip she requested round the premises. With what she described to us as . . . what was it? . . . 'a handsome young hunk with a hard on.' She had a remarkable memory for detail, and gave her handlers a virtual plan of the whole layout. What would need to be adapted or cleared out. Capacity of the wharves and loading bays. Then a useful trip to France, and information about contacts and activities in the UK. Nothing quite as rewarding as pillow talk, is there? Beats crude head-on assaults.'

'And you had to film it? Just to satisfy your own perverse tastes? No use for blackmail. I'd

312

left my wife before this whole thing started.'

'Useful for the record. Might come in handy. One can always discard what's no longer needed. And your precious Mrs Leith quite enjoyed performing for the benefit of the camera.'

'Her flat,' I said wretchedly. 'And that hotel. Was that so easy to wire up?'

'Very easy indeed. A lot of our technical consultants stayed there while the Heathwaters reconstruction was going on.'

'And planting that misinformation about me — juggling dates to fit evidence the police were looking for?'

'Easy enough nowadays to hack into anybody's computer. Insert anything you like. And remove it when it's done its job and you don't want to leave it lying around.'

'You planted that phoney September date *after* Fran had disappeared, to make it seem that I was with her at our old rendezvous. You set the dogs on me when it amused you.'

'But called them off just in time before they could do real damage.'

'When *that* amused you.'

'Life would be awfully dull if one couldn't mix business with pleasure.'

'But you hadn't banked on Frances Leith going a lot further than that?'

'Stupid bitch. Forgetting how to play it cool.'

'Just because she fell in love with me, you didn't have to — '

'Not because she fell in love with you. That was stupid, but we could have overlooked it. It was *you* falling in love with *her* that I couldn't stomach. For Christ's sake, what was so special about her?'

Impossible to tell her. Or anyone else in the world. That haunting smell in the corner of Fran's throat, the way she half laughed as if wondering whether to share something or to save it for another moment; the way she stared into the distance, sometimes wistful and sometimes challenging; most of all those silences which somehow told me she was glad I was there.

'You gave me the cold shoulder, Craig.' Her voice tightened like a violin string about to snap. 'Not once, but several times. That was bad enough. But to go and fall for that trollop Frances Leith . . . '

It was crazy. I was the one thing she couldn't get. She wasn't used to not getting what she wanted. She would never, ever, believe there was something she couldn't get if she wanted it enough. She was mad. So sure of her own infallibility, so much in control of any situation, twisting it to suit whatever she fancied at the time. But mad. And when she didn't get what she wanted, not just eccentric, but mad. Dangerously mad.

How could you tell a woman that, in spite of her almost flawless beauty, she gave you the creeps?

But, whatever resentment might be eating away at her warped mind, there was one question still taunting my own. 'That man Viney. Where does he figure in your sleazy set-up?'

'Yes, that must have hurt you.' She was smiling again. 'Seeing him enjoying the same favours you thought were on your exclusive patch.' She kept me waiting, then drew it out very slowly. 'We needed to know where the next demos at each of the reconditioned sites were going to be. Because we wanted to infiltrate them, make them bigger and noisier to attract a lot of publicity. While we developed our major facility elsewhere. Because that's what Heathwaters is, Craig: the heart of the whole operation.'

I said: 'Fran. Where is she? She's not dead at all.'

'Who says she isn't?'

'You know where she is. What the hell are you doing to her?' When she sat still, looking as if she was beginning to enjoy herself again,

I shouted: 'This is ridiculous.'

'It kept the game going until . . . well, until I could hope for a satisfactory resolution.'

'Hang time,' I muttered.

'What was that?'

'Hang time. A phrase used in the vineyards. Allowing the fruits of your labours time to mature until they have reached the peak of perfection, ready to be gathered in.'

'What a charming concept. Craig, I couldn't have put it better myself.'

'But in this case,' I said, 'the grapes have gone sour on you. And,' I went on, 'everything else is going sour. Your backers are going bust, the whole set-up is coming apart. So much for all those strings you've been pulling.'

The door was unceremoniously thrust open to admit Agnew again.

'There are two police cars at the main gate. Saying there've been reports of a disturbance. And they want to come in.'

'I never asked for police. They're not part of the programme.'

'They're here anyway. And there's a large gang trying to break through the perimeter fence on the town side.'

'Send the police round there,' I suggested. '*There's* their disturbance, all ready and waiting.'

I thought Agnew was going to go for me. Instead, he leaned menacingly towards Lisa. 'You set this whole thing up. For Christ's sake come and sort it out.'

He held the door open for her, and it wasn't out of politeness. She stormed past him. And before the door could close again, this time I grabbed it and went out fast.

'Stay right where you are,' yelled Agnew.

It was a ludicrous thing to say. He was bellowing at me while trying desperately to get Lisa moving towards what I supposed was the exit. Which meant that I had to make a dash in the opposite direction.

I was in a featureless corridor with a steel door at the far end, and above it what looked like a complicated spy camera, tilted to keep an eye on me. I went towards it. When I was within a few feet, all the overhead lights went out. For a moment I felt dizzy, in utter darkness with nothing to reach for, nothing to give me any sense of direction.

Slowly I groped to my right, and shuffled over until I could touch the wall. I went on forward, a pace at a time.

Somewhere a siren began shrilling.

I stopped for a moment to take a deep, self-encouraging breath.

A faint light ahead began to shape itself into the outlines of an opening door. I quickened my pace, unsure whether it was really there and whether it was going to slam in my face. But I went through, and down a corridor to my right there were brighter wall lights. I had gone only a few feet when they went out. And then came on again. It was as if Lisa was back at her desk console, playing malicious games with me. Or somebody was trying to familiarize himself with the system. Whoever it was, the lights stayed on until I reached a door at the far end and opened it without any trouble, to find the wind on my forehead and the sudden noise of a crowd ebbing and flowing across the car park.

I stepped outside. If I could find enough of the cars and vans belonging to locals we'd done business with, I could get them to form a powerful enough group to resist any tricks played by the gang running this scam, and let the police in. We had always been on good terms with the local police, and could give them some useful directions.

A crowd was wandering around the site, some of them looking a bit baffled. It was visitors' evening, after all. Some had been shepherded into the restaurant. But there was a more purposeful surge of men swinging round the end of the building. Maybe the raiding party had made their way successfully through the fence. As I began heading towards the cluster of cars a hundred yards away, three or four men detached themselves and came in at an angle to cut me off.

As they reached me, I took a wild swing at their leader, who went down, cursing. Two of the others grabbed my right arm and twisted it backwards. They were tough and strong, and knew what they were doing. But I knew, too. I ducked. Kneed one of them and headbutted the other.

'Hold it. Calm down, you silly bugger.'

It was a voice I knew. Or had known. Hadn't heard it for a long time. And anyway it was impossible.

He held on to my shoulder and wrenched me round to face him. And suddenly all the lights came on again, and there it was — a face I also knew. Just as impossible. Because he had died in Bosnia.

5

Mike Heriot was laughing that familiar boisterous laugh of his, and slapping me on the back and saying, 'Craggy, it's so good to see you. But a bit of a shock, I suppose, hey?'

'How the hell . . . ?'

'To the rescue in the nick of time, that's us.'

A small, orderly group of men were lining up behind him, obviously waiting for orders. Across the rest of the open space, as wide as a parade ground, a handful of men and women came wandering out of the restaurant, staring around like residents in a holiday camp waiting for the next instruction. One or two began heading for their parked cars. Half-a-dozen hefty marshals were trying to round them up.

'Not yet, folks. The show's not over yet. If you'll just be patient . . . '

I was still trying to take in the reality of Mike. 'And you — you're part of this deadly charade?'

'We were meant to be. But we changed our minds. You were right not to take up that appointment, Craggy. As usual, you old bastard. Just quietly, smugly, bloody well right. Only now . . . '

'Now?'

'It's quite a story. But first things first. We've go to get this situation under control before somebody lights the blue touchpaper.'

'Which means,' I said, 'getting to the control panel and broadcasting a message over those speakers up there. They'll override any other racket that's going on. Let me talk to the locals — '

'The way you did a little earlier? That little speech of yours triggered things off before the TLD were quite ready for their display, didn't it?'

'TLD?'

'Tactical Liaison Detachment. Yet another of the covert security branches. Part of Special Resources Division. They do love dreaming up gobbledegook, don't they?' He looked up at the surveillance cameras and the lights and the speakers clustered along the rear roof-line of the planned supermarket. 'But that's a good idea of yours, Craggy. To some extent you're a local. They know you, and I'd say they respect you. Can I sit in on it, at your elbow?'

'To shoot me if I say something out of turn?'

'To prompt you if you need it. Which I doubt.'

'Like I said, the main thing is to get to the control panel in that woman's office. You seemed to suggest she's capable of triggering an explosion or something out of sheer spite if things aren't going her way.'

'Meaning Lisa Maitland's on these premises? Dead right, Craggy. Lethal, that woman.'

There was no time to ask what he knew about Lisa and how he was involved with her. I felt in my bones, as old Walter might have put it, that we needed to move fast and take control.

I remembered the way in which I'd been hustled into the building. This time I was leading the way, hesitating at one corner inside, then remembering the dog-leg at one end of the corridor. I tried the first door to our left, and it opened to reveal what might have been the reception area of a small, expensive hotel, with double glass doors at one side and what looked like a small restaurant beyond.

'I'd guess plushy facilities for CIA agents,' said Mike, 'resting off their rendition flights.'

The next door had to be the one I'd been shoved through. If this one were locked . . .

It wasn't.

I led the way in. Lisa was back. If it were possible for her to look paler than ever, that was the way she looked. Some people, men or women, flush scarlet with rage. Lisa had become incredibly more livid. And she was holding a gun, incongruous in that smooth white hand, the hand of a smart, always self-controlled wheeler-dealer.

'Glad you've come back, Craig. I was thinking of sending someone to find you.' Then the gun hand wavered. She was looking past me. 'Newman. What the devil are you doing here? What right have you to be — '

One of Mike's men was past me, swiftly snatching the gun before she could regain her composure.

'Newman?' I said, baffled.

'Since my remuster, old cock. New job, new name. Probably the one they'd have given you if you'd fallen for their spiel.' He was moving round to stand above Lisa, while another of his men stood to her left.

'Right,' I said. 'Perhaps you'll let me have your chair.'

'Getting suddenly masterful, are we? I always knew you could do it, Craig. But haven't you left it a bit late?'

The two men lifted her bodily out of the chair and set her down on the one I had occupied during my last session here. They stood on guard, flanking her. Mike said: 'Right, all yours, Craggy.' And then, with a wry grin: 'One thing, old son. Apologies for lumbering you with Maureen. It was such a relief to be away from her. Away for good. I was horrified when I heard you'd taken her on.'

Lisa's laugh was the caricature of a witch's cackle. 'The two of you! Lumbered with inadequate women. But always so chivalrous. Except when it comes to . . . ' She was glaring at me, still struggling to maintain her dignity and not give too much away. Though she had already revealed more than enough.

'As a matter of interest, Craggy,' Mike went on, 'how did you suss out so many things and get the story off so pat?'

'The way anyone can do it if he concentrates hard enough. Why so much fuss about the Official Secrets Act and the rest of it? Everything you need to know is here in the everyday media and on line, if you know how to interpret the pieces and fit them together.'

'Fair enough.'

'But I haven't had time to work out where *you* come into it, and what's brought you here.'

'Treachery,' hissed Lisa. 'That's what's brought him here. We should have known he wasn't to be trusted.'

I found the VDU controls, and brought up a panoramic view of the space outside. People were milling to and fro, vaguely rather than menacingly.

'I'm going out there,' I said. 'I can talk to people I know.'

'No, Craggy. Better stay where you are, and let's combine our resources, right? And start by letting them hear your soothing voice. Call the shots, the way you used to.'

I put on my most authoritative voice, hoping it would come out commandingly at the other end. 'This is Craig Spencer Craig speaking. Most of you know me. I want to assure you that the disorder caused by the elements I named in my recent speech is being brought under control. Please follow these alterations to the programme . . . ' I rattled off a glib summary, hoping that what I visualized in my head would fit the realities. Then I turned to Mike. 'Have you got a second-in-command who could supervise things out there?'

'Freddy Allingham. Lieutenant Allingham. First-rate bloke.' He flipped out his mobile and barked a few words into it, smiled, and said: 'On stand by.'

'Tell him,' I said, 'to open the gates to the police, explain as much as he needs to stop them dashing about. Pull rank. Flatter them into cooperating with the military, sort of thing. Ask for their help in shepherding the crowd nice and neatly into the lecture hall, and keeping an eye on any difficult stragglers. And we've got to identify the operators who put this whole show on.' I glanced at Lisa. 'Too much to ask, I suppose, for you to order all your stooges to report to the main entrance and await further instructions?'

Her laugh grew wilder. Somehow she was hardly any longer in the room.

Mike was rattling off a few quiet instructions to Allingham. 'He'll be able to pick them out,' he reassured me. 'Recognize most of them himself, probably. We'll have met them — supposed to be on the same team, weren't we?'

'Yes,' spat Lisa. 'Only you've ratted, haven't you? Let the whole project down. But you won't get away with it. Mutiny. Not a nice word. And the answers won't be nice, I promise you that.' She produced a high, whining breath. 'Treason!'

Mike leaned back, almost leisurely now that instructions had gone out. Give it ten minutes, and we'd check on the results. If somebody didn't come looking for us first, showing their strength and wrenching things back into their own deadly pattern.

But Mike was reading my thoughts, and

Lisa's along with them.

'Don't you realize the whole thing's collapsed? Buywise and its backers, military and commercial, are done for. Under Congressional investigation. Like Enron, like so many cosy deals between the Pentagon and big business, destroyed by your own greed.'

'Greed?' said Lisa. 'I never wanted money.'

'You wanted power,' said Mike, 'just as greedily as some folk want money. Only when the currency ceases to be valid . . . ?' He turned towards me. 'You've been wondering where our group fits into this shindig, right? You must have seen last year's newspapers already warning that too close an alliance with the US was becoming a threat to our national security. A good few of us were aware of that long before the Press got on to it. After all, we were at the sharp end. We couldn't help realizing that our own superior officers in Iraq, Afghanistan, and all round the fringes of trouble spots had been brainwashed into giving orders which were in fact only instructions relayed from their American ringmasters. So we felt it was time to form our own little resistance cadre. They were planning to send our key under-cover personnel back to this country to take part in the gradual takeover. We were in on plans for the dummy run here. We'd received all the necessary bumf, learned every movement for when someone pressed the button. But you spurred someone into pressing a button too soon — and the wrong button, at that. High time to intervene. So here we are.'

His mobile trilled a brief summons. He raised an eyebrow, muttered a command, and then looked down on Lisa's stiffly arrogant shoulders. 'Some of your hotheads were opening up a rather vicious-looking armoury. We've clobbered them. But how do those little items show up on the inventory of a supposed theme park? Definitely not play-things for the public.'

'There are plenty more where those came from.' The words came out like a sorceress's cantrip.

'No doubt.' Another message came through. Mike smiled more happily. 'All going smoothly. Our blokes in the other centres — High Rigg, Skelmerby, and two more in the Midlands — are offering technical advice to the demon-strators. We've secured the strategic sites. But none as important as this place, eh, Miss Maitland? This is the master key to the whole network. And you've lost it.' When she sat there motionless, staring implacably straight ahead, he added: 'It's as good as over. But maybe your friends in the CIA can soften the blow for you. When they assess their operatives as being mentally damaged by their under-cover activities, psychotherapy is offered at a special rehab centre. I'm sure it would be easy to get yourself committed there.'

I was getting worried by the tension in every line of Lisa's body. Before she could snap, I said:

'There's one thing you've got to tell me. Where's Fran? What have you done with her?'

Lisa was smiling again, and it wasn't a pleasant smile. 'She's the one who's been sent away. For debriefing. Would you believe it, the stupid little slut was driving on her way to hand in her notice when we intercepted her. 'Hand in her notice'!' She repeated it with a snarl of indignation. 'Like some silly little secretary. So she had to be subjected to severe retraining.'

'Which would never work. She's way past that sort of thing.'

'Unfortunately, you were proved right about that. So we had to deactivate her.'

'What the hell does that mean? Damn you, where *is* she?'

'You'll never know now, will you?'

From being so still, her right hand moved swiftly. She clapped it to her mouth, and the smile became a grisly rictus. Her eyes rolled back. Her whole skull, with teeth clenched and blank eye sockets glaring, seemed about to tear through the stretched skin.

'Christ!' Mike exploded. He flung himself on her, grabbed her throat and tried to force her to be sick. But she curled up in his hands, jerking convulsively, then stiffened again until her sheer dead weight dragged her out of his grasp. He swore again, and looked over her slumped body at me in despair. 'I should have known. At her level, in that job, they're always trained what to do at the last moment. When they know it's the last moment.'

'She was mad, but I . . . mad enough to . . . ?'

'A future as a failure would never be good enough for Madame Maitland. At worst, a criminal found knee deep in a failed conspiracy. At best, a nonentity. No, she could never have faced being a nonentity.'

The deathly grin lingered on those twisted lips. As if she was still laughing at me.

How was I ever to find Fran now? Where was she, for God's sake? Where *was* she?

Lisa was laughing at me from the eternity into which she had plunged herself.

You'll never know now, will you?

6

DCI Plant's voice in my entryphone sounded as stolidly polite as ever, but somehow without that characteristic note of disbelief which could so easily drift on into a threat. Maybe he was genuinely looking forward to confronting me with something really solid that he had at last dug up. I let him in, expecting to see one of his usual stolid sergeants or constables bringing up the rear; but he was on his own.

'I suppose this is about that upset down at Heathwaters?' I didn't really suppose any such thing.

'Not my department, sir. Except that in the Missing Persons Unit we were planning to interview a Miss Lisa Maitland about her apparent involvement with that murdered woman — and possibly with Mrs Leith. Unfortunately we've been informed she had a fatal accident the evening of those disturbances.'

'An accident?'

My tone of voice alerted him. 'You were there at the time, I believe. Perhaps you've got something you'd like to tell me.'

'No,' I said hastily. 'Nothing. And since you've just said it's not in your department, perhaps you'll tell me what it *is* that's brought you here.'

'What I really came to see you about, Mr Craig' — self-satisfaction was beginning to ooze out of the haggard skin of his face — 'is your assailant, one Dominic Viney.'

'Is he beginning to make any sense?'

'He has confessed, sir.'

'To assaulting me? Difficult for him to pretend otherwise, considering one of your own officers witnessed him at it.'

'No, sir. He's confessed to murder.'

For a shivering, hideous moment I lost any grip on my surroundings. The room was no longer my room. Plant was an alien figure, suspended in space. I wanted him frozen there, not saying another word, not going on to utter that one name and tell me the facts I had been dreading and denying for so long.

'Murder?' I whispered.

'Of that woman we thought was Mrs Leith, until you gave us reason to think otherwise.'

'Since it wasn't Fran, where does he come into it?'

I was trying to steady the room, stop it pulsating.

Plant said: 'Viney broke down completely. Went on shouting that he had nothing left to live for, might as well tell us the lot and be done with it. A right extremist, that young man. Anti-nuclear, anti-American, preaching peace but lashing out whenever he was crossed. Seen 'em before on many a demo.'

'But the woman?' I had to know, had to have him spell it out for me that it definitely wasn't Fran we were talking about.

'He complained that the woman had been foisted off on him as a substitute. Disgusting, he thought it was. He'd been made a fool of by Mrs Leith, in ways he only learned later. But in spite of everything he was still besotted with her, thought he could sort it all out. Only then she disappeared, and your name was in the news, and he thought you must have murdered her. Then when this other woman cropped up and started . . . um, going through the motions, if I can put it that way . . . making up to him in just the same way and trying to pump him about forthcoming demos, he was . . . well, it sounds way out, but he felt *insulted*. How dare anyone suppose he could fall for such a slag, after someone as wonderful as Frances Leith? He got in a rage and killed her. And would have been happy for you to be lumbered with the blame.'

'Because he really did believe I'd murdered Fran . . . Mrs Leith?'

'Just so, sir. But now he's cracked. Conscience, maybe. It's odd how it works. Or doesn't work. The most unlikely people,' he said unexpectedly, 'have committed murder for a passion they really despise themselves for.'

I was beginning to realize that Plant wasn't just the caricature copper I'd tried to see him as.

The world was steadying. I could almost feel sorry for Viney. Whatever Fran might do, it was impossible not to fall in love with her. And the thought of being expected to play along with a cheap substitute was really repellent.

Still there was one question overriding every other sad, sordid little detail.

And still there was that derisive echo: *You'll never know now, will you?*

I had gone so far off into my own despair that I had almost forgotten Plant was still in the room. I was dragged back to reality by what he was saying.

'After further investigation, we've come across some interesting facts about Mr Toby Leith. I've got to admit that in spite of the supposed importance of his meetings in the States, I was still a bit surprised that he couldn't be bothered to come back to identify what we thought was his wife's body. And I came to an interesting conclusion.'

I remembered Fran's own summary of their relationship. 'His work really did matter more to him.'

'Possibly, sir. But equally, he didn't come back because he knew the body couldn't be Mrs Leith's. He knew his wife wasn't dead.'

'But when he came here to see me, he did think she was.' I remembered his anguish here on my doorstep. There had been nothing contrived in that. 'He wasn't shamming. He really thought I'd abducted her, and maybe killed her.'

'Originally, yes. But later, somehow or other he must have been told. By whoever it is he's in with. A great relief to him, I've no doubt.'

'But if he found out where she was, why . . . ' The taste of the whole situation was turning ever more sour. 'You reckon he knows where she is now?'

Plant assumed a statesmanlike look, emphasizing his reluctance to say anything which would commit him to a positive statement. 'We have been alerted to the fact that Mr Leith's premises in Pimlico, used during his times of attendance at Parliament, have for some weeks been supplied with a twenty-four-hour security guard.'

'But he's not a minister, or an ex-minister

from some sensitive post,' I objected. 'Only prime ministers and those involved with Northern Ireland or other hot spots are entitled to round-the-clock police protection.'

'In this case, not even orthodox policemen,' growled Plant. Clearly his sense of the proprieties was shocked. 'There's some indication of a confidential secondment from a Special Branch sideline, but even that may have been a bluff. None of my contacts in the Met were told, even though it's on their patch. Even now, nobody has tipped me off or given a nudge to any of my colleagues in the Missing Persons Unit, even though Mrs Leith's disappearance was in the news at the time and they knew the case is still open. This could be some group setting up a sort of safe house of their own. Too many private enforcers and semi-private security services around nowadays.'

'You've never been tempted? The pay's a lot better.'

'No, Mr Craig. I haven't.'

I recalled the advances made to me at one time and another. 'Nor me.'

'And that doesn't surprise me, Mr Craig.'

'Why are you letting me in on all this?' I asked.

'I felt I owed you one, sir. After what I put you through. We were both of us misled by someone. Or some agency.'

'Some people,' I agreed, 'have been playing some very dodgy games with the rest of us.' I knew he had to play his own official line; but it was time he dotted a few i's and crossed a few t's. 'Just what is the situation right now? Are you suggesting . . . Good God, man, you think that Mrs Leith is being kept in the Pimlico flat?'

'It's a possibility.'

'Then what are you going to do about getting her out?'

Plant looked deplorably smug. 'I have a warrant to search those premises, sir. Which we are proposing to do as soon as we have driven to Pimlico from here.'

'Do her guardians know that you're aiming to trespass on their territory?'

'There's always the danger of leaks, and precious little loyalty. But we've done our best to keep wraps on it till the last minute.'

'Either way, couldn't it get a bit rough?'

'We'll have to see, sir.'

'Look, Chief Inspector, if she *is* there . . . '

'You'll be one of the first to know, sir. I reckon I owe you that, too.'

I saw him to the door. There was a dark blue Espace at the kerb, with three men waiting patiently in it. Plant's cronies looked about as attractive as the bruisers in the

Heathwaters lecture hall.

As soon as they had driven off, I phoned Mike.

★ ★ ★

We parked, the four of us, round the corner from the cul-de sac. Its cobbled quaintness suggested it had once been the cramped stableyard of an inn, long since tarted up as a brief row of flats, each with a narrow alley separating it from its neighbour. Two police cars were parked across the end of the cul-de-sac. Young Allingham, casually dressed in jeans and a lumberjack's shirt, sauntered along the far side of the street to the end of the enclave, leaning against a lamp standard to light a cigarette while he glanced down the row.

When he came back he said: 'Friend Plant seems to be having a bit of an argument with two bruisers. A certain amount of waving documents about. I'd say Plant and his back-up are just about ready to risk giving battle.'

I said: 'Come on, Mike. While they're stalling for time, I think . . . '

He needed no explanations. We both sprinted round the nearest police car and down the alley beside the Leiths' flat. A side door was opening, and two men were edging their way out, with a woman pinned between them. One of the men was Toby Leith, the other a hefty character in a blue uniform with shoulder flashes reading G#PROTECTION.

Their captive was Fran.

There wasn't much room for a fight. To get enough swing behind a punch you were liable to crack your elbow against the brick wall. It was a matter of grabbing, holding on, and heaving. I left Toby Leith to Mike, got the other man by the upper arm, and wrenched it back from his shoulder so that he cursed and had to let Fran go. I flung the man towards Allingham, coming up behind me, and let Fran fall into my arms.

A few minutes later we were grouped outside the front door, confronting DCI Plant and his team.

'Here's your missing person,' I said.

Toby Leith tried to struggle free from Mike's grip 'My wife . . . '

'There are some questions to be answered on that subject,' said Plant. 'Including possible charges of the lady being held against her will. Attempts to pervert the course of justice, withholding information from the police, and a few other related matters.'

'Nonsense. My wife is coming back home into our flat with me. Right now. I shall of course be reporting this outrageous intrusion to higher authority.'

'She's coming home with *me*,' I said, more to Plant than to Leith. 'After she's thoroughly rested, I'll guarantee that she reports to you with any answers you need.'

Plant looked doubtful; but then looked at Mike and the rest of my team, and was obviously assessing the odds in any unseemly punch-up.

He said: 'I shall hold you responsible, Mr Craig, for presenting Mrs Leith to my divisional office within the next twenty-four hours.'

'No problem, Chief Inspector. I do indeed intend to be responsible for Mrs Leith's welfare from now on.'

7

She lay back in my arms on the couch with her eyes shut, taking long, shuddering breaths and then laughing in a half-incredulous way, her head burrowing in under my chin as if to find a secure resting place where nobody else could get too close. When I let my hand drift across her swollen belly, she made a purring sound and put her hand over mine, pressing it down.

For a long time we had no need to talk. Sitting here together was enough. She was here, I was here, we were touching but without any immediate rage of desire, because the real deep desire was fulfilled just by our being together.

At last she said: 'Have you forgiven me?'

'For what?'

'Spying on you. Pretending.'

'Just pretending to love me?'

'No, damn you. I told you that wasn't meant to happen.'

'But it did?'

'You know it did. That's why . . . this.' She moved languorously under my hand. And then, thrusting herself upright, out of my arms, she said desperately: 'You do believe it's yours, don't you?'

'Yes.'

'How can you be so sure?'

'Aren't *you*?'

'Yes. Because I took precautions with' — she winced — 'the others.' Her voice sank again to a sad murmur. 'With you as well, at first. But not later.'

'Which says something about you,' I said happily. 'And about us.'

'It says I'm a cheat. Even cheating on myself.'

'No. Being honest with yourself.'

'No, I'm a fraud. Since early on, I've been a fraud. Saying I didn't want the child, telling you things had to stop and I'd have to do something about it.'

'But then why did you tell me about it, rather than keep quiet and . . . and go away for an abortion, which is what I thought you were doing?'

'I was even cheating on myself. I half *wanted* things to happen. I wanted you to know, wanted it all to add up to something. And at the same time I was scared. Don't you despise me?'

'Stop it. I love you. Isn't that enough? Never mind the post-mortems. We're here.' There was a long, warm silence. Then I simply had to come out with it: 'Just one thing, though.'

'I knew there had to be something.'

'Why did you never get in touch? You must have known I'd be worried sick. And then you must have heard about the accusations they were chucking at me. Couldn't you have come forward? Or got word to me somehow?'

'Oh, dear.' She let herself sink back into my arms, very tentatively, as if unsure of her welcome. 'I didn't know about it for ages. They'd shut me away. For being a naughty girl.'

'They couldn't just — '

'They were capable of doing anything. I knew I was working for a very unscrupulous lot. Knew it too late.'

'How did you get involved in the first place?'

For a long minute or more I thought she wasn't going to say anything. Sooner or later it all had to come out between us. But if she wanted to wait, couldn't bring herself to spoil this contentment between us, this time out of time after so much confusion, then I would wait.

When she began to talk, it was in a subdued voice like a murmured recital of transgressions in a confessional.

'It started out with me trying to help Toby.

He asked me casually enough, thought it might entertain me — a sort of game for which he knew I was well equipped. Casual, no commitments. And by the time I began to find how shady the whole operation was, it was too late. I felt sick of it . . . but there didn't seem to be any antidote. Until you came on the scene.'

Her story, blurted out in unhappy, self-accusing bursts, became a script I could almost have written myself. Or could have delivered as a speech to a receptive — or sceptical? — audience.

Fran admitted shamefacedly that Lisa's first assessment of her had been right. Just as she had told me, for a long time she had fought shy of any lasting relationship. Her sexual appetites could be satisfied by the occasional self-indulgence, given an added frisson when she could use the man not merely for physical pleasure but also to rob him of useful secrets.

'Some prostitutes steal their client's wallet, or credit cards, or whatever he's left lying around,' said Fran bitterly. 'I just stole his business or political knowledge — and handed it on to the pimps who were running me.'

Industrial espionage proved not only amusing but profitable. She knew that her handlers were somehow involved in a military/business tie-up, but she felt no compunction in playing the games she had already come to accept as normal after her career in image consultancy. The counters in that game were indeed just counters, not real human beings with real feelings and backgrounds. You nudged them about on the board, enjoying your own subtleties, marvelling at the naïveties and clumsiness of some, the stark ambitions of others.

Until she began to get a sour taste in her throat and around the edges of her mind. It dawned on her that she was being manipulated, just as she had been manipulating others to draw their secrets out of them. And there was somebody in charge who was so much more ruthless and determined that if it was all a game, the game had become detestable.

She made up her mind to quit. Making an appointment to see her controller, she was ambushed on the way and bundled into a van which took her to a house so bleak and featureless that she was sure she wouldn't recognize it again. There they tried to coax her, then laugh her, into recanting. The pay was good, she had been enjoying herself, hadn't she? They flattered her that she was too good to lose.

But all the time there was an indescribable element of contempt and even downright hatred in the supposed persuasion.

'That woman,' said Fran, hushed and still frightened. 'She was obsessed with you.'

'What did she say?'

'Very little. Not in so many words. Your name kept cropping up, but she would never actually . . . Craig, what had you done to her?'

'Nothing,' I said. 'That was the trouble.'

There was another long pause. I was happy to move away from the realities of the past and accept the fact that Fran was here, the waiting was over, we did not need to talk until we were ready to talk about the future rather than the past.

I kissed her in that fragrant softness of her throat.

★　★　★

Mike Heriot — or Newman, if he was going to cling to that renaming — arrived at a suitable time for opening the bottle of champagne I'd had in the fridge for some months now, unsure of it ever being of use. He sat facing us, grinned companionably at Fran and then at me, and raised his glass.

'Here's to the two of you. And may things

sort themselves out without too much hassle.'

'I do seem to have got Craig into a mess,' said Fran remorsefully.

'If you ask me, he's contributed more than a fair share of getting himself into the mess. Very high profile stuff, that rant at Heathwaters. Bound to bring them down on him a lot more heavily than they'd been doing so far. Especially Madame Maitland.' Mike leaned back in the armchair and studied the room, almost as I might have done, assessing the possibility of a swift exit. But at the same time he was relaxed, weighing things up calmly. 'Are you up to telling us where that woman was keeping you, before you were shifted out to Pimlico?'

I said: 'Look, does she have to — '

'Yes,' said Fran, 'I do. Let's get it all straight, and be done with it.'

Her usual meetings with her handlers took place in a drably functional set of offices above building society premises in Victoria. She never knew whether the society downstairs ever traded in the normal way. She made an appointment in their usual code, and was on her way to tell them she was finished with the whole shabby set-up when she was intercepted. There must be no record or even the most casual mention by a passer-by of her being seen at the place where

347

she usually reported. She supposed that her car must then have been driven to Suffolk, supplied with those pieces of apparent evidence, and left where it could be found and fitted into their framework — or, rather, into Lisa's pulling of strings in her humiliating puppet show.

'But where were you all that time?' I asked. 'You couldn't have been in Toby's flat right from the start.'

She began to shiver, so that I wanted to withdraw the question and tell her it didn't matter, it was all over. But she gulped and went on:

'That house I told you about. Out in the sticks somewhere. But not far from an airfield. There was a lot of activity every now and then. Not Heathwaters. Somewhere closer to a motorway, I thought. Only I was never allowed to look out.'

What did they do to you? I sensed that Mike was asking the same question too, but not daring to do so out loud.

Fran must have known what was nagging at us. 'At first they seemed to be trying to brainwash me into getting back into business. But there was something missing, as though . . . as though . . . ' She faltered, and I took her hand to tell her it was all right to stop. But again she forced herself on: 'As though they were simply marking time. I said I wanted to get in touch with you, and they — *she* — just laughed and said that . . . how did she put it . . . oh, 'That little episode's over. Forget it.' '

'I remember reading about one of those Victorian murder trials in Manchester,' said Mike, 'when the defence counsel asked the jury 'Who is more jealous, venomous and savage than a woman who has been jilted?' '

I wondered if DCI Plant numbered that one among his collection.

Fran went on: 'For a while they didn't let me have any newspapers to read, or let me watch television except for some trashy quiz shows. I had a feeling . . . ' She looked puzzled rather than jarred by past fear. 'Somehow I felt I was being kept in reserve. For something. Just in case. Only I had no idea what might happen.'

'Neither had they, I think.' Mike reached for the champagne bottle and refilled our glasses rather than wait for me to let Fran go. 'But why were you transferred to your husband's flat?'

'I've no idea. It was only a few days ago. Toby tried to make out he'd only just heard of what had happened to me, and he wanted to take care of me, but we had to play it carefully.' She smiled a wan smile. 'More familiar, reassuring surroundings. Cosier. Only it wasn't cosy at all. Somehow even more horrible than the other place. I was still a prisoner — for my own safety, Toby said. The phone was cut off, though when he was in the flat he was forever on his mobile. I could tell he was desperate, sweating over something that was going wrong in all his dealings with some political group here and a much tougher one in the States. I'd always suspected that there was an element of bribery and double dealing in those so-called consultancies of his. He's going to lose his Parliamentary seat in the next election, but there've been promises of work in a new consortium if he cooperates. It was the wheeler-dealers over there who were calling the tune.'

'Not any longer,' said Mike. 'The game is up. It's not going to be like a rebellion in a Third World country. No machetes at dawn, and all opposition exterminated. There'll be 'discussions at high level', the US ambassador will be recalled, and some NATO bigwig will be appointed to investigate a breakdown in relations. Here there'll be a Parliamentary inquiry, a report which will take two or three years to finalize, a few reprimands as a result, and life will go on as normal.'

'Unless some of them fight back.'

'They may. But they're the ones who'll get the severest reprimand. Departmental heads are cunning enough to see where the future lies, and who's going to provide them with their creature comforts.'

Fran laughed. It was a fresh, exhilarating laugh. Mike did have that effect on one. He had woken her from sombre memories, and you felt that whatever might lie ahead, there would be ways of coping. Even of enjoying life again.

Mike went on: 'Just as there were operatives in the Intelligence sections on both sides of the Atlantic who warned Bush and Blair that there were no WMDs in Iraq, and have since been feeling angry about their reports being deliberately distorted to suit the warmongers, so now there are plenty of them coming over to our side before any more lies are promulgated. We need a counterbalance to the American hegemony — loyal types within our own forces, checking on who's issuing the orders and whose hand is in the till. It'll all depend on whether some key figures will be too scared to risk being chucked out of their snug little sinecures. But I think there are enough to tilt the balance.' He stared across his glass at me. 'After your peroration at Heathwaters,

Craggy, I take it you're with us?'

'I don't think I'm cut out to be an MI5 or MI6 type. 'Bond . . . James Bond.' Sounds impressive. But 'Craig . . . Craig Craig.' Hasn't got the same ring to it.'

'I wasn't thinking of espionage. You made it clear long ago that you weren't going in for that sort of thing. I had in mind the notion of sorting out the Buywise mess, for a start. Right up your street. A smooth transition, no bloodshed. Like any board of directors who've made a godawful mishmash. Not facing a firing squad, or even a prison sentence for fraud. Pay them off with a few million quid and slide discreetly into their directorial chairs.'

'Aren't we in the land of dollars rather than pounds?' I kept it flippant, stalling until I could work out what on earth he had in mind.

'No, we're not. The Buywise operations weren't nominally administered from the States. There had to be a UK holding company backed by a London commercial cartel to get round the Monopolies and Mergers boys. All right, so we know the Dreghorn associates were really regulating the whole thing from the US, but legally the whole enterprise in this country is run by the London headquarters. The easiest thing in the world now to hive that off — take it over just as is, but genuinely administer it from the UK, not just as a façade. At the moment it's ready to go into receivership. We get some investment bankruptcy adviser — '

'Not Toby!' said Fran quickly. We all three laughed absurdly.

'A quick round-up of your reliable colleagues, Craggy. Bring 'em back into the fold, get them on side. The present CEO will stand down — '

'How can you be sure of that?'

Mike grinned wickedly. 'After it's been made clear to him just what sort of can he'd be left carrying if he tried to tough it out, I reckon he'll be glad to slip away without a stain on his character. And then we negotiate with the Government for subsidies to keep the company afloat.'

'You're a wonderful optimist.' Fran was beginning to enjoy herself.

'Here again, they'll be anxious to hush up what they've been involved in with their friends across the ocean.' He leaned towards me, serious now. 'It's all yours, Craggy. Take over the existing network, but use it for the good of your suppliers. Your friends in this country and in France. Global logistics supplier, a truly European combine of brewers, vintners, distillers. With all the clout to give a fair deal both to suppliers and customers.'

'And wouldn't it all end up just the same sort of racket as the original? Undercutting, squeezing the small-time companies until they drop dead? The same sort of executives squeezing their way in, calculating what's good for themselves, ironing out individuals, pressing them all into the same mould?'

'It'd be up to you to make sure it didn't turn out that way.'

We had finished the champagne. My arm was getting stiff, but I didn't want to draw away from Fran even for a moment.

Mike was grinning again, looking at her. 'Besides,' he said, 'you've got a lot of family responsibilities that'll need paying for. Not to mention the cost of extricating yourself from some embarrassing leftovers.'

Fran chose this moment to sit upright. 'It's all my fault. Ever since I met you' — she smiled wryly at me — 'I had a hunch things could never be simple and straightforward.' Yet she sounded quite unrepentant. 'Do you really want to get involved in this shake-up, my love?'

'Top priority,' I assured her. 'Now, where do we start? Mike, since you're not dead, I don't really need a divorce. Maureen's a bigamist.'

'True. But . . . puts me in an awkward position. I know I owe it to you, after lumbering you with her; but honestly, old chap, it'd be a bit too complicated, letting her into why I did what I did. I suppose I could see her in confidence, tell her not to make difficulties, or else. But it wouldn't be fair to upset her too much.'

'I'm not sure she'd be all that upset,' I said. 'She'd make such a drama. She'd wallow in it. But I don't think publicity is what you want.'

'Not yet. Not until we've decided when to come out into the open.' He nodded. 'Much better for you to go ahead, Craggy, with a simple divorce.'

I looked warily at Fran. 'And Toby? Hasn't exactly been a caring husband, has he?'

'That wouldn't stop him expecting me to play the loyal wife when he was up against it.' This was the old, competent, professional Fran, coolly analysing the image of a client and making a decision.

'And we do have to decide exactly how much to tell DCI Plant when he starts grilling you. Don't want you sent to prison for wasting police time.'

Mike got to his feet. 'I think I'll leave that to you.' He leaned over Fran and kissed her, then gripped my hand and for a few moments looked more ill at ease than I had ever known him, as if afraid to speak. When words came, they were forced out unhappily.

'Maybe you're right, Craggy.'

'About what?'

'Our mutiny. It's going to be quite a fight. A long-drawn-out one. Dirty tricks time. The grubby folk who've been running things till now are winded, but they'll get their breath back. There'll be official inquiries, but large buckets of whitewash will be kept handy. Buywise and the Dreghorn finance set-up will be blown away. Tidily written off. But the CIA and the NMD won't give up gracefully. Too much at stake. The gravy train has to be kept rolling. There'll be other commercial conglomerates to make up the package. And they'll set to work undermining everybody else. Here in the UK we can expect some diplomatic meetings, and some disciplinary hearings and compulsory retirements. An odd court-martial, maybe, that the public never get to hear about. No, with all the personal problems you've got on your plate right now, I reckon you'd be wise not to get involved.' He smiled an oddly uncertain smile at Fran. 'Talk him out of it, my dear.' Somehow there was an underlying question.

Just as I was about to open the door to see him out, the entryphone buzzed.

Barry was on the doorstep. 'Going to let me in, old son?' He glanced uncertainly at Mike. 'Not interrupting anything, am I? Just thought it was time for a celebration, surely?' He waited until Mike had gone away along the pavement towards Gloucester Road, and said eagerly: 'I mean, it's true, is it?'

'Depends on what you — '

'Fran. She's shown up, hasn't she? I mean, congrats. And after all, it was Rhona and me wot done it — brought you together in the first place. Don't keep me dithering here on the doorstep.'

I said: 'Sorry, I'm busy.'

'For Christ's sake, old lad. We do really need to sort things out.'

Hadn't I heard something like those words before, in that same voice, just inside this very front door?

'I mean,' he was chattering on, 'I never did trust those Keating types. There's something fishy about that whole shower, and we do have to see where we stand.' Barry took his glasses off, polished them with a handkerchief from his top pocket, and blinked knowingly at me. 'And while we're at it, mind how you go, old son. You never know. Wherever Fran's been, can you be sure she hasn't been brainwashed? Programmed to

357

assassinate you, or at any rate to do you down somehow?'

'You've been seeing the wrong sort of movie.'

'Don't say I didn't warn you.' He was peering past me, but I wasn't going to let him in. 'Remember, way back, I told you she could be murder, that one.' Then he laughed uproariously and tried to slap me on the arm. 'But the main thing is us getting together soon. Sort things out,' he repeated.

'Yes,' I said. 'I'll let you know when I'm ready to sort you out.'

I closed the door on him and went back to make sure that Fran was really still here, misshapen not just at the hip but beautifully so in that swelling, heavily laden body.

Before I could say a word, she said: 'Let's get one thing straight. I've no intention of trying to talk you out of getting involved in your friend's strategy. Afterwards, you'd never forgive me.'

'If you did try,' I said, 'I wouldn't be listening. Of course we've got to have a go at it.'

'Good.' She was staring into the distance at something I couldn't identify. Then she patted the couch beside her. 'Sit down, darling. Darling Craig. We've got a lot to talk about.'

We had indeed.

We do hope that you have enjoyed reading this large print book.

Did you know that all of our titles are available for purchase?

We publish a wide range of high quality large print books including:
Romances, Mysteries, Classics
General Fiction
Non Fiction and Westerns

Special interest titles available in large print are:
The Little Oxford Dictionary
Music Book
Song Book
Hymn Book
Service Book

Also available from us courtesy of Oxford University Press:
Young Readers' Dictionary
(large print edition)
Young Readers' Thesaurus
(large print edition)

For further information or a free brochure, please contact us at:
Ulverscroft Large Print Books Ltd.,
The Green, Bradgate Road, Anstey,
Leicester, LE7 7FU, England.
Tel: (00 44) **0116 236 4325**
Fax: (00 44) **0116 234 0205**

Other titles published by
The House of Ulverscroft:

WRONG TURNINGS

John Burke

When Detective Inspector Lesley Gunn married Sir Nicholas Torrance, she might have expected this to be the end of her career as a sleuth. But returning from their honeymoon, they find themselves involved with the flamboyant Chet Brunner. The brash film and TV entrepreneur Brunner has surrounded himself with enemies, along with an ex-wife lurking in a nearby cottage with her criminal second husband. Added to that, Brunner's current wife and latest mistress are battling over him and with him. And a young widow has some startling things to learn about her dead husband and the bumptious Brunner. Then a killer strikes, and Lesley cannot help offering her own theories . . .